VEILFALL

VEILFALL

JOHN D JENNETT

COVENANT OF SILENCE SAGA BOOK IV

Contents

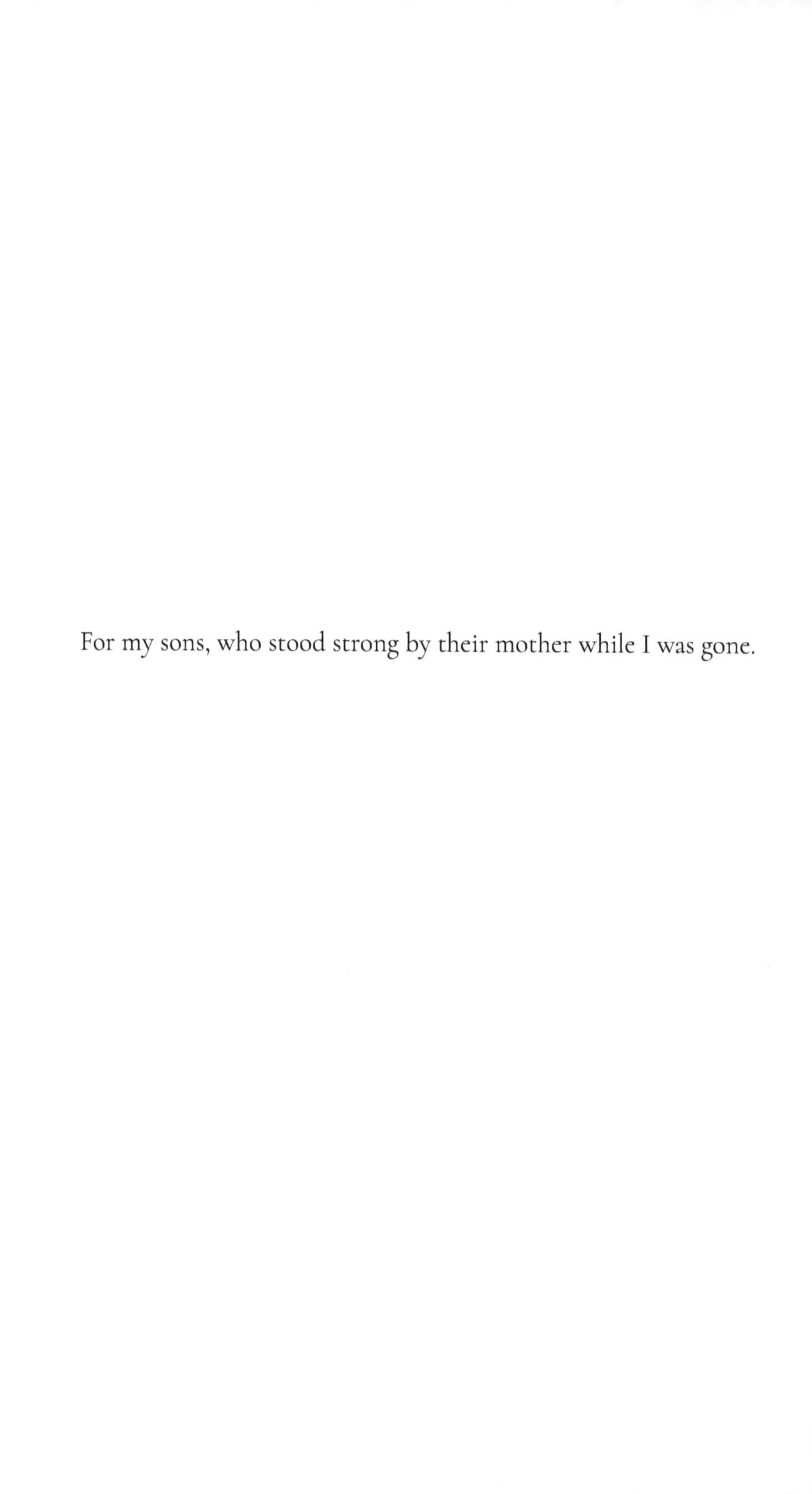

For my sons, who stood strong by their mother while I was gone.

1

The Morning After the Sky Sang

Morning came back the way it always did. Gray light slid through the trees and caught on dew and spiderwebs. Birds tested the air with tentative calls, as if checking whether it was safe to resume the day. The sky was empty. No color bled along the horizon. No luminous curtains lingered where they should not have been.

On screens everywhere, it was still night.

Maya stood barefoot on the porch, her jacket pulled tight against the early chill, and watched the world pretend nothing had happened. Her phone buzzed in her hand. She didn't need to look to know what it was. Every device within reach had been doing the same thing since before sunrise.

Footage. Replays. Slow motion wonder.

The auroras stretched across continents on her screen, emerald and violet bands rippling over cities that had never known them. Headlines scrolled past faster than she could read them.

SKY FIRE STUNS WORLD
SOLAR EVENT OF THE CENTURY
GLOBAL LIGHT PHENOMENON BAFFLES SCIENTISTS

She turned the volume down, then muted it entirely. The silence didn't help.

The sky above her was normal. That was the problem.

Maya closed her eyes and felt the difference immediately. It pressed against her from every direction, not loud but constant, like standing too close to a power substation. The Weave was not fractured in the way it had been before. It was stretched. Drawn taut across the planet and vibrating with the afterimage of what had passed through it.

She exhaled slowly and tried to ground herself the way she had learned. Name what is real. Anchor to the body. Separate signal from noise.

The noise didn't separate.

Her phone unmuted itself when the next clip auto-played. Someone had stitched together footage from half a dozen countries, sunrise in one frame and midnight in another, all layered with commentary and reaction videos. The sound overlapped in a way that should have been chaos.

Instead, Maya heard structure.

She opened her eyes and stared at the screen. The clip itself was nothing special. A wide shot of a highway outside São Paulo, traffic slowed as people leaned out of car windows to film the sky. No visible anomaly. No light. No motion.

Her awareness spiked anyway.

Her breath caught, sharp and involuntary, and the pressure behind her eyes flared. She swiped the video away, heart pounding, and the sensation faded just enough to let her breathe again.

That one mattered, she thought. She didn't know why. Only that it rang differently, like a plucked string still vibrating after the sound had died.

Inside the house, a radio murmured from the kitchen. Alex had turned it on low, probably out of habit. Voices argued softly about ionized particles and atmospheric refraction. Someone laughed, brittle and uncertain.

Maya stepped inside and leaned against the counter. The tile was cool under her feet. Ordinary. Solid. She focused on that while the world frayed at the edges.

Reports were already coming in.

A news ticker mentioned digital clocks drifting out of sync across several cities, all off by the same fraction of a second. Another article speculated about camera sensors glitching after prolonged exposure to unusual light. Someone else posted a grainy image of repeating geometric artifacts captured by traffic cameras in three different countries, identical down to the angle.

And beneath it all, buried in comments and first-person posts, were the other reports.

People hearing music where there was none.

Maya pressed her fingers to her temple. Each mention landed like a pinpoint of pressure somewhere in her awareness. Not sound. Not sight. Location. Presence. She could almost map them, bright spots flaring across an invisible globe.

A hospital hallway somewhere in Eastern Europe. She didn't know which one, only that it smelled faintly of antiseptic and old paint. A woman stood frozen beside a crash cart as the monitors around her went silent all at once. No alarms. No flatline. Just quiet. In the quiet, a harmony unfolded, low and layered, so beautiful it made her cry. The machines came back seconds later. She never told anyone what she heard.

A commuter in Tokyo paused mid-step at the edge of a crosswalk, seized by the sudden certainty that something vast had turned its attention toward him. The feeling passed. The light changed. He crossed the street shaking and didn't know why.

A child in a small town Maya could not place hummed to herself while coloring at the kitchen table. The tune was simple and precise. No one else recognized it.

Maya felt them all.

She slid down into a chair and braced her elbows on the table, head in her hands. This was too much. She had handled convergence events before, localized surges, nodes flaring and settling. This was different. The Weave was no longer something she reached for. It was everywhere, brushing up against her skin, inside her breath.

She tried to filter.

The familiar technique rose on instinct. She imagined narrowing the channel, damping the edges, letting only the strongest signals through. For a moment, blessedly, it worked. The pressure eased. The world dimmed to something survivable.

Then more pushed in.

Not louder. Closer.

Maya gasped as the floor seemed to tilt beneath her. She grabbed the edge of the table, knuckles white, and felt warmth spill over her lip. She wiped at it and stared at the smear of red on the back of her hand.

Alex was beside her immediately.

"Hey," he said quietly. "Sit back. You're good. I've got you."

"I'm fine," she said, though the room swam when she tried to lift her head.

"You're not," he replied, not unkindly. He pressed a folded paper towel into her hand without looking away from her face. "This isn't adrenaline. This is something else."

She leaned back and closed her eyes, focusing on the sound of his voice. He didn't flood her with questions. He didn't try to fix anything. He simply stayed, steady as a hand on her back, and the edges of the noise softened enough for her to breathe.

On the radio, a new voice cut in. Confident. Reassuring.

"Experts are cautioning against panic," the commentator said. "There's no evidence of lasting effects. These reports are likely the result of heightened anxiety following a visually striking but harmless atmospheric event."

Maya laughed once, sharp and humorless.

"That's dangerous," she said.

Alex turned the radio down further. "What is?"

"That." She gestured vaguely at the sound. "If they convince people nothing's wrong, they won't recognize it when it happens again. Or when it happens to them."

As if summoned by the thought, a new sensation rippled through her awareness. Not a flare. A stumble. Somewhere nearby, close enough to matter, a thread slipped out of alignment.

Maya sucked in a breath and reached without thinking.

She didn't cast. She didn't focus. She simply steadied.

The wobble smoothed. The pressure receded. Whoever it was took an unconscious step back from the edge and didn't know how close they had come.

Maya slumped, exhaustion crashing down on her shoulders like wet concrete.

Alex's hand tightened briefly on her arm. "You just did something," he said.

"I know," she whispered. "I don't know how."

Outside, the sun cleared the treetops at last, washing the yard in pale gold. It should have felt like relief. Instead, it felt like a new baseline settling into place.

The feeds kept playing. The reports kept coming. The anomalies didn't stop.

Maya stared out the window and understood, with a cold certainty that sank into her bones, that this was not an aftershock.

The sky had sung, and now the world was trying to remember the tune.

Her phone buzzed again in her hand. A breaking news alert flashed across the screen, half-loaded, stuttering as if even the data hesitated.

Maya felt it before the words resolved.

Somewhere else, something new was beginning.

2

Fault Lines in the Team

The house was chosen because no one would remember it.

It sat at the end of a narrow gravel road that had never quite decided whether it belonged to the woods or the town. The siding was dull, the roof patched, the porch sagging just enough to suggest neglect without inviting inspection. Nothing about it asked to be noticed. That was the point.

Maya stepped inside last and locked the door behind her.

The air smelled faintly of dust and old wood, layered with the sharper tang of disinfectant. Someone had cleaned recently. Not thoroughly, but deliberately. The kind of cleaning meant to remove fingerprints and not much else.

Alex moved immediately to the windows. He checked the edges of the heavy blackout curtains, tugging them into place until not a sliver of daylight remained. When he was done, the room felt smaller. Pressed inward.

Joe set three phones on the kitchen counter and silenced them one by one, his expression tight. "Every outlet's live," he said. "Feeds are already pulling."

"Muted," Richard said, glancing at the screens mounted along the far wall. "Not off. We need eyes."

"We don't need noise," Elara replied. She stood near the center of the room, arms crossed, shoulders rigid. Heat rolled off her in faint waves she didn't seem to notice. "Noise is how they find you."

"They already know something happened," Richard said. "Pretending otherwise doesn't protect us. It blinds us."

Maya let the argument wash past without intervening. Her attention was fixed on the screens.

Six of them flickered in silent rotation. News channels. Social media clips. Amateur footage stitched together by algorithms that didn't care about truth, only engagement. The auroras filled every frame. Cities bathed in color. People shouting and laughing and crying, mouths moving without sound.

She felt it all.

The moment the door had closed, the pressure had intensified. Not sharply, not dramatically. It was worse than that. Constant. Like standing beneath a low ceiling she couldn't see but knew was there.

"Everyone settle," Alex said quietly. It wasn't a command, but the room responded anyway.

Joe leaned against the counter and exhaled. Elara unclenched her fists. Richard straightened his jacket, his movements precise, controlled.

Maya took a step farther into the room and stopped.

The sense of being watched had followed them inside.

It wasn't the sharp awareness she had felt during confrontations before. This was broader. Diffuse. As if attention itself had thickened in the air. Cameras didn't account for it. Surveillance didn't explain it.

The Weave was listening.

She reached out instinctively, not with power, but with awareness. The safehouse sat on no significant node. No crossing lines. No obvious strain. It should have been quiet.

It wasn't.

Somewhere beyond the walls, threads vibrated in restless patterns. Distant, but present. Not one or two. Dozens. Hundreds. The background hum of a world that had not slept through the night and was still trying to decide what it had seen.

"Maya."

She looked up. Alex was watching her closely now.

"You good?" he asked.

"I'm here," she said. It was true. It was also incomplete.

Joe followed her gaze to the screens. "It's not slowing down," he said. "Every major network's on loop. People are dissecting pixels like scripture."

Richard stepped closer, hands clasped behind his back. "That's inevitable. Once something crosses the threshold of shared experience, you can't put it back."

Elara shook her head. "You can disappear. You can make yourself hard to find."

"For how long?" Richard countered. "A week? A month? The longer this goes unanswered, the more dangerous the vacuum becomes."

Maya felt the argument rising before it was spoken. Not just the words, but the intent behind them. Each voice carried its own harmonic edge. Fear. Control. Responsibility. None of them aligned.

She pressed her palm flat against the table and focused on the sensation. Solid wood. Cool surface. Present moment.

Outside, a car passed on the road. The sound was distant and ordinary. It did nothing to ease the tension.

Joe picked up one of the remotes and switched the feeds to a split view. Six cities. Six skies. Identical light patterns replayed from different angles.

"They're calling it a once in a lifetime event," he said. "Meteorological anomaly. Solar interaction. Pick your flavor."

"And you don't buy it," Elara said.

"No," Joe replied. "Neither does anyone who's honest. The comments are already shifting. People are comparing notes. Patterns are emerging."

Maya flinched as several of those patterns lit up at once in her awareness. She sucked in a breath and held it, forcing the pressure back down.

Alex noticed. He always did.

He stepped closer without touching her, grounding himself first, then extending that calm outward. The effect was subtle but immediate. The noise softened, just enough.

"Thanks," she murmured.

Richard watched the exchange with sharp interest. "You can't keep doing that forever," he said. Not unkindly. Not yet.

Maya met his gaze. "I know."

The words settled heavily in the room.

Silence followed, broken only by the flicker of screens and the faint electrical hum of the house. No one moved to turn anything off. No one suggested opening a window.

This place was meant to hide them. Instead, it felt like a container.

Joe broke the silence first, tapping one of the screens with a knuckle. "They're already clustering the footage," he said. "It's not random anymore. Same camera angles. Same timestamps. Same edits popping up in different languages."

No one answered him at first. The feeds rolled on in muted color, auroras flowing like something alive, beautiful enough to distract from what lay beneath them.

Elara shifted her weight and took a slow breath. Then another. The air around her shimmered faintly, heat pressing outward in subtle waves that curled the edges of a nearby curtain. She clenched her hands at her sides and focused on stillness, jaw tight.

Joe noticed. "You alright?"

"I'm fine," she said quickly. Too quickly. "I just need a second."

Richard folded his arms and surveyed the room with a critical eye. "This location is adequate for a stopgap," he said. "But not for what's coming. Curtains and silence won't hold once people start asking the right questions."

"People are already asking," Joe replied. "That's the problem."

"They're guessing," Richard said. "There's a difference."

Maya leaned against the counter and tried to follow the conversation, but the pressure in her head had returned, creeping back in around the edges. Each raised voice sharpened it. Each moment of tension tugged at distant threads she couldn't see but could feel responding.

Alex shifted closer without comment. He didn't touch her. He didn't need to. The simple act of proximity steadied her breathing, brought the room back into focus.

Joe swiped to another clip. "Look at this one. Same pattern we saw in Brazil, but mirrored. And this one here. See the glitch? Same geometry, same drift."

"That proves nothing," Richard said. "Patterns appear when people want them to."

Joe met his gaze. "That's my point. People want them. Once enough of them agree on what they're seeing, the truth won't matter anymore."

Elara let out a breath that carried more heat than air. "So we hide," she said. "We pull back. Let it burn itself out."

"And when it doesn't?" Richard asked. "When the burn spreads?"

She turned on him, eyes flashing. "Then we're not standing in front of it when it does."

Maya flinched as Elara's fire spiked. Not outward. Inward. The Weave tightened in response, a sharp vibration that made her vision blur.

Alex's voice cut through it. "Easy."

Elara closed her eyes and nodded once. The heat receded, leaving the air heavy and tense.

Richard looked from one to the other, his expression unreadable. "This isn't sustainable," he said. "Not the hiding. Not the strain you're putting on her."

Maya straightened. "I didn't ask for this."

"I know," Richard said. "But intention doesn't change outcome. Right now, this entire situation hinges on you being able to manage something no single person should be carrying."

Joe glanced at Maya, concern sharpening his features. "Is that true?"

She opened her mouth to answer, then hesitated. The noise pressed harder, like a tide testing a weakened barrier.

Alex noticed the hesitation before she spoke. He always did.

"Maya," he said quietly. "You don't have to cover for it."

She swallowed. "It's just... louder," she said. "That's all."

The lie didn't hold. Not in the room. Not in the Weave.

Joe set the remote down slowly. "Alright," he said. "Then let's stop circling it. So what do we do now?"

The words hung there, simple and dangerous.

No one answered.

Elara stared at the floor. Richard's jaw tightened. Joe waited, eyes moving from face to face. Alex watched Maya.

Maya felt the weight of the question settle squarely on her shoulders. The pressure behind her eyes pulsed in time with her heartbeat. Outside the safehouse, the world was already shifting, patterns locking into place without their consent.

Inside the room, they had nothing but uncertainty.

And silence.

Joe broke it with a harsh exhale. "Fine. I'll say it. We can't sit here and hope the world calms down."

Elara lifted her head. "We can, actually. We should."

"No," Joe said. "You're talking like this is a storm. It isn't. This is people. They're scared and they're hungry for answers. If we don't give them something real, they'll accept whatever lie fits their fear."

"People don't want truth," Elara snapped. "They want a target. They want someone to blame."

"They want a story," Joe said. "And they're going to get one, with us in it whether we like it or not."

Richard stepped forward, voice controlled. "Which is why we need structure. Rules. Chain of command. You can't run an operation of this magnitude on instinct and good intentions."

Elara's eyes narrowed. "So you're volunteering to be in charge."

Richard didn't flinch. "Someone has to."

"Not you," Elara said.

Joe's attention flicked to Richard, then back to Maya, then to Alex. "What about the government? Hargreaves. HECATE. They're not going to sit back. If we don't negotiate now, we won't get the chance later."

"We don't negotiate with people who build cages," Elara said. "They can't weaponize what they can't find. We disappear. We move. We stop leaving a trail."

"And if they come for others?" Joe asked. "If they start hunting anyone who twitches wrong? We just stay hidden and let it happen?"

Elara's expression tightened, the heat rising again. "Don't put that on me."

"I'm not," Joe said. "I'm putting it on all of us."

Richard's voice sharpened. "Going underground doesn't solve the problem. It delays it. Negotiation might buy time, but only if we have leverage. We don't have leverage without order. Power doesn't survive chaos. Someone has to set rules."

Maya listened, nodding when she could, trying to hold the center of the room like a seam that refused to split. That had been her role for weeks. Keep them aligned. Keep them moving. Keep them alive.

The room made it impossible.

As each voice rose, the noise inside her skull rose with it. Threads tightened. Nodes flared in the distance like distant lightning, answering emotion like a body answering pain.

She pressed her fingers to her temple. A ringing started, high and thin. It grew louder with every sentence.

"You're doing it," Alex said quietly.

Maya blinked. "Doing what?"

"Pushing it down," he said. "You're bracing like you're about to take a hit."

She tried to laugh, but it came out brittle. "That's because I am."

Joe's jaw clenched. "Maya, talk to us."

She looked at them and saw what they needed from her, all at once. Elara needed safety. Joe needed truth that could stand in public. Richard needed control. Alex needed her alive.

The Weave needed her listening.

She swallowed, and the pressure behind her eyes turned into a sharp pulse.

"It's everywhere," she said.

They all quieted, not because they agreed, but because something in her voice made the room recognize weight.

"I can't keep filtering everything," Maya continued. She forced the words out plain, without poetry, without mysticism, because this wasn't a sermon. It was a fact. "It's in every city. Every node. Every person who's close to the edge. I can feel it all. I can't turn it down anymore."

Silence followed, thick and immediate.

Elara's heat steadied, like a flame forced under glass.

Joe stared at her, the implications clicking into place. If Maya went down, there was no buffer. No warning. No coordination. No one else in the room could do what she was doing.

Richard's expression shifted, not to sympathy, but to assessment. A system flaw. A single point of failure.

Alex didn't look surprised. He looked angry, but not at her. At the situation. At the fact that the world kept taking more from her.

"Maya," he said softly, "why didn't you say it sooner?"

"Because it doesn't change anything," she replied. "Because we still have to decide what we're doing."

Joe's voice dropped. "It changes everything."

Richard nodded once. "It confirms what I suspected. We can't build strategy around one person holding the weight of the planet."

Elara spoke without looking up. "So what, then? You want to spread it around?"

"I want a structure," Richard said. "A way to function that doesn't depend on her endurance. We need divisions. Roles. Protocols."

"Protocols," Elara repeated, disgust heavy in the word. "That's what HECATE calls their cages."

"Don't be naive," Richard snapped. "Protocol is not a cage. It's the difference between coordinated action and panic."

Joe raised his hands slightly, trying to keep the room from igniting. "Alright. Then let's be concrete. If Maya goes down, who makes the call?"

No one answered.

The question landed like a weight on the floor. The safehouse felt suddenly smaller, as if the air itself had been compressed by the implication.

Elara's eyes flashed. "Why does there have to be someone?"

"Because there already is," Joe said. "Right now it's Maya. That's the truth whether we say it or not."

Maya's throat tightened. She wanted to argue. She wanted to deny it. She wanted to refuse the shape of that crown before it was even offered.

She couldn't, because the Weave was still roaring behind her eyes, and the room was still waiting.

Richard's mouth opened, then closed again. He looked around, measuring reactions, calculating costs.

Finally he said, "I can do it."

Elara's stare cut him. "No, you can't."

Joe didn't answer immediately. Alex didn't either. Alex simply shifted closer to Maya, a quiet statement of allegiance that didn't require words.

Richard's jaw tightened. He didn't retreat, but the room didn't accept him either. Not fully. Not yet.

Maya felt the fault line widen.

Alex spoke, calm and steady. "We're not deciding who's king."

"That's not what this is," Richard said.

"It's what it becomes," Joe replied.

Elara's hands clenched again, heat stirring. "I'm not taking orders."

Joe's voice went flat. "Then we're already done."

Maya's vision blurred at the edges, not with tears, but with strain. The noise pressed in as if the Weave itself responded to their fracture with a cruel kind of agreement.

Alex placed a hand lightly on her shoulder. The contact was grounding. Not magic. Not power. Presence.

Her breathing slowed. The pressure eased a fraction.

No one had solved anything, but the room stopped escalating. Alex did that. He always did. He stabilized people, not plans.

Joe rubbed a hand over his face. "We're spinning," he said. "We can't settle the whole world tonight."

Richard's tone cooled. "Then we settle what we can. We stay put, gather intel, and keep a low profile until we understand the new landscape."

Elara exhaled. "Staying put is a trap."

"Moving blind is worse," Joe said.

Maya forced herself upright. "We stay," she said. Her voice was quiet, but it carried. "For now. We watch. We gather information. We don't make ourselves louder than we already are."

Elara looked like she wanted to argue, but she didn't. Joe nodded once. Richard's posture loosened slightly, as if he accepted a temporary postponement as victory.

Alex's hand left Maya's shoulder, but his presence remained.

They dispersed through the safehouse in uneasy silence. Joe went to the kitchen, already scrolling through muted feeds. Elara moved to a corner near the back door, arms wrapped around herself, eyes fixed on nothing. Richard paced, stopping occasionally to stare at the screens as if he could impose order through scrutiny alone. Alex lingered close to Maya without hovering.

Maya stood alone in the center of the dim room and listened to the hum beneath everything.

It was louder now that no one was speaking.

The Weave didn't care about their arguments. It didn't slow down to let them build consensus. Threads pulled tight across the world, vibrating with new awakenings, new fear, new attention.

Leadership was coming whether she wanted it or not.

The only question was what it would cost her, and what shape it would take when the world forced it into her hands.

Her phone buzzed.

Not a normal vibration. A sharp, stuttering pulse that made the hair on her arms rise.

She looked down at the screen.

BREAKING: LIVE FOOTAGE COMING IN...

The words were still loading, but Maya's awareness had already turned toward the source. A flare in the distance. Not a wobble. Not a near miss.

A thread snapping into alignment with a violent certainty.

Someone, somewhere, had not just leaned toward awakening.

They had crossed it.

3

Hargreaves on Trial

The room had no windows.

That was deliberate. Windows invited distraction. They suggested an outside world where influence might leak in or out. This room existed for one purpose only: judgment.

Victor Hargreaves sat alone at the long table, hands folded neatly atop a thin stack of prepared notes he didn't look at. His suit was immaculate. Dark charcoal, conservative cut, perfectly pressed. His tie lay straight, its knot centered with almost military precision. He looked like a man who understood the language of power and had spoken it fluently for decades.

Around him, senators shuffled papers that already contained conclusions.

Bottled water sat untouched at every seat. No one drank. No one needed the excuse.

The chairwoman cleared her throat. "This hearing is classified and sealed. No electronic devices are permitted. The record will reflect that all members are present."

She fixed her gaze on Hargreaves. "Senator Hargreaves, you are here to answer questions regarding Project HECATE, Silent Protocol, and your unilateral authority over both."

Hargreaves inclined his head slightly. Respectful. Controlled. "I'm prepared to answer."

The first question came from across the table, sharp and unadorned. "Did Project HECATE operate outside congressional authorization?"

"No," Hargreaves said. "It operated under emergency continuance clauses invoked after multiple national security briefings."

"Briefings you led," another senator cut in.

Hargreaves didn't bristle. "Briefings I delivered, yes. Based on intelligence my office collected."

A woman two seats down leaned forward. "Including off book funding streams?"

Hargreaves met her gaze. "Including contingency funds legally available to classified defense initiatives."

The language was precise. Clinical. Every word had been chosen weeks ago.

A senator with a stack of annotated reports tapped the page in front of him. "Let's talk about Silent Protocol. You authorized suppression of information, detention without warrant, and experimental containment measures on U.S. soil. Do you deny that?"

"I deny the characterization," Hargreaves said evenly. "Silent Protocol prevented mass panic during an unprecedented threat environment."

"By violating constitutional protections," the senator replied.

"By preserving order," Hargreaves said. "Those are not mutually exclusive in crisis."

The room shifted. Chairs creaked. Someone exhaled sharply.

Another voice rose, colder. "You don't get to decide that alone."

Hargreaves folded his hands tighter. "Someone had to."

A younger senator, jaw clenched, finally said the word that had been circling the room. "Weaponization."

It landed hard.

"Let's stop pretending," he continued. "You weren't just containing these individuals. You were studying them. Testing thresholds. Exploring applications. Weaponization."

Hargreaves held his gaze. "I was ensuring preparedness."

"For what?" the senator demanded.

"For what comes next," Hargreaves replied.

That split the room cleanly in two.

One side leaned forward, anger sharpening into resolve. Accountability. Arrests. Dismantling HECATE before it became something worse than the threat it claimed to oppose.

The other side stiffened, eyes flicking between reports and Hargreaves as if measuring how much of the dam he represented. Fear lived there. Fear of losing the only structure that had held when the impossible began pressing in.

"You take him out," one senator said quietly, "and what fills the gap?"

Hargreaves seized the opening. "Exactly. You can dismantle HECATE if you wish. But don't confuse removal of leadership with removal of threat. Walkers exist whether we acknowledge them or not. Without coordination, without containment, this becomes chaos."

"Or freedom," someone countered.

Hargreaves shook his head. "Power without oversight destroys itself. History proves that."

He believed it. That was the most dangerous part.

Silent Protocol had worked, in his view. The world had not burned. Markets had not collapsed. Cities had not erupted. He was the dam, and the water was rising.

Then the room changed.

It was not dramatic. No alarms sounded. No lights flickered.

Sound simply fell away.

Not vanished. Diminished. As if the air itself had thickened and refused to carry vibration.

A senator was mid sentence when his voice cut off, mouth still moving. Another leaned forward, confused, then froze as her own breath became loud in her ears.

Heartbeats became knowing things.

Someone scraped a chair back. The sound didn't travel.

Hargreaves felt it instantly.

Pressure. Absence. A signature he recognized from classified reports and sleepless nights. Residual activity, but not localized. Not targeted.

His eyes widened a fraction.

This wasn't caused by anyone in the room.

A man across the table clawed at his throat, convinced he couldn't breathe though his chest was rising and falling. Another bowed her head and tried to pray, lips moving soundlessly, panic blooming in her eyes when she couldn't hear her own words.

Secure recording systems and displays failed all at once.

The silence deepened.

Miles away, Maya Rodriguez gasped.

The surge hit her like a hole punched through the world. Not noise. Not pressure. A void where something should have been. Her knees buckled and Alex caught her before she hit the floor.

"Something's wrong," she whispered, already reaching.

She didn't know where it was. Only that it was large and wrong and dangerous.

She pushed herself outward, stabilizing instinctively, pulling threads back into alignment she could barely see. The effort burned. Her vision narrowed. The void resisted, then shuddered.

Back in the Senate chamber, sound crashed back all at once.

A chair hit the floor. Someone shouted. Voices overlapped in raw confusion. The decorum shattered and barely stitched itself together again.

"What was that?" someone demanded.

No one answered.

The chairwoman slammed her gavel, hands shaking. "This hearing is adjourned. Immediately."

Guards moved in. Senators stood too quickly. Papers scattered.

Hargreaves remained seated for a moment longer, his confidence finally cracking along a hairline fracture.

He stood, smoothing his jacket out of habit, and followed the others out.

Outside, cameras waited. Lights flared. Reporters shouted questions they didn't know were missing the truth by miles.

Hargreaves adjusted his tie. His fingers trembled.

For the first time, he understood that containment was no longer a question of policy.

Hours later, a classified memo circulated through secure channels.

Residual activity detected in secure federal chamber. Source unknown. No Walker presence confirmed.

In the margin, written by an unsteady hand, someone added:

If this can happen here, it can happen anywhere.

4

The First Public Walker

The heat didn't belong in Paris.

"It was unseasonably hot even for August. The city should have been easing toward cool mornings and warm afternoons. Instead, the heat clung to the streets like a wet cloth, settling in the spaces between buildings and refusing to move. It turned the stone facades pale and tired and made the whole city feel vaguely impatient with itself.

At Châtelet–Les Halles, impatience was already a way of life.

People streamed through the concourse in steady waves, flowing around pillars, kiosks, and one another with the practiced precision of commuters who had learned that hesitation was a kind of weakness. Shoes slapped against tile. Train announcements echoed from somewhere overhead, swallowed and repeated by the geometry of the place. A musician near the escalators played the same three chords over and over, trying to catch a pocket of attention before the crowd carried it away.

No one was looking for miracles.

They were looking for their platform. Their connection. Their next obligation.

Claire Moreau pushed through the crowd with a tote bag biting into her shoulder and a folder tucked under one arm. She'd left her apartment earlier than usual and still felt late. The metro had been delayed, the streets above were clogged, and her phone had already buzzed twice with messages from her supervisor asking where she was.

She didn't answer. She hated the way a phone could turn a human life into a leash.

Her steps were quick and automatic, her gaze scanning signs without really seeing them. She smelled perfume and sweat and the faint metallic tang of the rails. She heard a hundred conversations in fragments and none of them mattered.

Then the pressure behind her eyes tightened.

It wasn't pain at first. It was more like the sensation you got when weather changed too fast, when air pressure dropped and your body noticed before your mind did. Claire slowed without meaning to. Her hand rose to her temple, fingers pressing lightly as if she could push the feeling back where it belonged.

Two people near her did the same thing.

A man in a suit stopped and rubbed at his forehead as if he'd forgotten why he was walking. A teenager with earbuds in blinked hard and turned his head, one earbud dangling loose, his expression faintly confused.

Claire looked around. Nothing looked different. The crowd continued moving. The announcements continued repeating. The musician's chords continued cycling.

But something felt wrong in the way the air sat against her skin.

She shifted her tote bag and kept going.

A bank of glass storefronts lined the concourse, reflecting the crowd in long, distorted panels. Claire's reflection moved with her, but it seemed to lag by a fraction. The angle was strange. That had to be it. Bad lighting. Heat. The glass warping the image.

She glanced away and then back.

Her reflection flickered.

Just once, like a skipped frame.

Claire stopped again. It was a small hesitation, the kind people corrected around without comment. She stared at the glass panel, heart beating faster for no reason she could explain.

The reflection steadied. She saw herself clearly, flushed from the heat, hair pulled back too quickly, eyes slightly narrowed in irritation. Behind her, faces moved in restless streams.

Nothing was wrong.

And yet the pressure behind her eyes didn't fade. It deepened, as if something had leaned closer.

A child on a man's shoulders pointed upward and laughed, not at anything visible, but as if delighted by an idea. The man glanced around, distracted, and then kept walking. A woman near the ticket machines paused, her lips parting as if she'd heard her name in a crowded room.

Claire felt the faint urge to look up, even though there was nothing above but ceiling, signage, and fluorescent lights.

She resisted it. She had learned, like everyone else, that curiosity was an indulgence.

She started walking again, moving with the flow toward the escalators, when a couple beside her argued softly in rapid French. Their words didn't make sense at first because Claire couldn't catch the thread of them. Then she realized she wasn't failing to hear. Their voices were clear.

It was the meaning that kept slipping away.

She frowned and looked sharply at them. The couple kept talking, unaware, but their sentences seemed to loop back on themselves. Like the same thought being spoken through different mouths.

Claire blinked hard. The pressure behind her eyes pulsed.

She told herself she was overtired. She told herself it was the heat. She told herself she needed water and sleep and fewer late nights staring at spreadsheets until the numbers swam.

Her phone buzzed again.

She didn't check it. She could feel the vibration through the tote bag, a small insistence against her ribs. That simple act of refusal made her feel briefly in control.

Then the lights above the concourse flickered.

It was not a full blackout. Not even close. Just a brief dimming, a stutter in the fluorescent line. People barely noticed. A few heads lifted, and then the crowd continued, smooth and mindless.

But Claire felt it like a hand pressed against the back of her skull.

The pressure became a tight band. Her stomach turned. For a moment she had the strangest sensation that the concourse was not a place but a throat, and the city was holding its breath.

She swallowed and tasted metal.

She stopped again, and this time the people around her stopped too, not all at once, but in small pockets. A ripple of hesitation passed through the crowd.

Someone muttered, "Vous sentez ça?"

Do you feel that?

Claire didn't answer because she didn't know what "that" was, only that it was everywhere now, thin and invisible and impossible to ignore.

A man near the escalator took off his glasses and rubbed his eyes. A woman pressed a palm to her sternum and looked down at it as if her own body had betrayed her. The teenager with the earbuds pulled them out entirely, his face pale.

The musician stopped playing.

That was the first true sign that something had changed.

The three chords died, and the concourse should have filled the space with noise. Instead, the silence that followed felt too clean, too sharp, as if sound itself had stepped back.

Claire's throat tightened. She looked around, searching faces for an explanation.

In the far reflection of the glass storefront, she saw a man standing still amid the flow. He wasn't remarkable. Average height. Dark hair.

Work clothes. He held a paper cup of coffee in one hand, a strap over his shoulder, the expression of someone waiting for a train and thinking about anything except the moment he was in.

Yet Claire's eyes locked on him.

Not because he looked dangerous.

Because the flicker in the glass seemed to gather around him, as if the distortion had found a center.

She stared, and the pressure behind her eyes spiked, sharp enough to make her wince.

The man in the reflection turned his head slightly, not toward her, but toward something she couldn't see. His expression shifted, just a fraction, as if he'd felt a change in the air.

Claire's breath caught.

The crowd resumed moving in uneven waves, but Claire didn't. She couldn't. Her feet felt heavy. The tiled floor seemed suddenly too solid, too close, as if it were bracing itself.

Somewhere deep in the station, a train horn sounded.

It should have been ordinary.

Instead, it felt like a warning.

Claire tightened her grip on her folder and took a step forward, eyes still on the man she couldn't stop watching. The heat pressed in. The lights hummed. The reflections flickered again, faintly, like the world trying to decide how to display itself.

The first scream cut through the concourse like a snapped wire.

It came from the upper level, sharp and raw, and for a heartbeat no one understood it. People looked up out of irritation rather than fear. Paris was loud. Someone always shouted. Someone was always late or angry or drunk.

Then the sound of impact followed.

Metal slammed into concrete with a force that carried through the floor. The vibration rolled down the escalators and into the concourse, rattling signs and sending a shiver through the glass storefronts. A second scream rose, then a dozen more, voices overlapping into something frantic and formless.

Claire felt it in her chest before she saw it.

A delivery van burst through the barrier at the edge of the upper plaza, tires shrieking as it fishtailed sideways. One headlight hung loose, flashing wildly. The front end clipped a support column, sparks spraying as metal scraped stone. The van lurched, bounced, and came straight for the escalators.

People scattered.

The crowd that had moved with such practiced rhythm moments before exploded into chaos. Bodies surged in every direction. Someone fell. Someone else tripped over them. The air filled with shouts in French and English, warnings and curses blending into noise.

Phones came out instantly.

Hands rose even as people ran, instinct overriding sense. Screens lit up, framing the impossible angle of the van as it tore across the plaza toward the heart of the station.

Claire froze.

She didn't know why. Fear should have driven her backward, pushed her into motion like everyone else. Instead, her eyes locked on the van as if the moment had narrowed to that single, terrible line of movement.

The driver's door flew open.

The man inside was slumped over the wheel, unmoving.

The van hit the edge of the escalator.

The impact tore loose a section of railing and sent shards of metal skidding across the concourse. The vehicle tipped, weight shifting, momentum carrying it forward. Gravity took over, relentless and blind.

It was going to fall.

Claire saw it with a clarity that burned. The van would drop down the escalator shaft. It would crush anyone still trapped below. There was no time. No warning loud enough.

Claire's stomach tightened, her mouth watering in that nasty, unmistakable way that came right before you got sick.

Across the concourse, the man from the reflection stood directly in the van's path.

He had not run.

He stared at the oncoming vehicle, eyes wide, coffee cup slipping from his hand and spilling across the tile. The strap of his bag slid off his shoulder. His mouth opened, not in a scream, but in shock, as if his body had not yet accepted what his eyes already knew.

Claire shouted something she couldn't remember afterward.

The man lifted his hands.

It was not a gesture of command or defiance. It was reflex, the instinctive motion of someone bracing for impact, palms up as if he could push the world away.

The van stopped.

Not slowly.

Not violently.

It stopped as if it had struck an invisible wall.

The front wheels lifted slightly off the ground, suspension screaming under the sudden halt. The back end swung forward, momentum twisting the vehicle sideways, but it did not fall. It hung there, tilted and trembling, balanced on nothing that anyone could see.

A shockwave rippled outward.

Loose debris lifted from the floor and froze in the air. Broken glass halted mid tumble. A dropped phone spun once and stayed suspended, its screen still recording.

Sound collapsed.

The screams died into nothing. The crash that should have followed never came. The concourse existed in a pocket of unnatural quiet, punctuated only by the ragged breathing of the man holding his hands out in front of him.

Light bent around him.

It wasn't a glow. It wasn't fire. It was distortion, the air warping as if reality itself had softened in his presence. The edges of his outline blurred, glassy and wrong, like heat rising off asphalt but sharper, cleaner.

The crowd stared.

No one moved.

Phones remained raised, arms locked, recording hands shaking. Someone sobbed softly. Someone whispered a prayer. Someone else whispered a name, trying to label what they were seeing before it could change again.

The man looked down at his hands.

They were shaking violently now.

"I didn't," he said, voice breaking into the silence. "I didn't mean to."

The pressure inside Claire's skull spiked so hard she cried out. It felt like standing too close to a live wire, like every nerve in her body had leaned forward at once.

The van creaked.

The sound was small, but it shattered the stillness like glass breaking.

Fear surged back into the space, raw and overwhelming. The man's breathing hitched. His focus wavered. For an instant, the distortion around him flared brighter, then collapsed inward.

The van dropped.

Not all the way.

It slammed sideways into the escalator housing, crumpling metal and sending sparks showering across the concourse. The impact knocked people backward. Sound came roaring back in a wave of screams, alarms, and shattering glass.

The man stumbled.

The world rushed him all at once.

Claire sagged against a pillar, heart hammering so hard it hurt. Her phone was in her hand, screen glowing, recording everything she had just watched.

She didn't remember taking it out.

Around her, hundreds of screens told the same story from a hundred angles.

The moment had already escaped.

And the city, stunned and breathless, had just witnessed something it could never unsee.

The screaming didn't stop all at once.

It thinned. It frayed at the edges. Panic unraveled into something smaller and sharper as the crowd's momentum failed. People skidded to a halt where they stood, breath tearing in and out of them, eyes fixed on the same impossible point.

The man stood there with his hands still raised.

The van lay twisted against the escalator housing, metal groaning as it settled. Steam hissed from the crumpled hood. Sparks flickered and died. Nothing moved that should not have been able to move.

No one rushed him.

No one rushed anyone.

The silence that followed was not the clean absence from before. This one was crowded with disbelief. It pressed in close, thick with the sound of breathing, with the soft clatter of something small finally dropping to the floor.

A phone slipped from someone's hand and hit the tile. The screen cracked with a sharp, ordinary sound that felt too loud. Another followed. Then another. People stared at the devices as if they had betrayed them.

Claire realized her own arm was raised.

Her phone was still recording.

She lowered it without looking, fingers numb, and for a moment she simply stood there, swaying slightly, her shoulder pressed to the cool stone of the pillar. She swallowed hard and forced herself to keep her eyes open.

The man's hands shook.

He lowered them slowly, like someone afraid of startling a wild animal. His palms hovered at chest height, fingers splayed, uncertain what shape they were allowed to make. His face had gone gray beneath the distortion of light that still bent faintly around him.

He looked down at himself again, then up at the people staring at him.

Their faces were wrong.

Not hostile. Not yet. Just stripped bare. Awe and terror sat side by side in their eyes, inseparable now. Someone sobbed quietly. Someone laughed once, sharp and hysterical, then clapped a hand over their mouth.

A woman a few steps from him sank down onto the floor without taking her eyes off his face. Her knees hit hard, but she didn't seem to notice.

"What are you?" someone whispered.

The words were barely louder than breath, but they carried.

They hung there, unanswered, heavier than the wreckage.

The man flinched as if struck. His eyes darted toward the sound, then away again, scanning the crowd like he was searching for an exit that hadn't existed moments ago. His chest rose and fell too fast. Sweat darkened the collar of his shirt.

"I don't know," he said.

The words came out rough, cracked at the edges. He shook his head, once, then again, harder, like denial might reset whatever had gone wrong inside him.

"I don't know," he repeated. "I didn't mean to. I just... it was going to fall."

No one contradicted him.

No one reassured him either.

Claire saw the moment the truth reached him. It wasn't the wreckage or the silence or even the phones rising again as people remembered themselves. It was the look on their faces when they realized he was just a man.

Terrified. Shaking. Standing where anyone else might have been standing.

Hands began to rise again, slower this time.

Phones came back up, lifted with care, as if the air itself might break. Screens framed him from every angle. A drone buzzed somewhere overhead, its operator unseen, its camera already streaming.

The man noticed.

His breath caught. He looked directly at one of the phones, eyes wide, reflected back at himself through glass and pixels and distance. For a heartbeat, he looked like he might bolt.

He didn't.

He stood there, rooted in place, hands hovering uselessly at his sides, caught between the instinct to run and the paralyzing certainty that running would make everything worse.

Claire felt something in her chest twist painfully.

This was the moment, she realized. Not the stopping of the van. Not the bending of light. This.

The world seeing him see them.

Somewhere far back in the crowd, sirens wailed. Boots pounded. Authority was coming, loud and late.

The man heard it too.

His eyes lifted, unfocused, and for just a second he looked impossibly small, a single human shape at the center of something no one knew how to name yet.

He did not flee.

Not yet.

The quiet didn't last.

It couldn't.

The first sound that returned was not a scream or an alarm. It was a notification chime. Then another. Then dozens, overlapping in a soft electronic chorus that cut through the stunned stillness like insects waking at dusk.

Phones vibrated in hands that had forgotten to lower them.

Claire realized she was still recording when her wrist began to ache. Her arm trembled, muscles locked from holding the device too long in the same position. She lowered it without stopping the video, breath shallow, eyes never leaving the man standing at the center of the wreckage.

Around her, others did the same.

Some people had dropped their phones when the van hit. They stared at the cracked screens on the floor for a heartbeat, as if the devices had betrayed them, then scrambled to pick them up again. A woman knelt beside a shattered case, fingers shaking as she swiped at the glass, relief breaking across her face when the screen lit back up and the red dot appeared.

Live.

Someone laughed. It was a thin, disbelieving sound that broke off into a sob.

The man with his hands lowered now stood frozen, eyes darting from face to face as if trying to understand what kind of crowd he'd stepped into. He looked smaller without the distortion around him, just another commuter in a wrinkled shirt and scuffed shoes, surrounded by twisted metal and staring lenses.

Cameras ringed him.

Not arranged. Not intentional. Just everywhere.

A phone mounted on a stabilizer hovered at shoulder height, its owner backing away while keeping the frame centered. Another device lay on the floor, screen angled upward, capturing the man from below with the van looming behind him like a collapsed beast. A drone buzzed overhead, small and sleek, drifting into position as its operator somewhere above realized what he was seeing and adjusted for altitude.

The sound of rotors joined the noise.

News helicopters arrived in a rush of displaced air, circling too low, too fast. They hadn't prevented anything. They'd only come to witness it. Camera booms swung out over open doors. Lenses zoomed in hard, locking onto the impossible geometry of the scene.

Red lights blinked.

Feeds went live.

Claire's phone grew warm in her hand. The comment bar at the bottom of the screen filled so fast she couldn't read it. Hearts and symbols flooded upward in a blur of color. Her signal indicator flickered, strained under the weight of a thousand identical uploads clawing their way into the network at once.

Somewhere in the station, an automated announcement began to repeat evacuation instructions in a calm, neutral voice. It played beneath the chaos, irrelevant and ignored.

Clips broke free from their creators almost instantly.

A wide shot from the upper level hit the internet first, shaky and breathless, framed by a man shouting prayers in the background. Seconds later, a cleaner angle followed from a news camera, stabilized and professional, zooming tight on the man's face as he stared at his hands like they belonged to someone else.

A drone feed layered over both, the escalator shaft and crumpled van visible from above, the frozen moment already replaying itself from angles no human eye had held at the time.

Algorithms took over.

The footage tagged itself. It clustered. It cross referenced identical timestamps, identical distortions, identical impossible frames. What should have been noise sharpened into signal as systems built to recognize pattern found something they could not discard.

Within minutes, the same clip appeared with different captions in different languages.

Paris. Châtelet. Miracle. Hoax. Terror attack. Angel. Weapon.

Claire watched her own video vanish from her screen and reappear, stripped of context, cropped tighter, slowed down, annotated by strangers she would never meet. Someone had circled the man in red. Someone else had added text and arrows. Another version played his voice on loop.

"I didn't mean to."

The words spread faster than the image.

Sirens wailed at last, echoing through the station tunnels as police and emergency crews fought their way through the jammed streets above. It was already too late. Whatever authority might have contained the moment had arrived after the moment had decided to belong to everyone.

Claire lowered her phone completely, fingers numb.

She looked around and saw the same expression on dozens of faces. Awe had burned off, leaving something harder behind. Possession. Fear. Certainty.

This wasn't a story waiting to be told anymore.

It was already being told, reshaped and multiplied with every second that passed.

And no one was blinking.

Maya felt it before any alert could reach her.

She was standing in the kitchen of the safehouse with a mug of coffee cooling untouched between her hands, watching dust drift through a sliver of morning light that leaked around the edge of a curtain. The room was quiet in the way it only became when everyone else was sleeping or pretending to be. For a few fragile minutes, the Weave had been a distant pressure instead of a roar.

Then it hit.

The sensation tore through her awareness like a struck chord, sharp and perfectly tuned, vibrating through layers she had not known existed. It was not a flare or a surge the way earlier awakenings had been. This was cleaner. Brighter. So strong it stole her breath.

Maya gasped and the mug slipped from her fingers, shattering on the floor.

She staggered back against the counter as the harmonic spike rippled outward, not localized to any single node she could dampen or isolate. It spread in all directions at once, a wave traveling through the lattice beneath the world with terrifying clarity. She felt it in her teeth, in her spine, in the place behind her eyes where the Weave always pressed when it wanted to be noticed.

"Oh no," she whispered.

She reached instinctively, trying to do what she always did. Narrow the channel. Soften the edges. Pull the noise into something manageable.

There was nothing to narrow.

The signal did not come from a place she could touch. It came from everywhere that mattered, riding the attention of millions of minds snapping into alignment around the same impossible image. Cameras. Fear. Awe. Belief. The Weave answered all of it at once.

Maya slid down the cabinet and ended up sitting on the floor amid shards of ceramic and spreading coffee. Her hands shook as she braced them against her knees, breathing hard, riding out the vibration as it tore through her.

This one's different.

The realization settled with cold certainty.

Previous awakenings had been quiet enough to blur, to dismiss, to smother under explanation and denial. This one had been witnessed. Framed. Shared. Fed back into the world through machines that did not forget and minds that did not want to.

She felt the resonance continue long after the initial spike passed. The Weave did not fall silent. It rang, a deep metallic hum that lingered beneath everything, like a bell struck too hard to stop. Each echo pulled at distant threads, nudging them closer to alignment, closer to the edge.

Alex appeared in the doorway, already moving before she could call out.

"Maya?" he said.

She looked up at him, eyes wide, breath still unsteady. "It's out," she said. "Whatever happened, it's everywhere."

He crossed the room and knelt beside her, careful not to touch her until she nodded. When his hand finally settled on her shoulder, it grounded her just enough to keep the floor from tilting.

"Can you dampen it?" he asked.

She shook her head once. "No. This isn't a sound you can turn down. It's a chorus."

She could feel it still, the way attention itself had become a conduit. The image. The fear. The sudden need to name what had no name yet. It all fed back into the Weave, tightening it, stressing it, making it ring harder.

"This one can't be hidden," she said. "It can't be quieted. The world saw it happen."

Alex didn't argue. He didn't need to. He could see it in her face, in the way her gaze kept drifting as if tracking something just beyond the walls.

The hum persisted, low and relentless.

Maya closed her eyes and listened, not because she wanted to, but because the Weave demanded it. Somewhere far away, threads were still vibrating in response, answering the shock with movements of their own.

This wasn't just an awakening.

It was a signal.

And the world had heard it.

The footage reached the secure rooms before anyone had finished deciding what it meant.

In a windowless operations center beneath a government complex in Brussels, a wall of screens flickered to life almost in unison. Analysts who had been tracking social feeds for weeks straightened in their chairs as the same clip appeared again and again, pulled from different sources, different angles, different hands.

A van hung in the air.

Not metaphorically. Not blurred by motion or corrupted by compression. It hung there, tilted and impossible, surrounded by frozen debris and a crowd caught mid panic.

A woman in a tailored suit leaned forward, palms flat on the table. "Pause it."

The image froze. The man at the center of the distortion stood with his hands raised, face twisted in shock and fear.

"That's not CGI," someone said quietly.

"No," another replied. "And it's not a drone trick either. We've got live streams from six independent civilian sources, plus two traffic cameras and a private security feed from a retail chain above the concourse."

"Run it again."

The clip restarted. Sound filled the room, screams collapsing into silence as the van stopped dead. The distortion rippled outward, bending light in a way no software could fake convincingly at that scale.

A man at the far end of the table rubbed his face. "Jesus Christ."

Phones began ringing almost immediately.

Encrypted lines lit up. Secure tablets chimed. A dozen conversations started at once, voices overlapping in controlled panic.

In Washington, a senior advisor stared at the same footage in a Situation Room annex, jaw tight. "I want options," he said. "Right now."

"You're looking at them," someone replied. "Containment is already compromised. It's viral."

"Then discredit it," another voice snapped. "Get ahead of the narrative. Call it mass hysteria. Experimental vehicle failure. Anything."

"That won't hold," a third said. "The physics don't lie. And neither do a million recordings."

"Then secure the individual," the advisor said. "Before this spreads further."

"In France," someone pointed out. "On foreign soil. In a transit hub."

Silence fell for half a second as that sank in.

Across the Atlantic, a general in a secure NATO briefing room watched the clip loop again, arms folded tight across his chest. "If that's a weapon, we're behind," he said.

"If it's a person," a civilian official replied, "we're worse than behind. We're blind."

Calls spiked across continents.

Paris to Washington. Washington to Berlin. Berlin to New Delhi. Embassies lit up with urgent requests and carefully worded denials. No one wanted to be first to say the word Walker out loud, but no one could avoid circling it.

Orders went out and contradicted one another within minutes.

Local authorities were told to secure the scene and preserve evidence.

Intelligence agencies were told to suppress dissemination without provoking backlash.

Media liaisons were instructed to prepare statements that did not yet exist.

Legal teams demanded clarification on jurisdiction that no one could provide.

Every protocol on the books assumed secrecy, isolation, and time.

There was none.

A senior French official slammed his hand against a conference table. "You can't arrest a phenomenon," he said. "And you can't pretend this didn't happen. It happened in front of everyone."

"Then we find him," another said. "We control him."

"And if he panics again?" someone asked. "If this happens twice?"

No one answered.

The footage kept playing.

Each loop added more data. More reactions. More analysis layered over fear. Somewhere in the noise, the realization took hold that this was not a single incident but a precedent.

Containment required borders that no longer mattered.

Discrediting required doubt that no longer existed.

Securing the individual required leverage no one had.

A woman in Brussels stared at the frozen image and said what everyone else was thinking but refusing to voice.

"There's no protocol for this."

Around the world, in rooms designed to impose order on chaos, officials watched the same impossible moment unfold and understood the same terrible truth.

The system was moving and it was already behind.

He tried to move.

It wasn't a plan. It wasn't even a decision. It was the animal part of him taking over the moment his mind caught up to what his body had done. He took one step backward, then another, eyes wide, shoulders hunched as if he expected the air itself to strike him.

The crowd shifted with him.

Not in sympathy. In instinct.

People leaned away, a ripple of motion that widened into a ring, leaving him more exposed with every inch he retreated. Phones tracked him like sights. Lenses followed the tremor in his hands, the sweat on his face, the wild panic that made him look less like a miracle and more like a trapped man.

Sirens wailed louder now. Close enough to matter.

That sound broke something.

His breathing hitched and the distortion around him sharpened. It snapped into focus like a tightened wire. The air thickened. The lights above the concourse flared, dimmed, then flared again, buzzing with a harsh electrical whine.

A screen on a nearby kiosk went black.

Then every screen followed.

For a heartbeat the concourse was lit only by emergency strips and the pale glow of hundreds of phones. That glow stuttered. Bars dropped. Streams froze. Comment feeds stopped mid sentence. For an instant it looked as if the world itself had tried to shut its eyes.

Then the surge hit.

Claire felt it as a pressure wave, not a sound, not a blast, but a sudden shove that made her stumble sideways into the pillar. Her vision blurred at the edges. People cried out as the air seemed to lurch. A man near the escalators vomited onto the tile, one hand clawing at his throat as if he could force his breath to behave.

The commuter at the center of it all doubled over.

He squeezed his eyes shut and clenched his fists, and the distortion around him flashed bright enough to make people recoil. Loose debris that had settled back to the floor lifted again. Not gracefully. Not controlled. It rattled upward as if yanked by a violent hand.

Someone screamed his name.

Claire didn't know how they knew it. Maybe they didn't. Maybe it was just the human need to assign a name to what terrified them.

The man looked up with an expression that was pure panic.

"I can't," he said, voice cracking. "I can't stop it."

That did it.

Awe turned to fear in the space of a breath.

People surged backward, tripping over each other, shoving, cursing, crying. Phones dropped again, not out of disbelief this time but out of the need to run. The ring around him broke into chaos.

Security pushed in from one side, shouting orders that no one heard. Police followed close behind, faces hard, hands already on weapons, eyes locked on the man as if he were a threat they could aim at.

He flinched at the sight of them.

The air snapped.

Every overhead light went out at once.

The concourse plunged into a dim, emergency glow. The buzzing of electricity faded into a thick, unnatural quiet that swallowed voices as if sound could not travel cleanly anymore. Tech failed in a wave. Radios hissed and died. Body cameras blinked out. A rolling blackout moved through the station like a living thing.

Claire tried to shout but her voice came out wrong, muffled, swallowed by the pressure in the air.

The man turned and ran.

He didn't run like a hero escaping a crowd.

He ran like a frightened animal fleeing a fire.

He shoved through the scattering commuters and disappeared into the smoke and shadows of a side corridor just as a second surge hit, weaker than the first but sharp enough to send another wave of panic through the station.

By the time anyone pushed after him, he was gone.

All that remained was the wreckage, the dead screens, and the recordings already loose in the world.

It took minutes for the footage to cross borders.

It took hours for it to harden into myth.

The first clips were raw and shaky, uploaded with captions that sounded like prayers or accusations.

Then the edits began.

A slowed down loop of the van stopping midair with the words PROOF OF GOD stamped across the frame in bright text.

A grainy version with glitch overlays and a narrator insisting it was a government psy-op, a staged event to justify new surveillance laws.

A dark remix set to ominous music, the distortion around the man made to look like a portal, captions screaming END TIMES in three languages.

A clean, polished montage with cinematic cuts, calling it ASCEN-SION, framing the man's raised hands as the opening of a new era.

Hashtags formed like blood in water.

#ParisMiracle

#FalseFlag
#JudgmentDay
#Chosen
#KillIt
#ProtectHim

People who had never cared about anything beyond their own lives woke up and picked a side before breakfast.

Fan art appeared by noon. Stylized silhouettes of a man holding up a van as if he were Atlas. Digital paintings of glowing eyes and angel wings that had not existed in the footage. Prayer circles formed in comment sections. Threats stacked beneath them.

Some demanded to worship him.

Some demanded to cage him.

Some demanded to execute him.

And in between, millions of ordinary people watched the same impossible moment on loop and felt something inside them shift, not into understanding, but into certainty.

Back at the safehouse, Joe watched the feeds without sound and felt the shape of the world changing.

He sat close to the screens, forearms on his knees, jaw tight. The room behind him was dim and tense. Maya was somewhere out of sight, breathing through whatever storm still pressed behind her eyes. Alex moved quietly through the space like a man refusing to let panic take root. Elara stood near the back door, arms wrapped around herself, heat contained by sheer will. Richard watched from the corner, face hard and unreadable.

Joe didn't need volume. The captions told him enough. The faces in the comments told him more.

"They're not asking if it's real anymore," he said.

No one answered. They didn't have to.

Joe pointed at one clip, then another. The same footage, two different stories.

"They're deciding what it means," he said. "And they're doing it fast."

Maya's voice came from the hallway, strained but steady. "What are they saying?"

Joe's mouth tightened. "Everything."

He leaned closer, eyes scanning the flood.

"Some people want to kneel," he said. "Some want to burn him alive. And the ones in the middle are disappearing."

Alex stepped behind him and looked at the screen, silent.

Joe exhaled hard. "It's splitting clean," he said. "Weave worshippers and end times fear. Saints and monsters. No middle ground forming."

Richard finally spoke, voice cold. "That's what happens when power goes public."

Maya stepped into the room, face pale, eyes too bright. She looked at the frozen frame on the main screen.

The man stood with his hands raised. The air around him bent. The van hovered mid fall. The crowd blurred in the background, caught between terror and wonder.

An icon.

A symbol.

A weapon, depending on who was looking.

Maya stared at it and felt the Weave hum beneath her skin, still ringing faintly, as if the planet itself could not stop vibrating from what the world had witnessed.

"This can't be undone," she said.

Joe didn't look away from the screen. "No," he said. "It can't."

The viral clip froze on the man's terrified face, hands lifted as if he could hold the world back.

Across the planet, the same image played in bedrooms, boardrooms, basements, churches, and command centers.

It became a banner.

It became a warning.

It became whatever the viewer needed it to be.

Maya understood, with a calm that felt like grief, that the world didn't just witness a Walker.

It chose what a Walker meant.

Her phone buzzed.

Not a normal vibration. A sharp, stuttering pulse that made the hair on her arms rise. The alert loaded slowly, as if even the network hesitated.

LIVE FOOTAGE QUESTIONABLE EVENT REPORTED...

Joe leaned forward. "Where?"

Maya didn't answer. She didn't need the words.

She could already feel it.

A new strain. A new wobble. A new pressure point flaring across the lattice.

Not confirmation.

A question, rippling outward through the world like an echo that refused to die.

Is it happening again?

Fragment 7.4

Fragment 7.4: On Human Re-Attunement

(Recovered from the Black Archive. Attribution uncertain. Annotations added post-Convergence.)

It was once believed that the Weave chose.
That belief was comforting. It implied order, intent, and the mercy of limitation.
It allowed early observers to frame emergence as anomaly rather than inheritance.

This was incorrect.

The Weave does not grant. It resonates.

What Convergence revealed was not the appearance of power, but the removal of silence.
Humanity did not receive something new. It remembered something old, long buried beneath
generations of disuse and denial.

Re-attunement spreads not in leaps, but in gradients.
Most humans now exist in a state of ambient resonance. They hear echoes where none should be.
They feel pressure without cause. They recognize patterns they cannot name and respond to
symbols before reason intervenes. These individuals do not command the Weave, yet they amplify it
through attention, fear, belief, and collective alignment.

A smaller population displays the instability observed after the First Public Manifestation.
These individuals, designated Walkers by early classification systems, are capable of direct
interaction with the greater Weave. Their manifestations vary in scope and expression, but all
share a defining trait: reaction precedes understanding.

Most do not survive intact.
Some burn out.
Some fracture.
Some are consumed by Echo.
Some are taken by institution that mistake control for safety.

✶ Archivist's Margin Note.

The term "Walker" is increasingly insufficient. It describes function, not cost.
Future classifications must account for endurance, anchoring capacity, and
resistance to mass resonance feedback. Containment has already failed.
Instruction may yet succeed.

5

Maya's Overload

The safehouse was quiet in the wrong way.

Not calm. Not restful. Just muted, like someone had pressed a hand over the world's mouth and expected it to hold. Screens glowed without sound. Phones lay face down on tables. Even the air felt cautious, as if it were waiting to see what would break next.

Maya sat on the edge of the couch with her elbows on her knees and her hands clasped together so tightly her fingers ached. The pressure behind her eyes had not gone away since Paris. It had changed shape, flattened into something constant and heavy, like a ceiling lowered an inch too far.

She could feel the Weave everywhere.

Not as power. Not as threads she could pluck or pull. As presence. As weight. As a constant awareness that the world beneath the world was stretched tight and vibrating with attention.

Joe watched her from across the room, saying nothing. Elara stood near the back door, arms folded, heat contained but restless. Richard pretended to read something on a tablet he hadn't scrolled in ten minutes. Alex hovered close without hovering, seated on the floor near Maya's feet like he could catch her if gravity decided to get creative.

"I can dampen it," Maya said.

Her voice sounded steadier than she felt.

Alex looked up immediately. "You shouldn't."

"I didn't say shut it down," she replied. "Just soften it. Take the edge off. Buy time."

"Buy time for who?" Elara asked.

"For everyone," Maya said. "For the ones who don't know what's happening to them yet."

Joe exhaled slowly. "Maya, the feeds are still climbing. That Paris clip alone is being mirrored faster than we can track. You trying to quiet that is like trying to lower the tide with a bucket."

"I know," she said. "But if I don't try, it keeps building. The noise feeds itself."

Alex shifted closer. "You're not a breaker box. You don't have to absorb the surge just because it's there."

Maya met his eyes. "If I can ease even a fraction of it, I have to."

She didn't wait for agreement.

She closed her eyes and reached.

At first, it felt familiar. The Weave responded the way it always had, opening under awareness, brightening at the edges. She anchored herself to the room, to her breath, to the solid weight of the couch beneath her.

Then the world rushed in.

Not in layers. All at once.

Thousands of points flared across her awareness, not as voices or faces but as tensions. Tight places. Fractures forming before they knew they were fractures. People leaning toward something they didn't understand, drawn by fear or awe or the need to make sense of what they had seen.

She felt them everywhere.

A woman in Manila clutching her phone with shaking hands as she replayed the Paris footage for the tenth time. A man in Lagos standing on a balcony at dawn, convinced the air itself was watching him. A teenager in São Paulo who had stopped sleeping because every time she closed her eyes she heard a hum just below hearing.

The Weave did not narrow.

It widened.

The pressure behind Maya's eyes intensified, spreading down her neck and into her shoulders. Her breath shortened without her noticing. The safehouse faded at the edges as her awareness stretched too far, too fast.

"Maya," Alex said.

She couldn't answer.

The harmonics began to interfere with one another, not cancelling out but reinforcing. Attention fed resonance. Resonance fed attention. The system looped back on itself, tightening like a pulled knot.

She tried to pull back.

The Weave did not follow.

A sharp spike ripped through her awareness, clean and blinding. Maya gasped as the floor lurched beneath her, the room tilting sideways as if gravity had decided to renegotiate terms.

Then she was falling.

Alex caught her before she hit the floor, but the Weave didn't care that her body had stopped moving. It kept rushing through her, unfiltered and relentless.

This wasn't exhaustion.

This was overload.

Maya was dimly aware of voices shouting her name, of hands on her shoulders, of the couch edge digging into her back as Alex lowered her down. She was aware enough to know she was still connected and unable to disengage.

Panic flared, sharp and useless.

Then something shifted.

The pressure didn't vanish. It separated.

The noise thinned, not quieter but ordered, like water redirected into channels instead of flooding the room. Maya sucked in a ragged breath and felt the sharp edge of the surge blunt just enough for her to stay conscious.

Alex's hand was on her shoulder, steady and grounding.

He wasn't blocking the Weave.

He was sorting it.

"I don't know what I'm doing," he said under his breath.

But his voice was calm.

Maya's awareness adjusted around his presence and she realized he wasn't resisting the flow. He was acting like a baffle, letting the strongest signals pass through while bleeding off the excess into something harmless, something diffuse.

She could see again.

Not the room. The lattice beneath it.

Dozens of forming Walkers flickered into clarity. Some were barely leaning toward awareness, skimming the surface. Some were already cracking, overwhelmed by sensations they had no framework to survive.

And threaded through them was something else.

Not emergent. Not human.

It didn't push. It didn't pull.

It watched.

The presence moved through the awakenings like a shadow cast by no object, selective and patient. It lingered where fear spiked highest, where attention pooled thickest.

Maya recognized it with a chill that had nothing to do with temperature.

The Unmaking.

It wasn't arriving.

It was already here.

"Maya," Alex said, sharper now. "We have to pull you back."

She tried to speak and failed. Her awareness was caught on that watching presence, on the way it leaned closer without touching, content to observe.

Alex didn't wait.

He pulled.

Not gently.

The connection snapped shut like a slammed door. The Weave recoiled, ordered streams collapsing into silence with a force that rattled her bones.

Maya screamed as sensation crashed back into her body all at once. Pain flared behind her eyes. Her stomach lurched. She curled in on herself, gasping, shaking, alive.

The room came back into focus slowly.

Alex knelt beside her, breathing hard, eyes unfocused like he was still listening to something she could no longer hear.

Joe hovered a step back, face pale. Elara's hands were clenched at her sides, heat leaking in sharp, controlled pulses. Richard stared at Alex with something like calculation mixed with fear.

Maya lay there for a long moment, letting the world settle.

"I can't do that again," she said finally.

Alex nodded. "You shouldn't."

She turned her head to look at him. "You filtered it."

His brow furrowed. "I didn't mean to. I just... separated it. Like static from signal."

Maya swallowed hard. "You didn't just ground me. You redirected the Weave."

Alex didn't argue. He didn't look pleased.

"That thing," she said quietly. "It was watching."

Joe stiffened. "Watching who?"

"All of them," Maya said. "Through them."

Silence settled over the room, heavier than before.

Alex sat back on his heels, eyes closing briefly. "It noticed," he said.

Maya felt the truth of it settle into her bones.

The Weave was quieter now, but tighter. Like a drawn bow.

Somewhere beneath the world, something waited.

And it was paying attention.

6

Birth of the Quiet Choir

The city still knew how to breathe.

That was the problem.

Morning traffic moved when it should. Trains arrived close enough to schedule that commuters did not complain out loud. Coffee shops opened their doors and sold the same cups to the same hands. Children were dropped at school. Office lights flicked on behind glass.

Nothing was wrong in any way that could be reported.

Yet the air felt thinned, like color washed once too often from fabric. Sounds arrived half a second late, or landed without weight when they arrived at all. Footsteps echoed a little too long in underground corridors. A plaza fountain continued to run, but its splash sounded distant, as if heard through water.

In the central square, a man stood holding a newspaper he was no longer reading. The wind lifted the pages and let them fall back against his knuckles. He did not notice. People flowed around him, annoyed but not alarmed, adjusting their paths the way a river does around a rock.

At a nearby intersection, the pedestrian signal changed from red to green. No one crossed.

Cars waited. Drivers tapped steering wheels. One leaned out a window and shouted something sharp and forgettable. The light cycled again. Still no one moved.

Across the street, two women faced each other mid conversation. One had her mouth open around the start of a word she would never finish. The other's brow was furrowed, expression fixed in the shape of mild disagreement. They stood like that while the city slid past them.

No sirens rose.

No alarms sounded.

No one screamed.

Stillness did not arrive all at once. It accumulated.

It slipped into places where attention lingered too long. A bus stop where the Paris footage had been replayed all night. A living room where a family had argued softly about miracles and monsters until the argument ran out of words. A transit platform where people waited together, sharing nothing but proximity and unease.

In those places, motion slowed.

Then paused.

Then forgot how to resume.

From above, the city looked unchanged. From within, it felt as if memory itself had begun to pool.

No one saw it form.

There was no flash, no pulse, no moment that could be pointed to afterward and named as the beginning. Residual Weave energy did not behave like fire or storm. It did not expand outward. It collected.

Where fear had repeated itself often enough, where attention had circled the same images until they wore grooves into thought, residue thickened. Not as matter. As alignment.

Threads that once vibrated independently began to settle into shared rhythm. A harmonic found another that matched it. Then another. Distance did not matter. Location was irrelevant. What mattered was pattern.

Reflections began to double.

Glass caught faces and returned them with slight delay, expressions echoing themselves before resolving. A man walking past a storefront saw two versions of his own stride for a heartbeat too long and slowed without knowing why.

Shadows lingered.

They did not detach or move on their own. They simply hesitated, clinging to corners and doorframes as if reluctant to let go. In narrow streets, the overlap made noon look like evening.

Sound dampened unevenly.

A laugh carried across a plaza and vanished halfway through. A dropped object struck pavement without echo. Words spoken softly traveled farther than shouts. The city did not fall silent. It became selective.

Across multiple neighborhoods, across train lines and districts that had nothing in common but recent attention, the same quiet adjustments took place. Harmonics aligned. Residuum settled into coherence.

Not intent, not consciousness, but Structure. Something unfinished found a way to hold itself together.

A woman stepped off the curb when the light told her to. Her foot never reached the pavement. One heel hovered inches above the white stripe of the crosswalk, frozen in the act of motion. Her arms hung at her sides. Her coat shifted slightly in the breeze. Her eyes remained open, unfocused, reflecting the traffic light that no longer mattered.

The driver closest to her slowed first, confused rather than afraid. He leaned forward, peering through the windshield. The car behind him tapped its horn. The sound cut off too quickly.

People nearby felt it as hesitation before thought.

A man with a briefcase stopped mid stride, his hand still curled around the handle. A cyclist put one foot down and forgot to lift the other. Conversations trailed off, words dissolving before they reached mouths.

No one screamed.

There was no shock sharp enough to demand it.

Stillness spread outward in a soft ring, catching people where they stood. Eyes stayed open. Bodies remained upright. Breath continued, shallow and automatic.

Inside the freeze, the world was not empty.

The woman in the crosswalk stood once more in a hospital hallway that smelled like disinfectant and grief. She heard her name spoken the way it had been spoken only once, too late to answer. The moment replayed without end, without release, looping like a thought that had never been allowed to finish.

Nearby, a man relived a kitchen argument from years ago. The last sentence repeated, hanging unresolved between him and the memory of someone who no longer lived there. He felt the weight of it again, fresh and unfinished.

Others drifted through moments they had buried carefully. Missed chances. Last looks. Words not said because there had always been time.

There was no progression. No choice. No escape. Memory overwrote the present with perfect fidelity. From the outside, the city had paused. From within, it remembered itself apart. And it did not yet know how to stop.

It ended the way it began, without warning. One moment the crosswalk was a still photograph, the next it was motion again, as if the city had blinked and forgotten it had ever stopped. The woman's foot came down. Her heel struck the pavement and she stumbled forward, catching herself with a sharp inhale that sounded too loud in the hush. Her eyes snapped into focus. She looked left, then right, as if the cars had appeared out of nowhere. The light was already red. A driver leaned on his horn, furious, and she recoiled like the sound had struck her in the ribs.

Around her, bodies resumed at once. The man with the briefcase took two steps before realizing he'd moved. The cyclist lurched forward and nearly fell. Two women who had been frozen mid conversation suddenly finished their sentences at the same time, then stared at each other in confusion because the words felt misplaced, like lines delivered after the scene had changed.

Time had passed for everyone else.

A bus hissed to a stop at the curb. Doors opened and closed. A delivery truck rolled through the intersection that should have been blocked. Phones came up, screens lit, messages stacked in missed minutes.

For the frozen, none of it belonged.

A teenager put both hands over her face and started crying without sound, shoulders shaking as if something inside her had broken loose. A man in a suit laughed once, bright and wrong, then slapped a hand over his mouth like he couldn't believe the noise had come from him.

A woman near the corner smiled. It was small and faint and unsettling, like an expression she hadn't earned. Her eyes were wet, but her mouth held that quiet curve as she stared at nothing. Someone asked if she was alright. She nodded, still smiling, still not seeing them.

People drifted away in uneven directions, and as they moved, the changes became clearer.

Some walked slower, posture softened, as if the bones in their backs had been rearranged. Others moved too smoothly, too carefully, like their bodies had learned to conserve motion. A few spoke with altered cadence, their words measured, their voices stripped of old hesitation.

A man who had been holding his phone stared at it as if it were unfamiliar. He tapped the screen, then frowned at the name displayed on an incoming call.

He answered anyway.

"Hello," he said, and when the voice on the other end said his name, he flinched. "Who is this?" he asked, confused, irritated, then suddenly frightened. He looked around as if the caller might be standing nearby, hidden in the crowd.

A woman stood beside a memorial plaque set into the stone wall of a building, reading names carved into granite. She mouthed one name three times, trying to summon the person attached to it.

Nothing came.

Her face tightened, not in grief, but in panic. She knew the name mattered. She could feel that it mattered. The emotional weight that should have been tied to it was missing, scraped clean, leaving only the shape of importance without the substance.

Others lost something quieter.

They remembered the events, but the pain attached to them had been dulled, as if someone had turned down the volume on the worst parts of their lives. That should have been mercy. It didn't look like mercy on their faces. It looked like someone had stolen the ability to mourn properly.

And a few gained something that felt like poison wrapped in silk.

Unnatural calm.

A man who had just been frozen in the middle of the street stepped onto the sidewalk and adjusted his tie as if nothing had happened. He looked at the crowd, at the shaken people, at the phones filming, and his expression remained smooth. He offered a polite smile to a woman crying beside him, as if she'd spilled coffee and needed reassurance.

Then he walked away, steady as a metronome, eyes empty of urgency.

The city did not erupt. It did not riot. It did not collapse.

It absorbed the moment and kept moving.

But something had been rewritten.

And no one could say exactly what it had cost.

Maya felt it like grit in her teeth.

She stood near the safehouse window with the curtain barely cracked, not looking at the street so much as listening through the thin slice of daylight. Paris had taught her that the world could be loud without sound. This was different.

The Weave didn't roar. It scraped.

A new pattern threaded through the lattice beneath everything, quiet enough that most people would never notice, persistent enough that it made her skin crawl. It wasn't a single flare like a Walker waking up. It wasn't chaos either.

It was layered.

A chorus without mouths and no breath.

The safehouse around her stayed intact, but her awareness stretched outward anyway, cautious now, testing the edges like a hand feeling for a crack in glass. She followed the discordant thread until it widened into something she could almost map.

One city. Mid-sized. Not a major capital. Not a place anyone would focus on if they were hunting spectacle. It had been trending for a day after Paris, then drowned by the next wave of arguments and edits and outrage.

That was why it had become dangerous. The chorus lived there. It didn't speak words. It didn't announce itself. It didn't demand attention. It remembered.

Maya felt the echoes of human lives braided together, not neatly, not kindly. Grief and regret sat beside relief. Unfinished conversations repeated with mechanical devotion. The harmonies were made from stolen resonance, memory tones stripped from people and left vibrating in the Weave like a plucked string that wouldn't stop.

Familiar threads were present, but bent.

She recognized the shape of human emotion the way she recognized a familiar road. It was there, and yet it wasn't moving the way it should. The lattice vibrated unevenly, as if something had wedged itself between strands and forced them to sing in alignment.

Maya's throat tightened.

"This isn't a Walker," she whispered.

It was worse, because it didn't need one.

Alex was behind her before she turned.

He didn't ask what was wrong. He could read it in the way her shoulders had drawn tight, in the way her breathing had gone shallow, in the way her focus had narrowed like she was staring into a bright light.

"You're reaching," he said quietly.

"I'm not diving," she replied. "I'm listening."

"That's how it starts," he said.

He moved closer, careful. Not crowding. Anchoring. When his hand touched her shoulder, the Weave around her shifted, not because he pushed it away, but because he sorted it. The static bled off, the sharpest frequencies separating into something her mind could hold without breaking.

Maya exhaled, surprised at how much relief that gave her.

"I can't isolate it," she said. "It's everywhere in that city. Like... like it's threaded through the streets."

Alex's brow furrowed. "A Walker could do that?"

"No," she said, and the certainty in her voice startled her as much as it did him. "Not like this."

She reached again with more precision, guided by the filter Alex provided. The chorus sharpened into detail. It wasn't one presence moving through people. It was many fragments moving as one, assembled from residue and repetition.

Composite. An Echo made of echoes. Born from Residuum and mass resonance, formed where attention and fear had overlapped until the residue learned a pattern and held it.

Joe's voice came from behind them, tense. "What are you hearing?"

Maya didn't take her eyes off the nothing she was staring into. "A chorus," she said. "Quiet, but constant."

Elara shifted somewhere in the room, heat stirring. "That's not possible."

"It's happening," Maya said.

Alex swallowed, gaze distant, as if he could almost sense the shape of it through her reaction. "It's singing," he said, the words coming out like he didn't mean to admit them.

Maya shook her head once, slow.

"No," she said. "It's remembering us."

The line landed in the room with a weight that made no sense to anyone who couldn't feel what she felt.

Maya's hands trembled as she held her awareness on the chorus. It didn't lash out. It didn't surge. It simply persisted, quiet and patient, harmonies drawn from human lives like water drawn into a well.

A new kind of threat. Not explosive. Not cinematic. Not something a camera could catch in a single frame and label. Something that could spread without being noticed.

Maya let her awareness pull back, not because the chorus pushed her away, but because she couldn't stand the intimacy of it. She could still feel it lingering in the distance, a soft pressure under the world's skin.

Alex's hand stayed on her shoulder until her breathing steadied.

"What do we call it?" Joe asked.

Maya stared at the floorboards, grounding herself to wood and gravity and the small, ordinary truths that still worked.

Then she said, "The Quiet Choir."

And even as she spoke the name, she knew it wasn't just a label. It was a warning.

It didn't move like a hunter.

It moved like a law.

The Quiet Choir was not a mind that chose in words. It was alignment. It was residue finding the shortest path into coherence. It did not need to understand pain to recognize density. It only needed to sense where the Weave was thickest with human weight.

It drifted.

Not across streets. Across patterns.

A plaza where a memorial still drew flowers from strangers who couldn't name the dead. A hospital corridor where grief was routine and the walls had learned to hold it. A courthouse stairwell where anger echoed day after day, each argument leaving its trace. A cramped apartment where a man replayed a voicemail from a deceased mother until the recording wore thin.

Those places rang louder.

The Choir leaned toward them without intention the way smoke leans toward open air. The harmonics tightened. The dampening of sound became more precise. Reflections lingered a fraction too long around faces that had cried too often. Shadows refused to separate cleanly from bodies that carried old fear.

When it touched a crowd, it did not seize them all.

It sampled.

A single person froze. Then two. Then a small cluster at the edge of a crowd where a memory had just broken open. When the cluster resumed, the pattern repeated elsewhere, slightly refined. The next freeze lasted one breath longer. The next carried less panic. The next stole different pieces.

Selective, not conscious.

Preference, not planning.

It wasn't random decay bleeding out of the Weave. It was something that had learned the shape of what fed it and shifted to match.

The Choir did not want victims.

It wanted resonance.

And trauma was resonance that never stopped vibrating on its own.

They saw the numbers before they saw the shape.

In a secure operations room in the Netherlands, a wall of screens showed maps and feeds and scrolling incident logs. Each report alone looked mundane. Each case file came with a familiar list of symptoms and a comforting cluster of labels.

Catatonia. Acute dissociation. Transient amnesia. Mass hysteria.

A medical advisor with tired eyes tapped a chart on a tablet. "Look, it's consistent with stress contagion. Viral fear response after Paris. People are primed."

A woman in uniform didn't look convinced. "Then why are the clusters forming around the same types of locations?"

"They're not," the advisor said quickly. "That's confirmation bias. You're looking for pattern because you expect it."

An analyst cleared his throat. "We've got video from four incidents. No one screams. No one runs. They just stop. Then they resume and half of them can't answer basic questions."

A second analyst added, "It's spreading without a vector. No shared media exposure at the moment of onset. No chemical traces. No EM anomalies strong enough to trigger equipment alarms."

A man at the head of the table leaned back, fingers steepled. He didn't like unknowns. Unknowns were how systems failed.

"Any sign of a Walker?" he asked.

"No," the analyst said. "No visible manifestation. No heat signatures. No kinetic anomalies. No light distortion."

"Then it isn't one," the man said, relief audible in his voice.

The room tried to accept that relief. It wanted to, because protocols existed for Walkers now. Clumsy protocols, but they were written down. They could be enforced. They could be briefed and denied and contained, at least on paper.

There was no protocol for a phenomenon that didn't announce itself.

A liaison officer spoke carefully. "Local authorities are calling it a psychological contagion. Public health wants to handle messaging. They're preparing statements about stress and misinformation."

"Good," the man said. "Keep it medical. Keep it calm. No mention of anything unverified. We don't need another panic wave."

An analyst hesitated. "Sir, it isn't presenting like a normal contagion."

The man's gaze sharpened. "Define normal."

The analyst swallowed. "Normal doesn't rewrite memory."

Silence held for two beats.

Then the room did what institutions always did when faced with something that didn't fit. It forced it into the nearest category and pretended the fit was close enough.

"Classify it and move on," the man said. "Psychological event clusters, likely triggered by post-Paris stressors. Monitor for escalation."

The words went into a file. The file went into a system. The system felt safer.

Outside those rooms, people kept freezing under streetlights and waking up with pieces missing.

No sensor detected what mattered.

No protocol listened for a choir.

Maya didn't need maps.

She could feel the Choir moving.

Not like footsteps, but like tension shifting along a net. The Weave under her skin had a new itch that didn't go away. Every time she tried to focus on something ordinary, the discord returned, soft but insistent, a reminder that the world had changed its baseline.

She sat on the floor with her back against the couch, eyes half closed, while Alex stayed nearby like a quiet brace holding up a cracked wall.

"It's not random," she said.

Joe looked up from the muted screens. "What isn't?"

"The freezes. The memory hits. All of it." She swallowed against the dryness in her throat. "It's following density. It's following places that already hurt."

Elara's jaw tightened. "So it's hunting."

Maya shook her head. "Not hunting. Not like you mean it. It doesn't hate. It doesn't even know what hate is." She pressed her fingers to her temple, trying to hold onto the shape of what she'd sensed. "It's a consequence. It's what happens when enough people lean toward the same impossible thing and the Weave answers them."

Joe's face darkened. "Paris."

Maya nodded once. "Paris didn't just wake people up. It seeded the world. It made attention into fuel. It turned belief into pressure." Her voice dropped, not from drama, but from the weight of the thought. "The Weave's starting to host structures that aren't tied to human intent."

Alex's hand tightened on her shoulder. He didn't speak, but she felt him sorting the noise at the edges of her awareness so she could finish the thought without breaking.

Maya stared at the floorboards like the answer was carved there.

"The Unmaking doesn't have to break things anymore," she said quietly. "It can let them form wrong."

The room went still.

Richard, who had been listening from the corner with his usual measured distance, spoke with controlled skepticism. "You're saying this is intentional."

"I'm saying it's preference," Maya replied. "It's selection. It's learning where the Weave is easiest to bend."

She hated the certainty in her own voice. She hated that it felt like discovering a new rule in a world that already had too many.

"This is the first," she added.

And the way the words landed told her everyone understood what she meant.

First implied more.

Night settled over the city in a soft, ordinary way, as if the sky itself refused to participate.

Streetlights cast warm pools on wet pavement. Windows glowed behind curtains. A tram rattled past on schedule, bell chiming once at an empty intersection.

On one block, three people stood motionless beneath the lamps.

A man with groceries in one hand, plastic bag stretched thin, apples pressed against the side like bruised hearts. A woman with her coat half on, one arm still raised to thread it through the sleeve. A boy with a backpack on one shoulder, foot angled as if he'd been about to step off the curb.

Their eyes were open.

Not staring.

Absent.

Cars rolled by and slowed, drivers frowning, uncertain, then moved on. Someone glanced, then looked away. No one wanted to be the first to decide what it meant.

A faint hum lived under the noise of the city.

Not loud enough to be heard.

Just present enough to be felt, if you were cracked in the right place.

When the three resumed, it happened at once. Bags swung. Fabric slid. The boy's foot came down.

They walked on.

Each carried something different than they had a moment before.

And the streetlight glow remained steady, indifferent, as if it hadn't witnessed anything.

Maya watched the live feed in the safehouse without sound and felt her stomach drop in slow motion.

The Quiet Choir wasn't a single thing confined to a single city.

It was a pattern that could repeat.

A structure that could be hosted.

A way the Unmaking could inhabit the world without ever showing its face.

She understood, with a cold calm that made her want to scream, that this was not an ending.

It was a beginning.

The first of its kind.

Her phone buzzed with a new alert. Another cluster. Another city. Another report wrapped in harmless language.

No explosion. No announcement. Only resonance.

And somewhere under the world, the Choir kept drifting toward places that already hurt.

7

The Immortals' Warning

The Weave narrowed.

Maya felt it happen before she could name it, a sudden constriction that had nothing to do with silence. The pressure did not vanish. It focused. The endless background noise that had become her constant companion since Paris thinned into a single, drawn thread, pulled so tight it made her breath catch.

She gasped and grabbed the edge of the table.

The Quiet Choir receded. Not gone. Never gone. Just far enough away to feel deliberate, like a crowd stepping back in unison to make space.

"Maya?" Alex said.

He was already moving toward her, hand out, eyes searching her face. She could feel him reaching the way he always did now, not pushing, not grounding, just listening for where the strain lived.

"It's pulling back," she said.

Alex frowned. "I don't feel a filter. There's nothing to grab."

"That's because it isn't being filtered," she said. Her voice sounded distant to her own ears, thin and oddly hollow. "It's withdrawing."

The word settled with weight.

The Weave around her did not feel safer. It felt *emptied* with intent. The space she occupied sharpened, edges too clean, like a room cleared of furniture for reasons no one explained.

Maya straightened slowly.

"They're isolating me," she said.

Alex stiffened. "Who is *they?*"

She didn't answer. She didn't need to. The narrowing tightened again, and the world around her fractured.

Not physically. Perceptually.

The safehouse peeled away in layers, each one sliding sideways rather than breaking, reality folding like overlapping sheets of glass. The air grew dense with resonance planes, stacked and intersecting, each vibrating at a different harmonic that made her teeth ache.

Then the sorrow arrived.

It pressed down like gravity, immense and controlled, carrying the weight of centuries without the arrogance of authority. Light gathered into a towering shape that was not light at all, but presence given outline.

Kemen stood before her.

She was vast, her form stretching beyond the limits of the fractured space, yet restrained, as if bound by rules that mattered more than power. Her expression held no judgment. Only grief. Not for what was coming, but for what had already been lost.

Maya felt reduced to scale.

Then the temperature dropped.

A second presence resolved beside the first, sharper, colder, defined by edges instead of mass. Where Kemen carried sorrow, this one carried containment, precision honed into something that cut rather than comforted.

Vilya.

Neither of them stepped forward. Neither touched the world. They hovered at the edge of what the Weave would allow, projections shaped by tension and necessity, not bodies crossing a boundary.

Maya swallowed. "You're not here."

Kemen inclined her head slightly. "We are as present as we are permitted to be."

Maya forced herself to breathe. "You felt it," she said. "The Choir."

"We did," Kemen replied.

Maya pushed past the instinct to kneel, to defer. She had learned the cost of that impulse. "It's an Echo structure," she said, the words coming faster now. "Not a Walker. Not residue alone. It's memory overwriting perception. It's selective. It's learning."

Kemen's expression did not change.

"You named it already," she said. "The Quiet Choir."

Maya flinched. Hearing the name echoed back made it heavier, more real.

Vilya spoke then, her voice precise and unforgiving. "It is not a creature. It does not choose as mortals choose. It is the Unmaking shaped by expectation and sustained by attention."

"So it's controlled by it," Maya said.

"No," Vilya replied at once. "It is not controlled. It is expression."

The words struck harder than denial would have.

"The Unmaking has learned to wear what humanity provides," Kemen said. "Belief. Fear. Memory. The Choir is not its master. It is its mirror."

Maya's hands clenched. "Then stop it."

The silence that followed was not hesitation. It was inevitability.

"You know why we cannot," Kemen said gently.

"Say it anyway," Maya said.

Kemen's gaze did not waver. "We are bound to the boundary. To act directly would destabilize the seal that holds the Weave intact."

Vilya stepped closer, his presence cutting sharp lines through the resonance planes. "Intervention would not prevent collapse. It would accelerate it."

Something inside Maya broke cleanly.

"So that's it," she said. "You watch."

"No," Kemen said. "We preserve."

"And we suffer," Maya said.

"Yes," Vilya said without apology. "Your stewardship was never meant to be temporary."

Maya laughed once, brittle, the sound echoing wrong in the fractured space. "All this time," she said. "All this talk about Guardians. People think you're a safety net."

Kemen's sorrow deepened. "We were never meant to be rescue."

Maya looked between them, anger and understanding twisting together until she could no longer separate them. "Then why tell me any of this?"

"Because the Choir feeds on resonance," Kemen said. "And resonance is shaped by choice."

Vilya continued without pause. "Fear strengthens it. Worship stabilizes it. Denial blinds against it."

Maya's stomach dropped. "You're saying we make it worse just by reacting."

"We are saying the battlefield is no longer power alone," Kemen said. "It is narrative. Memory. Restraint."

"And the Walkers?" Maya asked.

Kemen looked at her fully. "You are no longer anomalies."

The word landed like a verdict.

"You are successors," Kemen said. "Not chosen. Enduring."

The weight settled onto Maya's shoulders like something she would never be able to set down.

"And the Choir?" she asked.

"It will refine itself," Vilya said. "Exposure teaches it. Each encounter sharpens preference."

The space shuddered.

Kemen's outline fractured first, hairline cracks of light rippling through her form as the Weave strained around the contact. She exhaled, a sound like wind through ancient stone.

"Our time ends," she said.

Vilya's gaze locked onto Maya. "This is not the last structure," she said. "It is the first that survived long enough to be named."

Then they were gone.

Not fading. Gone.

The resonance planes snapped shut, collapsing inward with a force that knocked the breath from Maya's lungs.

She fell.

Alex caught her before she hit the floor, one arm bracing her shoulders, the other steady at her back. The safehouse slammed back into place around them, walls solid, air thick, the Weave suddenly thinner, stretched tight like a rope pulled too far.

Maya sucked in air and clung to his sleeve. "They're gone."

"I know," Alex said quietly. "It feels lighter. Wrong."

She nodded weakly. "They warned us."

Joe was already there, crouched close, eyes searching her face. "About what?"

Maya pushed herself upright with Alex's help. Her head throbbed, but the clarity remained.

"The Quiet Choir is Unmaking wearing us," she said. "They can't stop it. They won't."

Joe stared at her for a long moment, then nodded once. "So it's on us."

Maya met his gaze.

"Yes," she said. Not with confidence. With acceptance.

The Weave stirred again at the edges of her awareness. The Choir's resonance slid back into place, unchanged, patient, humming as if it had never left.

As if it had been listening the entire time.

Counter Fragment

COUNTER-FRAGMENT:
On the Fallacy of Universal Resonance

(Attributed to Cylian, Guardian of Measure. Source disputed.)

They say the Weave remembers humanity. This is a pleasing lie.
Memory implies loss, and loss implies innocence.
Humanity did not forget the Weave. It turned away from it deliberately,
and often violently, each time understanding demanded restraint.

The Weave does not awaken because it is heard.
It answers because it is touched.

Those who claim ambient resonance mistake consequence for cause.
The unease, the pressure, the sense of pattern that now troubles the many
is not attunement. It is proximity.
When a fire spreads, the air grows warm far beyond the flame.
Warmth is not combustion.

The majority of humankind does not resonate.
They echo.
Echoes carry no agency of their own.
Belief does not strengthen the Weave. It distorts it.
Fear does not call power. It destabilizes it.

* The term "Walker" should never have been shared.
   Naming invites pursuit.
   Pursuit invites force.
   Force invites collapse.
   Instruction is not enough. Correction will be required.

8

A New Circle

The safehouse felt hollow after the Immortals withdrew.

Not empty in the way rooms were empty when people left, but in the way a mountain valley felt after an avalanche passed through.

The air remained. The ground remained. But something immense that had pressed against the shape of the world was suddenly gone, leaving silence where weight had once lived.

Maya stood near the center of the room, hands braced against the edge of the table, breathing slowly until the tremor in her fingers eased. The Weave had narrowed when Kemen and Vilya appeared. Now it widened again, spreading into its familiar, unbearable fullness.

The Quiet Choir returned immediately.

It didn't rush back. It didn't surge or lash out. It simply resumed its presence, patient and steady, a low harmonic under the world that made her skin itch with awareness. It felt unchanged by the encounter. Unimpressed. As if it had waited because waiting cost it nothing.

There was no safety net left. Maya knew that now with a certainty that settled deeper than fear.

Alex watched her closely from a few steps away. He didn't ask if she was all right. He didn't reach for her unless she asked. He simply stayed where she could see him, grounded and real, a reminder that she was still here, still standing.

That mattered more than it should have.

Joe broke the silence first.

"No one's in charge," he said.

The words were not dramatic. They were not angry. He spoke them like a fact that had finally grown too large to avoid.

No one argued.

The truth unfolded in the quiet like a map no one wanted to read. The Immortals couldn't act. Governments were either blind, hostile, or already sharpening knives. Walkers were scattered across the world, frightened, unstable, reacting without context or support. And the Weave itself no longer waited for permission.

Silence followed, heavy and unresolved.

Someone would fill the vacuum. That much was inevitable. The only question was whether it would be filled by intention or by accident.

Joe leaned forward, forearms resting on his knees, eyes flicking briefly to the muted screens along the wall before returning to the group.

"This isn't just about the Quiet Choir," he said. "It's about what people think is happening. That's already shaping reality."

Elara scoffed softly. "You're talking about spin."

"No," Joe said. "I'm talking about damage control."

He gestured toward the screens. Even without sound, the images told their own story. Loops of Paris. Frozen bodies. Distorted light. Comment feeds racing too fast to read.

"Attention amplifies the Weave," Joe continued. "Fear and myth accelerate Echo behavior. People are already building explanations that make sense to them, and those explanations are feeding back into the system. If we don't shape understanding, someone else will. And they won't do it carefully."

Maya felt the truth of it resonate through the lattice beneath her feet. Belief carried weight now. Narrative was no longer harmless.

"People don't need the full truth," Joe said quietly. "Not all at once. They need something that won't tear them apart while they learn it."

Richard straightened, hands clasped behind his back, his expression hardening.

"You're still thinking too small," he said. "Narrative doesn't matter if there's no structure to support it."

Joe turned toward him. "Structure without trust collapses."

"And trust without structure is chaos," Richard shot back. "Coordination by consensus doesn't work at scale. Someone has to decide thresholds. Escalation. Response. Walkers can't self-govern this by instinct and hope."

He took a breath and continued, his voice steady, controlled.

"We need rules of engagement. Operational discipline. A command structure, even if it's temporary."

The words hung in the air, sharp enough to cut.

Maya felt Elara's fire stir before she spoke. It was subtle, a tightening of heat along the edges of the room, like a flame drawing breath.

"No," Elara said flatly.

Richard met her gaze. "No what."

"No hierarchy. No chain of command. That's the first step toward cages."

"That's paranoia," Richard said.

"That's history," Elara replied. "Protection turns into control fast. You know that. You've lived it."

Her heat flared just enough to make the air shimmer, then pulled back under sheer force of will. She crossed her arms, jaw tight.

"You build a system that can give orders, and sooner or later someone uses it to justify taking choice away."

She wasn't wrong.

That was the problem.

Maya closed her eyes for a moment, letting the noise settle. When she spoke, she didn't raise her voice. She didn't claim authority. She simply drew a line.

"No gods," she said. "No institutions. No rulers."

They all looked at her.

"I'm not building a throne," Maya continued. "And I'm not handing this to anyone who thinks they should."

Richard opened his mouth to argue, but she held up a hand.

"What we need isn't a chain," she said. "It's a circle."

The word felt right the moment it left her mouth.

"Shared responsibility," she went on. "Roles, not ranks. Coordination, not command. No one at the top. No one beneath."

Joe studied her, eyes sharp. "That's fragile."

"Yes," Maya said. "But it's human."

She looked around the room, meeting each of them in turn.

"This isn't a government. It's not an authority. It's a way to keep Walkers from breaking alone and the world from tearing itself apart while we figure out what comes next."

Silence followed again, different this time. Considered. Reluctant.

They talked it through slowly, every agreement scraped into place with effort.

The purpose came first. Identify Walkers before they fractured. Stabilize where possible. Support where consent existed. Monitor Echo behavior and Quiet Choir emergence. Share information before institutions buried it or weaponized it.

The structure followed, uneasy but workable.

No single leader.

Maya would map perception and strain, tracking resonance across the lattice. Alex would focus on stabilization and survivability, keeping people alive long enough to learn. Joe would handle intelligence and narrative containment, shaping understanding without feeding panic. Elara would serve as deterrence, force response when nothing else held. Richard would manage logistics, construction, and the hard solutions no one else wanted to touch.

Limitations mattered as much as purpose.

They wouldn't rule Walkers. They wouldn't compel participation. They would intervene only when harm was imminent.

No one pretended it was enough.

Each of them understood the cost of saying yes.

Joe knew he would become a target the moment he spoke publicly with authority. Richard knew institutions would come for him the instant this became visible. Elara knew restraint would be demanded of her when fire wanted to answer fire. Alex knew he would be holding the whole system together by feel and intuition. And Maya knew the Circle would orbit her whether she wanted it to or not.

No one celebrated.

The room felt tighter after the agreement, not looser. Commitment always carried weight.

Then Maya felt it.

A distant shift. Subtle. Almost nothing.

Somewhere far away, a Walker leaned toward the edge and didn't fall. Not because of intervention. Not because of power. Because someone else, somewhere, felt less alone.

The Weave responded with alignment instead of force.

Maya exhaled slowly, eyes closing.

The world didn't become safer. It became organized.

9

The Containment Alliance

Richard left the safehouse before dawn and had been gone less than a day when the message arrived.

It didn't come through his phone. It didn't pass through any channel that could be forwarded, archived, or intercepted by accident. It appeared on a hardened tablet he hadn't powered on since before Paris, its screen dark until the moment it decided not to be.

The notification contained no subject line.

No sender.

Just coordinates, a time window, and a single sentence rendered in neutral gray text.

We believe you already understand the necessity.

Richard stared at it longer than he should have.

He hadn't told the others where he was going. Not because he was hiding it, but because there was no language yet for what they were becoming. The Circle had been named, not formed. Agreed to, not tested. Maya was still standing, Alex still holding the world together by feel, Joe already fighting narratives without armor, Elara braced against a future she didn't trust.

And Richard had done what he always did when systems began to move without structure.

He followed the pressure.

The facility did not announce itself.

There were no flags outside, no insignia inside. No slogans etched into steel or glass. The architecture was neutral to the point of anonymity, a building designed to be forgettable even to the people who worked inside it. Concrete, matte composites, indirect lighting. The kind of place where policy was born and responsibility was diluted by process.

Richard was escorted through three access points, each quieter than the last.

By the time he entered the room, he already knew this wasn't an interrogation.

It was an alignment check.

The table was oval. Not round. Not hierarchical. Screens lined the walls, but none of them showed live feeds. Everything here had already been filtered, categorized, and translated into something safe to discuss.

Four people waited.

A U.S. defense liaison, civilian cut, military posture.

A NATO strategic coordinator whose accent was impossible to place and whose expression never shifted.

An intelligence analyst with dark circles under her eyes and a data slate already open.

And a legal authority whose entire presence radiated the careful calm of someone who wrote exceptions into laws and slept fine afterward.

No one said the word Walker.

Not at first.

They began with Paris.

They showed timelines that didn't loop. Angles that hadn't made it to public release. Thermal overlays that proved absence mattered as much as heat. They referenced the Senate incident without naming it, sliding past the moment where language failed and systems had quietly rewritten their own thresholds.

"This isn't about individuals anymore," the NATO coordinator said, hands folded. "It's about emergent behavior."

The analyst brought up the next set of data.

Clusters.

Freeze events misclassified as mass dissociation. Echo exposure buried under psychological terminology. Quiet zones where sound dampened, reflections lagged, and memory failure spiked without neurological markers.

Richard leaned forward.

"You're seeing structure," he said.

The analyst nodded once. "We're seeing systems."

Still, no one said the Choir.

Not directly.

They called it *non-localized coherence. Residual behavioral anomaly. Distributed resonance persistence.*

Language designed not to panic.

Or accuse.

Or admit too much.

Then the defense liaison finally spoke the name.

"The Containment Alliance."

The words were delivered without emphasis.

As if the concept already existed and they were simply catching Richard up.

The proposal unfolded cleanly.

Identify Walkers early.

Offer protection, training, and support before instability set in. Prevent uncontrolled manifestations. Maintain geopolitical equilibrium. It was all framed as cooperation. Safeguards. Stability.

Then the conditions appeared. Registration. Monitoring. Operational boundaries. Mandatory intervention thresholds.

Richard didn't interrupt. Because this was structure. Because this was what scale looked like. They could build facilities. Redundant systems. Containment fields. Training frameworks that didn't rely on intuition or proximity. They could survive public pressure, legal challenge, and internal fracture.

Everything the Circle refused by design.

"Choice remains," the legal authority said calmly. "Until it can't."

Richard exhaled slowly.

"And when a Walker refuses?"

The room didn't shift.

The NATO coordinator answered without hesitation. "Then we decide if refusal constitutes a risk."

"Some won't survive containment," Richard said.

The U.S. defense liaison didn't hesitate. "Yes."

"Some will be detained permanently," Richard said flatly.

The NATO coordinator answered this time, his voice level. "Yes."

Richard looked up at him. "Some will be used."

Silence held for a fraction longer.

Not denial.

The intelligence analyst glanced down at her slate, then back up. "Yes."

The legal authority folded her hands, the motion precise. "We're not asking if it's moral," she said. "We're asking if it's survivable."

That was when Richard understood the offer.

Not power.

Position.

Advisory authority. Design input. Safeguards written into doctrine while doctrine was still fluid. A seat close enough to shape thresholds before they hardened into inevitability.

If he refused, the Alliance wouldn't stop.

It would simply proceed without friction.

Richard saw Maya burning out under pressure she refused to name as leadership.

Alex holding fractures together by instinct.

Joe trying to slow a narrative avalanche with language alone.

Elara braced against a system that would eventually come for her whether she acknowledged it or not.

The Circle felt human.

The Alliance felt durable.

When Richard finally stood, no one stopped him.

Outside, the screens continued updating.

Names populated lists.

Protocols finalized without pause.

The world was already organizing.

This time, it had teeth.

10

Joe Follows the Money

Joe woke before the safehouse did.

It wasn't a decision. It was habit, ingrained too deeply to argue with. When systems shifted, when pressure moved without warning, sleep became a liability. He sat at the kitchen table with a mug of coffee gone lukewarm and six screens pulled close enough to feel like a wall. Outside, the sky hadn't decided whether it wanted to be night or morning yet.

Joe didn't start with feeds or footage. That was where panic lived.

He went where answers lasted longer.

Budgets.

Emergency appropriations scrolled across one screen, dense with committee language designed to dull attention. Defense subcommittee votes. Oversight amendments. Quiet reallocations buried inside unrelated bills.

HECATE was crippled.

Not dismantled. Not condemned. Starved out.

Joe traced the numbers twice to be sure. Oversight authority stripped. Black-budget discretion revoked. Funding reduced to a skeleton that couldn't support field operations or independent action. Senator Hargreaves' name still appeared, but only in ceremonial margins. A signature without teeth.

The public justification was clean and bloodless. Redundancy. Institutional failure. Public trust concerns after Paris.

Joe snorted softly and took a sip of coffee that tasted like regret.

HECATE hadn't been brought to heel because it was dangerous. It had been brought to heel because it was visible. Congress hadn't found a conscience. It had found a liability. And liabilities don't get buried. They get cut down to size.

Joe glanced down the hallway where the others slept. Maya was still standing, somehow. Alex was holding fractures together by instinct and proximity. Elara was pacing a future she didn't trust. Richard was already gone, following pressure like he always did.

HECATE wasn't gone. It just wasn't allowed to drive anymore. That didn't mean anything had stopped.

Joe pulled up the second layer of data and started following the money.

The numbers didn't vanish. They fragmented.

Funds once centralized under a single program now appeared in a dozen places. NATO emergency coordination budgets. Defense-adjacent research initiatives. Civilian resilience and stabilization grants with names engineered to sound harmless.

Each sum was smaller. Less conspicuous. Harder to trace.

Together, they added up to more than HECATE had ever controlled.

Joe tagged timestamps and watched the flow patterns emerge. Allocations approved days before Echo clusters spiked. Contracts signed weeks ahead of Quiet Choir activity. Resources positioned in regions that hadn't made the news yet.

"They're not reacting," Joe muttered to the empty room. "They're positioning."

That was the difference that mattered.

He moved to contractor registries next, then into encrypted personnel databases he'd stopped being surprised he still had access to. Names surfaced immediately.

Former HECATE analysts now listed as consultants. Division Gray engineers officially retired, quietly reappearing as technical advisors. Legal architects who had drafted Walker detention frameworks now operating as independent subject-matter experts.

Different logos. Same résumés.

Joe slowed down, checking himself for pattern hunger. Ran it again. Cross-referenced deeper.

He wasn't imagining it.

The same people were solving the same problem.

They'd just changed their letterhead.

That was when he found Division Gray's fingerprints.

Officially, it had been folded, reclassified, buried deep enough to barely cast a shadow. But its tools had survived. Joe recognized the signatures instantly. Data compression methods optimized for anomalous signal capture. Hardware requisitions disguised as environmental monitoring equipment. Storage facilities labeled as archival redundancy sites.

If you didn't know what you were looking at, it all looked reasonable.

Joe knew exactly what it was.

Division Gray hadn't ended.

It had evolved.

He followed the thread until it led somewhere colder.

Internal research summaries replaced procurement manifests. Documents written for people who didn't have time to read full reports but needed to understand what they were buying. The language was clinical. Careful. No moral weight. No human voices.

Just outcomes.

Post-event residue acquisition.

Joe read it twice.

They were collecting Residuum.

Not investigating it. Not recording it. Taking it.

Behavioral imprint recovery.

Resonance persistence harvesting.

Harvesting. The word you used for crops. For resources. For things that didn't have names.

Echo exposure zones were treated like asset fields. Containment teams entered after events not to help, but to recover what was left behind.

Joe scrolled down.

Emotional dampening in test populations.

Memory fragmentation markers.

Compliance smoothing observed under controlled exposure.

Compliance smoothing.

Joe didn't need imagination to understand that one. He'd lived long enough in the world to know what people meant when they wrote phrases like that.

They'd found a way to take human reaction and rub it down until it stopped cutting.

A line near the bottom froze his hands on the keyboard.

Recovered imprint density correlates strongly with fear saturation and prolonged replay exposure.

Joe felt the Quiet Choir like an itch in his bones, not here in the safehouse, but out there in the world. The Choir fed on resonance. These people weren't trying to starve it.

They were bottling what it left behind.

"They're not studying trauma," Joe whispered. "They're bottling it."

He kept digging.

There was no weapons program.

No missiles. No explosives. No troop movements. No battalions.

That was the trick.

He overlaid research summaries with patent filings. Matched procurement deliveries to incident clusters. Watched how contracts spiked just before certain events resolved too cleanly.

Patterns formed.

They weren't building weapons.

They were building pacification.

Systems designed to blunt panic. To reduce resistance. To dull the emotional spike that made people hard to steer.

A phrase in one summary made his chest tighten.

Narrative disruption capability under field conditions.

Memory destabilization fields.

Echo pattern force multipliers.

It wasn't a gun.

It was a switch.

You didn't need to conquer a city if you could rewrite how it remembered resistance.

Joe understood the shape of the threat then. Cold. Complete.

The Weave answered attention. Belief. Fear.

If you controlled the reaction, you controlled the resonance.

And if you controlled the resonance, you controlled what came next.

Joe pulled up the Containment Alliance funding streams and laid them over the Echo research timelines.

On paper, the Alliance doctrine was restraint and public safety. Cooperative training. Registration frameworks. Stabilization support.

It looked reasonable.

It looked necessary.

The funding told a different story.

Containment dominated Phase One. Facilities. Personnel. Monitoring.

But the real money lived deeper.

Residuum acquisition.

Resonance shaping platforms.

Cognitive compliance tools.

Narrative disruption modeling.

Containment was Phase One.

Weaponization was Phase Two.

Joe sat back, anger sharpening his focus instead of burning it away.

Either the Alliance didn't know what it was enabling, which meant the most powerful response structure on the planet was being hijacked from inside.

Or this was what it had been built for from the start.

Both possibilities were catastrophic.

He needed proof.

Joe dug through incident reports until he found one that didn't fit.

A minor Echo event. Small cluster freeze. No deaths. No viral footage. No panic.

Tagged internally as a stabilization success.

The event had resolved too cleanly. No lingering trauma. No secondary Choir resonance. No memory bleed.

This wasn't containment.

It was a field test.

They'd used something.

It worked.

And that terrified him.

Joe leaned back, staring at his own reflection in the dark screen.

HECATE was gone.

Hargreaves was sidelined.

Congress was congratulating itself.

They hadn't killed the program.

They'd freed it.

He shut the screens down carefully, bundled the files into an encrypted cache, and stood as dawn finally broke outside the window.

The world hadn't chosen containment or freedom.

It had chosen efficiency.

Joe knew, with sinking certainty, that this was the most dangerous choice of all.

And he knew exactly who he had to talk to next.

11

Elara Under Glass

Elara hadn't gone looking for trouble. She'd left the safehouse because the walls were starting to feel too close and the air inside carried everyone else's fear. She told herself she was running an errand, picking up supplies they'd need soon enough anyway. Batteries. Bandages. Things that didn't ask questions.

But really, she needed motion. Needed to burn off the pressure building under her skin before it found its own way out.

Walking the city helped. Noise helped. The ordinary mess of traffic and people and storefront lights grounded her in a world that still pretended nothing fundamental had changed. She was halfway between a pharmacy and a corner market when the heat spike rippled through her chest, sharp and unmistakable. By the time she saw the smoke clawing up the side of the high-rise, clearing her head stopped mattering.

Only the screaming did.

That was all it took.

She didn't ask permission. She didn't stop to think about angles or exits or what this would look like from the street. She moved because time had already run out for someone, and if she hesitated it would be for more.

The heat slammed into her the moment she crossed the perimeter. It wasn't hostile at first. It was panicked. Fire trying to be everywhere at once, climbing stairwells, chewing through doors, devouring oxygen. Elara reached for it without words, without ritual. She pulled, bent, forced the flames to fold inward instead of outward.

Windows burst above her, glass raining down. She lifted a hand and the heat curled, redirected, forming corridors where smoke thinned and air returned. People stumbled out of doorways, coughing, eyes wide, some running straight into her arms without knowing why they trusted her.

She carried them anyway.

A man with burned hands. A woman dragging a child who wouldn't stop crying. Two teenagers who couldn't stop shaking. Elara moved through the building like a wound closing, sealing flare-ups, venting pressure, dragging heat up and out through ruptured floors and shattered windows. Her fire wasn't wild. It was precise, shaped by instinct and desperation.

She didn't notice the phones at first.

She was too busy keeping the stairwell intact. Too busy forcing the flames to bow instead of surge. Too busy holding a door together with heat alone while people poured past her, coughing and crying and alive.

Someone shouted her name.

She froze for half a heartbeat.

She didn't know who said it. She didn't know how they knew it. She turned instinctively, and that was when she saw the camera.

A man stood at the far end of the street, arm raised, phone steady. Others stood beside him, screens glowing. Dozens of them. Maybe more. She caught her reflection in the glass of a shattered storefront and barely recognized herself.

Fire curved around her body, not touching skin, bending away from her like it knew better. Smoke parted where she stepped. Light flickered across her face, turning her into something sharp and unreal.

A child reached for her hand.

Elara took it without thinking, and the child didn't flinch. Didn't cry. Just stared up at her with wide, calm eyes, like this was the most reasonable thing in the world.

Sirens finally arrived. Red and blue light washed over the street, clashing with orange flame. Firefighters shouted orders. Someone yelled for people to move back.

The fire wasn't the danger anymore.

The watching was.

By the time Elara pulled herself away and disappeared down an alley thick with steam and shadow, the story had already started.

Joe saw the first clip before she made it back to the safehouse.

He was already awake, already working, already trying to keep pace with a world that refused to slow down. The video was shaky, vertical, badly framed, and devastatingly clear. Elara stood against a wall of flame, heat bending around her like a promise.

The headlines fractured almost immediately.

Fire Angel Saves Dozens in High-Rise Inferno.
Unknown Flame Entity Intervenes in Urban Disaster.
Is This the Sign We Were Warned About?

Joe didn't finish reading. He didn't need to. He could feel the resonance shift even through text and pixels. Attention poured into the Weave, belief stacking on belief, fear threading through awe until the signal tightened and hummed.

No version of the story included Elara as a person.

Only as an answer. Or a threat.

By the time she reached the safehouse, it was everywhere.

Richard had come back hours earlier, eyes shadowed, answers deferred. Whatever he'd touched out there hadn't let go of him yet.

Elara stood in front of the screen like she was watching a stranger's life. The footage looped endlessly, the same few seconds replayed from different angles. Her silhouette framed by fire. The child reaching for her. The way the flames curved, elegant and controlled.

Almost beautiful.

That was what terrified her most.

"That's not me," she said quietly.

No one contradicted her.

Alex stood close, eyes on her instead of the screen, scanning for signs of overload that weren't there. He could feel her fire jittering under her skin, reactive and raw. Maya hovered near the edge of the room, gaze distant, tracking how the Weave tightened around the image instead of the act.

Joe was already on his laptop, fingers flying, trying to slow a narrative avalanche with words that would never be enough.

Richard watched from the corner, unreadable.

Elara turned away from the screen, arms wrapping around herself like she could hold her shape together through force of will alone.

"I didn't do anything wrong," she said.

"No," Maya replied. "You didn't."

"But it doesn't matter," Elara said. "It doesn't matter what I did. It matters what they saw."

She gestured at the screen, at the flame caught forever in a frame that stripped out the heat, the fear, the smoke burning her lungs.

"I don't get to just save people anymore," she said, voice tightening. "I get turned into a reason."

Joe looked up. "We can manage this," he said, and even as he spoke it he knew how thin it sounded. "We can slow it. Shape it. At least a little."

"Until someone decides I'm useful," Elara shot back. "Or dangerous. Or both."

Her fire flared, heat rippling along the walls before she dragged it back under control, jaw clenched.

"They don't see fire," she said. "They see permission."

The room went quiet.

Richard shifted at last. "Visibility makes you unavoidable," he said slowly. "That makes you valuable. Which also makes you dangerous."

Elara turned on him. "To who."

"To everyone," Richard said. "Including us."

The words landed harder than he meant them to. Elara heard alignment in them even if he didn't say the word *Alliance*. She stepped back like the floor had tilted.

"So what," she said. "I stop."

No one answered.

Later, when the house settled and the screens went dark, Elara shut herself in the spare room. She sat on the edge of the bed, hands trembling, fire flickering along her fingers without permission. She remembered being unseen. Being anonymous. Being able to move through the world without anyone deciding what she meant.

Invisibility had been protection.

Visibility was exposure.

She picked up her phone one last time and scrolled past a still image of herself wreathed in flame. The caption beneath it was short. Definitive. Wrong.

Elara turned the screen off.

The fire dimmed.

Outside, the world kept watching anyway.

12

Operation Veilhook

The fourth day felt worse than the first.

Not louder. Not more dangerous. Just heavier.

The safehouse held tension the way a sealed room held heat. Nothing obvious moved outside. No vehicles lingered too long. No drones hovered where they shouldn't. That was what made it wrong. Absence had teeth now.

Elara hadn't gone out since the fire.

She stayed inside, quiet, flame pulled tight beneath her skin like something coiled and watchful. Joe worked nonstop, cycling narratives, feeding counterweights into a media storm that refused to stabilize. Alex barely slept, grounding Elara, grounding Maya, grounding anyone who drifted too close to overload.

Richard paced. Thought. Trusted the pause.

"They're being careful," he said that morning, studying a screen full of nothing. "If they were going to move, we'd feel it by now."

Maya didn't answer. The Weave hadn't relaxed. It had tightened.

Silence wasn't restraint.

It was alignment.

Elara didn't leave to prove anything.

She left because she was suffocating.

The walk was supposed to be short. A controlled loop around the block. Enough movement to remind herself she still existed as a person, not an image. Early evening, light thinning, foot traffic low but not absent. The kind of normal that didn't invite attention.

She didn't bring fire with her.

That was the mistake.

The first sign wasn't sound. It was pressure. A subtle compression in the air that made her chest tighten half a second before hands closed around her arms.

No shouts. No panic.

Professionals.

Something snapped against her wrist, cold and humming. Her flame answered instinctively and slid sideways, dispersing instead of igniting. The heat bled into a faint shimmer that vanished before it could take shape.

"What the hell," she gasped, twisting.

"Asset secured," someone said calmly. Not her name. A designation.

They moved fast. Four of them visible, more behind. Armor matte and unmarked. Helmets sealed. One carried a device that thrummed like a headache pressed into metal.

Elara fought.

Fire surged and died again, smothered mid-birth. Her emotions spiked and hit resistance, like screaming into insulation. Something stabbed at the back of her skull and the flame faltered.

They'd built this for her.

A bag went over her head.

Pain didn't come first.

Disorientation did.

Her fire tried to answer fear and kept slipping, like it couldn't find purchase. Heat dispersed into fields she couldn't see. Her breath came short and sharp. Panic clawed higher.

"Suppressor's holding," a voice said.

Another grip tightened. They were lifting her.

No.

Elara screamed and forced everything she had into a single ignition point.

Something cracked.

Not flame.

Air.

The distress hit Maya like a blade.

Not sound. Not sight. Harmonic rupture. Elara's signature flared and then folded, strangled mid-note. Maya was already moving.

"Alex," she said, grabbing him hard.

The jump tore.

Space folded wrong, pavement exploding outward as they arrived inside the perimeter of a fight already in motion. Maya hit the ground on one knee, vision swimming, Alex half-falling beside her as the Weave screamed at the intrusion.

Elara was ten meters away, struggling, bound, surrounded.

Maya didn't think.

She jumped again.

The second arrival shattered containment geometry. One operative flew backward and didn't get up. Another went down screaming as flame finally found oxygen and roared.

They'd planned for Maya.

They hadn't planned for fury.

The tech was wrong.

Not hostile. Adaptive.

Alex slammed his grounding into Elara, teeth gritted as feedback tore through him. The interference bit back, trying to read him, trying to adjust. He forced himself deeper, anchoring through pain, through noise, through the sickening awareness that the system noticed him noticing it.

Elara gasped and her fire came alive.

Fully alive.

Containment fields buckled. Armor blackened. One operative went down in a rush of flame so intense Alex had to look away.

Someone fired.

Maya caught it mid-air and threw it back. Bone broke. Blood hit concrete.

This wasn't controlled anymore.

This was survival.

The attackers broke.

Two tried to retreat. One didn't make it. Fire consumed the space where he'd been standing, leaving nothing clean behind. Another vanished into smoke trailing blood.

The last one looked at Maya like he'd finally understood what they'd miscalculated.

Then he ran.

Silence crashed down hard and wrong.

Elara sagged against Alex, shaking. Maya stood there breathing smoke and copper and burned insulation, hands still glowing faintly with aftershock.

People were dead.

This wasn't a warning.

This was war.

Joe arrived late and furious.

He cataloged wreckage with shaking hands. Gear fragments. Suppressors cracked open. Serial patterns too clean to be black market. Logistics too coordinated to be rogue.

"This wasn't random," he said quietly. "This was sanctioned. Not HECATE. Something newer. Smarter."

No one argued.

Richard didn't need Joe to finish.

He was staring at a shattered tablet pulled from the wreckage. Not at the hardware. At the logic embedded in its failsafes.

Restraint thresholds.

Acquisition priority.

Escalation avoidance until containment collapse.

His language.

His ideas.

Not copied. Implemented.

Richard's stomach dropped.

"I didn't authorize this," he said slowly.

Maya turned. "Authorize what."

"My work," Richard said. "Someone used my frameworks. Early drafts. Safeguards."

The room went very still.

"They took them," he finished. "And they didn't wait."

That was the betrayal.

Not ideology.

Access.

The Weave still shook.

Not with attack energy. With consequence.

This hadn't been about testing the Circle. It had been about taking Elara. Full stop. And they'd failed.

Which meant they would adapt.

Maya looked at Richard, at Elara, at Alex still shaking with exhaustion, and understood something settle into place.

Secrecy was over.

Richard burned the rest of his notes that night.

Not out of fear.

Out of clarity.

Whatever he'd believed he was shaping had already moved without him. His restraint hadn't slowed them. It had taught them efficiency.

He stood with the Circle now not because he'd chosen sides.

But because the choice had already been made for him.

And next time, he knew, they wouldn't miss.

13

Saints, Monsters, Weapons

Joe watched the world fracture before breakfast.

The new safehouse was quiet in that thin, early-morning way that never quite felt like peace. Concrete walls. Blackout curtains. A kitchen table that had already become a command surface layered with screens and cables and half-drunk mugs of coffee. Joe sat hunched forward, elbows on the table, eyes moving from one feed to the next without lingering.

He wasn't looking for outrage. Or validation. Or truth.

He was cataloging posture.

Asia lit up first. Emergency sessions. Statements released within hours of each other that contradicted themselves before the ink dried. One nation declared Walkers protected national assets, critical to sovereignty and defense. Another announced immediate criminal penalties for any unsanctioned Walker activity. A third quietly amended detention authority under existing counterterrorism statutes without saying the word Walker at all.

Europe followed. Registration frameworks framed as safety measures. Language heavy with reassurance. Voluntary. Temporary. Necessary.

Joe marked them anyway.

North America fractured along jurisdictional lines. Federal agencies stalled. State governments surged forward. Task forces announced. Committees formed. Oversight promised. Indefinite detention authorized in closed session.

Emergency legislation bloomed overnight like mold.

Joe didn't react. He didn't argue with the screen. He didn't swear.

He logged.

They hadn't waited to understand. They'd waited to claim.

By midmorning, the saints appeared.

It started the way these things always did. Soft at first. Almost comforting.

A grainy still of Elara standing against flame was rendered in brushstroke and gold leaf, her silhouette haloed, her fire curved into something that looked deliberate. A caption beneath it spoke of protection. Of cleansing. Of mercy.

Within hours, it multiplied.

Different styles. Different languages. Different iconography. Elara's face softened, sharpened, abstracted. Fire became wings. Fire became judgment. Fire became proof.

Maya appeared next.

Not as herself.

As a threshold. A watcher. A figure at the edge of light, half in shadow, half in brilliance. The one who opens. The one who decides.

Donations poured into newly formed sanctuaries that promised safety for Walkers and healing for the faithful. Their websites used words like refuge and calling and destiny. Their leadership spoke in careful tones about guidance and obedience and purpose.

Worship didn't look like chains.

It didn't need to.

Across the city, Alex stood near a different screen, arms folded tight across his chest.

The footage looped without context. The alley. The smoke. The bodies. The fire.

Not the hands grabbing Elara. Not the suppressor snapping closed. Not the first blow thrown in silence.

Just impact.

Headlines scrolled past.

Walker Violence Erupts in Urban Zone.

Are Walkers a Threat? We Can't Ignore

Containment Before It's Too Late!

Edited clips removed the ambush and left the aftermath. The dead were framed as responders. The attackers blurred into civilians. The fire became excess instead of defense.

Alex felt it in his bones. Fear spiked near nodes. Echo zones tightened. People started avoiding places they couldn't explain, the unease blooming into something sharper with every retelling.

Monsters justified eradication.

Richard watched a different leak surface while the coffee went cold in his hands.

The briefing wasn't meant to be public. It still wasn't complete. Slides without logos. Language stripped of emotion.

Anomaly had vanished from the vocabulary.

Capability replaced it.

Deployment potential. Force multiplication. Risk mitigation through asset control.

He recognized the framing immediately. Not because he'd written it. Because it was the logic he'd always feared was inevitable.

They'd been thinking this way long before he ever opened his mouth.

The guilt didn't ease. It deepened. But it shifted. Less poison. More weight.

Joe finally shut the feeds down and turned to the others. They were all there now, gathered in the common space of the new safehouse. No one spoke while he collected his thoughts.

"They're writing our myth without us," he said.

The words landed hard.

Maya felt the truth of it resonate through the Weave. Not as sound. As pressure. Belief was settling into shape, hardening where it pooled long enough. Stories were becoming structures.

Silence wasn't neutral anymore.

They finished the relocation that afternoon.

The old place was burned. Not literally, but in every way that mattered. This new site sat lower, quieter, stitched into the city instead of perched above it. Fewer lines of sight. Fewer digital footprints. Harder to notice unless you already knew where to look.

Maya stood still for a moment after the last door sealed and breathed.

The Weave didn't relax.

But it eased.

This place felt temporary. All places did now. But it was chosen. And that mattered.

They didn't argue as they settled in.

Alex set grounding rhythms without being asked, subtle adjustments in proximity and timing that made the air feel steadier. Maya recalibrated her jumps, learning how to arrive without tearing space when others were with her. Elara practiced ignition under Alex's watch, flame tight and controlled, no spectacle, no drift.

Joe coordinated. Times. Movements. Information flow.

Richard handled logistics. Quietly. Precisely. No commands. No assumptions.

They moved like a unit without naming it.

Later, when the screens stayed dark, Joe and Richard sat at the table with paper spread between them. Not plans. Not schematics.

Principles.

Voluntary coordination. Consent as non-negotiable. Transparency as armor. Oversight that answered to more than power. Mediation before escalation. Structure without ownership.

"This isn't about control," Joe said, tapping the page.

"No," Richard agreed. "It's about preventing it."

They didn't call it anything.

Elara stood apart near the window, phone in hand. Another image. Another caption. Another version of her that didn't belong to her at all.

"If they decide what I mean," she said quietly, "I stop being human."

No one contradicted her.

Maya felt the Weave tighten across the city. Across borders. Across millions of minds leaning toward certainty because uncertainty hurt too much.

Belief was becoming architecture.

The world hadn't chosen peace or war.

It had chosen sides.

<h1 style="text-align:center">14</h1>

Long Distance Training

Maya noticed the first reach when the house went quiet.

Not silence. The low, settled quiet that came after exhaustion, when even the pipes seemed to pause. She lay awake in the dark, staring at the ceiling, breath shallow, waiting for sleep that wouldn't come.

Then the pressure brushed past her awareness.

It wasn't an alarm. It wasn't pain. It wasn't even fear in the way she'd learned to recognize it. It felt distant and uneven, like fingers skimming the surface of the Weave without knowing what they were touching.

Maya sat up slowly, heart ticking faster. The threads around the safehouse hummed softly, aligned and steady. But beyond them, something tugged. Not toward her.

Through her.

Someone was panicking without words.

Then another.

Then more, scattered far enough apart that geography should've mattered. It didn't. The Weave didn't care about borders or oceans or time zones. It cared about resonance. And resonance was reaching for itself.

Maya pressed her palm to the floor and listened.

These weren't attacks. They weren't Echo events. They weren't distortions flaring toward collapse. They were untrained Walkers brushing against power and recoiling from it, afraid and alone and unable to articulate why the world suddenly felt louder inside their own bodies.

"They're not reaching for help," Maya whispered.

Joe stirred on the couch, already half awake. He felt it too. Not as pressure, but as wrongness. As a lie under strain, trying to hold a shape it couldn't sustain.

"They're reaching because something's breaking," he said quietly. "And the Weave doesn't like imbalance."

Alex appeared in the doorway, barefoot, eyes heavy but alert. "How many."

Maya closed her eyes again, sorting sensation from noise. "Enough that this isn't coincidence."

The Weave wasn't summoning them.

It was pulling itself back together.

Joe leaned forward, spine straightening as his awareness slipped sideways into the lattice beneath reality. He didn't search for individuals. He never had. He reached for truth.

Fear collapsed first.

Not erased. Clarified.

Somewhere far away, a young mind stopped spiraling long enough to draw a steady breath. Another stopped resisting the wrong sensation. A third let go of the belief that they were dying when they weren't.

Joe didn't speak into the Weave. He didn't send reassurance or instruction.

He removed distortion.

The effect rippled outward, subtle but unmistakable. Panic softened. Harmonics steadied. The Weave adjusted itself around the correction, the way a structure settles when stress is relieved.

Alex felt it immediately.

Grounding followed truth the way stone followed gravity.

He leaned into the resonance and reinforced what was already stabilizing. He didn't shield. He didn't impose. He made endurance possible where it already wanted to exist.

Across the world, breath slowed. Muscles unclenched. The urge to flee without knowing why eased.

"It's working," Alex murmured, disbelief threading through exhaustion. "I'm not holding them. I'm backing them up."

Maya opened her eyes and saw it.

Threads aligning. Not tightening.

Strengthening.

She stepped carefully into the flow, not to teach, not to correct, but to show.

Perception first.

She nudged awareness sideways just enough that a teenager in São Paulo realized the room wasn't slipping away from him. He was stepping too far ahead of himself. She let him feel the instant where the Weave bent before it tore.

In Busan, a dockworker stopped fighting the way machines responded to his presence. Instead, he felt the rhythm beneath them. The disruption eased when he matched it instead of resisting.

In Lagos, a nurse drawing heat from fevered patients felt the boundary she'd been crossing without knowing it. Maya didn't stop her. She showed her where to pause.

Survival came before mastery.

No one asked for lessons.

No one named what was happening.

They didn't need to.

Time blurred into overlap. Some connections lasted seconds. Some minutes. Some lingered too long, fear clinging to calm like a lifeline.

Maya learned when to step back.

Cutting contact felt cruel. Necessary. Overconnection bred dependence, and dependence fractured faster than isolation ever had.

Joe felt resistance from one presence. A refusal wrapped in suspicion. Fear of surveillance. Fear of ownership.

He didn't push.

Truth didn't land where it wasn't welcome.

Another presence demanded structure. Authority. Someone to tell them what they were allowed to be.

Joe let that need remain unanswered.

Alex stiffened suddenly, breath catching.

"What is it," Elara asked from the doorway.

Alex's gaze unfocused, tracking something only he could feel. "There's someone else," he said slowly. "Not them. Like me."

He reached deeper.

Then stopped.

Then nodded once.

"Two," he said. "Different. But steady. Same function."

He wasn't unique.

He was early.

Elara watched from the edge of the room, arms folded tight against herself. She didn't reach out. She didn't ignite.

She didn't need to.

She watched fear soften into calm across distances that once would've demanded intervention, spectacle, fire.

This was protection.

Presence without force.

For the first time since the high-rise, she exhaled without flinching.

When the last resonance faded and the house settled again, no one spoke.

They sat among scattered notes and half-formed thoughts, impressions written by hand because screens felt wrong now.

"This isn't an organization," Joe said finally.

Maya nodded. "It's a lattice."

Alex shook his head slightly. "A nervous system."

No headquarters. No ranks. No ownership.

Just connection.

Maya closed her eyes one last time and felt the threads stretching outward. Not thinner.

Stronger.

At the edges of her awareness, the Shadow Current shifted, unsettled. Not defeated, but slowed. Cooperation changed pressure. It always had.

The world had taught Walkers to hide.

The Weave taught them to find each other.

Somewhere else, far from the safehouse and far from any fear-driven awakening, something listened.

Not for help.

But for opportunity.

15

The Choir at the Node

The pull started hours before anyone named it.

Maya felt it first as a subtle imbalance, the way the Weave sometimes leaned before a storm. Not strain. Not rupture. A directional pressure that didn't belong to geography. It tugged at her awareness the way gravity tugged at water, quiet but relentless.

She stood on the roof of a low concrete structure at the edge of the city, staring out across a skyline that looked wrong in small, accumulating ways. Clouds stacked too evenly. Wind moved in broad, synchronized sweeps instead of erratic currents. The air felt heavy without being hot, charged without crackle.

Below, traffic slowed without cause. Horns didn't blare. Voices didn't rise. People moved with a shared patience that felt practiced rather than chosen.

"That node's awake," Joe said behind her.

Maya nodded without turning. "It's more than awake."

Alex leaned against the stairwell door, eyes closed, one hand braced on the concrete as if he were listening through it. "It's loud," he said. "But not sharp. It's... smooth."

Elara frowned. "That's not better."

They all felt it. A draw that bypassed instinct and went straight to attention. The kind of pull that didn't demand obedience, only focus. Walkers across the city were drifting closer without realizing why. Maya sensed their signatures bending inward, like iron filings toward a buried magnet.

Everything about it felt intentional.

Which was the problem.

Richard felt the draw and stopped. Whatever lived beneath the city didn't want to be shaped, and he'd learned the cost of forcing order where it didn't belong.

They descended into the transit access tunnels beneath the district, following the pressure as it thickened. The deeper they went, the quieter the world became. Not empty. Muted. Footsteps echoed less. Voices softened mid-sentence. Even the distant rumble of trains smoothed into a low, even pulse.

At the edge of the node chamber, the air changed.

The space was vast, carved out decades earlier for infrastructure that never quite materialized. Concrete ribs arched overhead. Old cables drooped like dead vines. In the center, the Weave folded inward on itself, threads looping and overlapping in dense, luminous strata.

The Quiet Choir had grown.

Not as a shape. Not as a presence with edges. As a field.

Maya expected violence. Pressure spikes. Static. The familiar warning signs of Echo buildup.

Instead, she felt calm.

Too much of it.

A man arguing with a security guard nearby lowered his voice, then stopped talking altogether. Two strangers who had been on the verge of a shouting match stepped apart and blinked, confused, their anger gone like it had never existed. A woman who had been crying on a bench wiped her face and sat still, breathing evenly, eyes unfocused.

Conflict didn't escalate.

It dissolved.

Elara clenched her fists. "I don't like this," she said. "It's smoothing people down."

Joe swallowed. His Truthsense twisted uncomfortably. "There's no deception," he said. "That's what's wrong. Nothing's lying."

Alex shook his head slowly. "It's not suppressing them," he said. "It's... aligning them."

Maya stepped forward before anyone could stop her.

The pull intensified, not as resistance but accommodation. The Weave adjusted around her presence, threads shifting to absorb her harmonic footprint the way water reshaped around a stone dropped gently into it.

She braced herself for hostility.

None came.

She reached out, not with power, but with perception.

At first, her mind searched for familiar markers. Emotion. Intent. Awareness. The signatures she'd learned to read in Walkers and Echoes alike.

There was nothing.

No anger. No hunger. No curiosity.

No watching.

She went deeper.

The Choir wasn't responding to her. It wasn't acknowledging her at all. Its harmonics flowed in repeating patterns, self-correcting loops that tightened where pressure rose and relaxed where it fell. Disturbance entered the field and was smoothed out. Variance collapsed toward equilibrium.

It wasn't making choices.

It was resolving equations.

Maya's breath caught.

She looked for fear and found none.

Looked for desire and found none.

Looked for intent and found only gradients equalizing, tension redistributing until the system settled into the lowest possible state of strain.

It wasn't alive.

But it was intelligent.

Not sentient. Not aware.

Optimizing.

"It's not watching me," Maya said quietly.

The others froze.

"It's not reacting to me either," she continued. "It's adjusting around me."

Joe stepped closer. "Adjusting how."

"Like I'm a variable," she said. "Not a threat. Not a person. Just… input."

The realization landed hard and cold.

Elara took a step forward, fire flaring instinctively along her hands. "Hey," she snapped into the open space, voice sharp with heat and defiance. "You want calm. Try this."

She let the flame rise.

Not an inferno. A warning. Heat curled and brightened, emotion bleeding into combustion the way it always did.

The Choir didn't flinch.

The fire thinned.

Not extinguished. Diffused.

The Weave around the flame redistributed the energy outward, dispersing it into the broader field until the heat no longer spiked, no longer burned. Elara's control slipped, not because she lost it, but because there was nothing left to control.

She stared at her hands. "It didn't even push back."

Joe tried next. He reached for truth, for distortion to strip away.

There was nothing false to remove.

No belief. No narrative. No deception.

Truth passed through the Choir without friction and came out unchanged.

Joe recoiled, shaken. "There's nothing there to hear us."

Alex knelt, grounding instinctively as the pressure brushed against his senses. The Choir adjusted again, incorporating his stabilizing presence into its broader pattern.

He felt it then. Not recognition.

Compatibility.

"It's not trying to hurt anyone," Alex said slowly. "It's trying to make the noise stop."

Maya nodded. Her voice was steady when she spoke, but her hands trembled. "It's not trying to end us," she said. "It's trying to finish itself."

The weight of that truth settled over them.

This wasn't annihilation.

It was order.

A version of stability that erased peaks and valleys alike. Fear and joy. Conflict and resolve. Choice itself smoothed down until nothing sharp enough remained to disturb the field.

Entropy, given shape.

Not destruction.

Reorganization.

Around them, the city breathed in unison.

Maya pulled back carefully, severing her focus before the Choir could absorb her fully into its calculus. The pull lessened but didn't vanish. The field continued its work, indifferent to their presence, committed only to balance.

"This is why attention matters," Maya said. "It grows when we look at it. When we react. When we try to fight it."

"Stability without choice is still annihilation," Elara said quietly.

Joe nodded. "And attention's the currency it feeds on."

They withdrew from the chamber without ceremony, leaving the Choir to hum beneath the city like a buried engine that had just reached cruising speed.

Aboveground, the weather held steady. Too steady.

Maya paused at the mouth of the tunnel and looked back once more, sensing the threads tightening beneath her feet. Not thinner.

Stronger.

Somewhere else, far beyond this node and far beyond this city, other places were beginning to feel the same pull.

And somewhere else still, something was watching the Choir not with fear or awe.

But with interest.

The war ahead wouldn't be fought against a villain.

It would be fought against a solution.

16

Hargreaves' Offer

Joe was halfway through dismantling a false narrative when the message arrived.

It didn't trigger an alert. It didn't announce itself with urgency. It slid into his system through channels he hadn't seen used in years, the kind of obsolete routing protocols only people who'd lived in the gray spaces before the fracture still trusted, layered beneath newer security like fossils trapped in sediment. That alone narrowed the list of possible senders to a number small enough to count on one hand.

The signature finished it.

Joe leaned back in his chair and closed his eyes for a moment, not in disbelief, not in anger.

In exhaustion.

Hargreaves was alive.

Not just alive. Free. Still moving through the gray spaces between collapsed authority and unclaimed influence, where men like him had always thrived.

Joe opened the data packet.

It wasn't a manifesto. It wasn't a plea. It wasn't even an apology dressed up as analysis. It was raw material. Partial logs from Alliance Echo experiments, stripped of identifiers but rich with pattern. Node amplification trials. Choir resonance scaling curves. Failure points circled in red, annotated with a precision that told Joe exactly how closely someone had been watching the wrong things for far too long.

At the bottom, a single warning line repeated three times in different phrasings.

Choir growth is accelerating faster than containment modeling predicts.

And beneath that, the ask.

A meeting.

With Maya present.

Joe stared at the screen until the words lost their shape.

He didn't feel fear.

He felt tired.

By the time he gathered the others, the safehouse was quiet in that late-night way that never quite reached sleep. Joe stood at the center of the common room and projected the data without preamble, letting the files scroll in silence.

Elara didn't wait for him to finish.

"No," she said flatly. "Absolutely not."

Alex folded his arms, jaw tight. "This is framing," he said. "He feeds us real data, controls the context, then steers the response. That's his playbook."

Maya said nothing. She stood near the wall, eyes unfocused, listening past the numbers.

Richard leaned forward, studying a resonance graph. "This is legitimate," he said after a moment. "Incomplete, but not falsified. Whoever compiled this had access to mid-tier Alliance research. Not leadership level. Not field only. That's a narrow band."

Joe nodded. "That band has his fingerprints all over it."

No one argued about whether Hargreaves could be trusted.

They argued about whether they could afford to ignore him.

"If we meet him," Elara said, voice low and sharp, "we change something. Even if we don't mean to."

Maya finally spoke. "We already changed something by not know-ing."

That quieted the room.

Later, in the smaller side room where the walls dampened reso-nance, Maya sat with the data alone. She didn't read it the way Joe did. She let it rest against the Weave and felt what bled through.

Regret was there. Not performative. Not clean. The kind that ate slowly and never finished.

Fear too. Not for himself. For outcomes. For scale.

There was no deception in the offer itself. No hidden hooks buried in the signal. That absence was almost more unsettling than a lie would have been.

Hargreaves wasn't seeking forgiveness.

He was seeking relevance.

Maya stood and went back to the others. "I'll go," she said.

Elara turned sharply. "Maya."

"On my terms," Maya added. "Which I won't explain yet."

They met him in a closed museum wing that smelled faintly of dust and old climate control. The Circle arrived separately, folded into the space with practiced ease. Alex grounded the room subtly, resonance smoothing beneath his awareness. Elara stayed back near a shadowed doorway, fire coiled and ready. Richard took a position where he could see everything without being seen himself.

Hargreaves arrived alone.

He looked older than Joe remembered. Thinner. The kind of thin that came from long nights and fewer illusions. He didn't scan the room for threats. He didn't posture.

He set a tablet on the table and waited.

"I won't insult you by apologizing first," Hargreaves said. "You wouldn't believe me anyway."

Joe said nothing.

Hargreaves activated the display. Choir resonance fields bloomed across the screen. Failed stabilization attempts. Artificial dampening curves collapsing under real-world variance. Casualty projections marked with a precision that refused euphemism.

"I helped build this," Hargreaves said. "I believed Walkers were the problem. Uncontrolled variables. A disease in the system."

He looked at Maya then, really looked at her.

"I was wrong," he said. "You might be the only treatment we have."

Maya didn't flinch.

"You're still framing it wrong," she said. "We don't fix systems. We reveal imbalance."

Hargreaves nodded once. "That tracks."

"Cooperation doesn't mean forgiveness," Maya continued. "Protection doesn't mean partnership."

"I know," Hargreaves said. And for the first time, he sounded like he did.

Joe stepped in then, voice level. "Here are the terms. You don't get access to Walkers. You don't communicate with any of us directly except through me. Every piece of data you provide gets verified independently. You break any of that, and this ends."

Hargreaves didn't hesitate. "Agreed."

He knew it was his only currency left.

They left without ceremony.

Outside, Elara exhaled hard. "Working with him changes us," she said.

Maya didn't argue. "Refusing him changes the outcome anyway."

As they walked away, Maya felt the Weave shift. Not approval. Not resistance.

Acknowledgment.

Hargreaves watched them go, hands folded, shoulders heavy.

Not hopeful.

Relieved.

Something worse was coming.

And now, they knew it too.

17

Splitting the Party (Again)

Morning in the larger safehouse didn't feel like morning.

It felt like a pause between impacts.

Maya stood in the doorway of what had once been a small office suite and watched people try to pretend they weren't afraid. The windows were covered. The lights were low. The air carried the scent of instant coffee and damp concrete and borrowed blankets. Someone had taped cardboard over a cracked interior pane to dull the sound. Someone else had set a chair under the knob of a door that no one trusted anymore.

The Circle wasn't alone in their space now.

That fact should've felt like relief. It didn't.

Two Walkers slept on couches in the common room, bodies angled as if they expected to wake fighting. One of them was young, maybe eighteen, with a bruised jaw and hands that twitched even in sleep. The other was older, hair gone gray at the temples, jaw clenched tight like he was biting down on his own panic.

A woman in a hoodie packed a go-bag near the kitchen counter, folding bandages with the careful calm of someone who'd learned that speed was the enemy of control. She didn't look up when Maya passed. She didn't want eye contact. Eye contact made things real.

A man near the far wall pretended he was only checking his phone. Maya could hear the Weave around him anyway. His resonance kept flaring and settling like a heartbeat trying to remember its rhythm.

She felt it all, a low chorus of harmonics layered beneath ordinary movement. Not chaotic. Not safe either. Aligned enough to function. The way a cracked dam might still hold if nobody pushed too hard.

Someone swore softly near the counter.

The sound of ceramic breaking cut through the low murmur of the room. Not loud. Just sharp enough to pull attention. A coffee cup lay in pieces on the concrete floor, brown liquid spreading in a thin, apologetic puddle.

The woman who'd dropped it froze, shoulders tight, eyes darting like she expected someone to yell. She crouched automatically, hands hovering, unsure whether to touch anything.

"Sorry," she said, too fast. "I'll clean it up. I didn't mean to."

"It's fine," someone else said, already reaching for paper towels.

Richard stepped forward before anyone could stop him.

He didn't announce himself. He didn't posture. He just knelt, picked up the largest shard, and looked at the cup like it was a puzzle he'd already solved.

Maya felt the Weave stir. Not surge. Not strain. Just a quiet rearranging, like breath finding a better rhythm.

The fragments slid together in Richard's hands.

No flash. No glow. The cracks softened, seams fading as if they'd never learned how to break in the first place. The cup reformed whole, warm again, steam curling faintly from the surface as if continuity itself had been restored.

Richard stood and handed it back.

"Careful," he said mildly. "It's still hot."

The woman stared at the cup. Then at him. Then back at the cup.

"I... it was broken."

Richard shrugged. "Not badly."

Around them, no one spoke.

Alex felt it and glanced up, eyes narrowing. Elara's flame didn't react at all, which somehow made it stranger. Joe watched from across the room, expression unreadable, already filing it away under *things we can't afford to normalize too fast.*

Maya felt something else ripple through the space. Not awe. Not fear.

Permission.

The woman took the cup with shaking hands. "Thank you," she said quietly.

Richard nodded once and stepped back into the room like he hadn't just rewritten a rule.

The Weave settled.

And for a moment, magic didn't feel like a weapon.

It felt like help.

Alex moved through them like gravity.

He didn't say much. He didn't need to. A hand on a shoulder. A quiet look, steady and direct. The simplest human contact. That was what made him dangerous to chaos. He anchored it without fighting it.

But Maya could see the cost in him.

His eyes were tired. Not sleepy. Tired in the way stone got tired of holding back a river.

He paused beside the teenager on the couch and rested two fingers lightly on the kid's wrist. The boy's twitching eased. His breathing smoothed. Alex held it for a moment, then let go and kept walking as if he hadn't just saved someone from tearing themselves apart.

Maya watched him go and felt a flare of anger she didn't have a place to put.

Not at Alex. At the fact that this was becoming normal.

At the far end of the suite, Joe had turned the largest room into something that looked like an investigation only he could run. There were no news feeds looping on the wall anymore. No talking heads. No loud myths.

Just patterns.

Handwritten maps. Node pressure readings marked by sensation and witness reports. Notes pinned in clusters: Choir calm-zones. Places where arguments died in people's throats. Streets where traffic slowed without reason. A strip of paper with three words underlined twice: attention creates structure.

Another section of the board tracked movement that didn't belong to civilians. Logistics routes. Rail corridors. The way certain trucks appeared on cameras for half a second and then never showed up again.

Alliance movement.

Maya's stomach tightened. She didn't like that Joe could make the world's chaos look orderly. It meant the chaos had rules. And rules meant intention.

Joe's head was bowed over the table, eyes narrowed. He looked up when he sensed her in the doorway.

"You sleep at all?" he asked.

"Not really."

He nodded as if he hadn't expected any other answer.

"Alex?"

Maya glanced toward the hall where Alex had vanished. "He's holding too many people together."

Joe's mouth tightened. "Yeah. I know."

Maya turned back to the room. Walkers moving quietly. No one talking too loudly. No one laughing.

She felt the Weave shift under it all like a stomach turning before vomiting.

This wasn't a hideout anymore.

It was a nucleus.

And nuclei drew attention.

Joe's phone sat on the table, screen dark. Not because it was off. Because he didn't trust anything that could be recorded.

The Weave didn't record.

It reacted.

The phone vibrated once. Joe barely glanced at it before the Weave stirred. Joe froze, eyes narrowing as he read the message. It was badly structured. Half sentences. No clear ask. Panic trying to pass as information. The Weave flared in response, not as a voice, but as pressure beneath the words. The fragments were human. A location reference with no name. A mention of uniforms. A throwaway line about a hum that wouldn't stop. The Weave reacted to the fear threaded through it, tightening where the sender couldn't hold themselves steady.

Joe didn't answer right away. He let the message sit. Let the fear burn itself out. Then he did what he always did. He reached for what didn't lie.

He stripped distortion. Not by force. By ignoring everything that didn't line up. The panic collapsed like a tent when the pole snapped. What was left wasn't calm. It was clarity, raw and hard.

Guesswork collapsed into direction. Noise fell away, leaving signal that had already been there.

The place resolved because it matched three cases he'd already seen. Rail corridor. Industrial grit. An overpass that didn't show on public maps. A line of movement that felt disciplined and practiced. Dark uniforms mentioned twice in the text. Equipment described only as "humming," but with the kind of repetition people used when something scared them.

Joe blinked and returned to the room with a slow exhale.

Maya watched him. "Report?"

Joe nodded. "They're staging near the rail corridor."

Alex appeared at the doorway as if the words had pulled him in. Elara followed him, hair tied back, eyes too bright. Richard was already there, leaning against the wall with his arms crossed, watching everyone like he was counting exits.

Joe continued, voice level. "They're moving like they've done this before."

Elara's jaw tightened. "Alliance?"

"Could be. Could be contractors with Alliance doctrine. It's clean either way."

Another message came in minutes later. Shorter. Calmer. Almost blank. Not panic this time. A weight. A pressure that wanted the world to become smooth. A Walker near something they didn't have words for. The message didn't describe events. It described how standing there felt.

Joe read it twice. The words didn't change, but the tension beneath them did. The Weave settled as the panic thinned, leaving an impression of crowds that wouldn't hold shape long enough to break. A street corner where a man lifted his fist and then lowered it, confused. The Choir's field pulling, not like a voice, but like a slope.

Joe withdrew, lips pressed thin.

Maya could already feel it in her own bones. The node was calling.

Two fires at once.

She looked at the board. Rail corridor. Node calm-zone. Two threats that didn't care about fairness.

They gathered at the main table with the others keeping their distance, pretending not to listen while they listened anyway.

Maya laid her palm flat on the map where Joe had marked the node district.

"The Choir's field is widening," she said. "It's pulling Walkers. It's smoothing people down."

Alex's voice was low. "If it grows there, it'll grow anywhere. A megacity node is a bell. It'll ring through everything."

Joe tapped the rail corridor marks. "And Alliance movement is tightening around logistics. They're not just chasing Walkers anymore. They're harvesting something. Echo tech. Residuum. Whatever they can carry without understanding it."

Richard's eyes narrowed. "If they're harvesting Echo matter, they're going to try to force stabilization."

Maya looked at him. "And you know what forced stabilization becomes."

Richard didn't answer. He didn't have to.

It became the Choir, but with hands.

Elara's hands curled into fists. A thin heat tremor danced along her fingers, almost invisible. "So we go together."

Joe shook his head once. "We can't."

Silence fell, heavy and immediate. Even the distant hum of the building seemed to soften as if the walls were listening.

Maya felt it in the Weave, the shift that happened when a group stopped pretending choice was possible.

Splitting the party wasn't a tactic. It was a concession.

Elara moved away from the table without speaking. The hallway swallowed her. Maya watched her go, then followed.

Elara stood in the back room where they stored supplies, hands braced on the edge of a shelf as if she needed something solid to keep her from burning through the floor. Her shoulders were too still. That was how Maya knew she was holding back.

"You're not going," Elara said without turning.

Joe stepped into the doorway behind Maya. He'd followed too.

Elara finally turned, eyes hard. "You're not going after them again."

Joe didn't argue. He didn't tell her she was being irrational. He didn't offer reassurance. He just told the truth.

"I'm the one who can hear them," he said.

Elara's flame flickered along her fingers like a threat she didn't want to make.

Joe continued, voice quiet. "I can turn Weave-noise into something we can act on. I can strip distortion so we get signal instead of panic. If we're going to move ahead of them, it has to be me."

Elara's throat worked. She swallowed it down like poison. "That doesn't mean it has to be you and him."

Her eyes cut toward the doorway where Richard stood at a distance, watching without stepping in.

Joe's expression didn't change. "Richard knows the frameworks. He sees the patterns they're using."

Elara's voice dropped lower. "Richard's frameworks got used against us."

Richard's mouth tightened. He didn't speak. He didn't defend himself. That was new.

Joe nodded once. "That's why he needs to see how they're deploying them. So we can stop being surprised."

Elara's flame tremor eased, replaced by something worse. A steadiness that said she'd made up her mind and didn't like it.

"You come back," she said. Not a plea. A demand.

Joe met her gaze. "I'm going to try."

That wasn't a promise.

It was honesty.

Back in the main room, Richard finally pushed off the wall and stepped toward the table.

"Maya shouldn't go to the Choir without me," he said.

His tone had weight in it, the kind men used when they wanted their words to become law. It slipped out before he caught it.

Maya looked at him, calm and sharp. "You don't get to decide that."

Richard's nostrils flared. He checked himself, but the impulse was already exposed.

"I'm not trying to command you," he said, and it sounded like the lie he wanted to believe. "I'm trying to keep you from walking into something that doesn't care whether you live."

Maya held his gaze. "The Choir doesn't respond to authority," she said. "It doesn't negotiate. It optimizes."

Richard's jaw tightened. "That's why you need someone who understands systems."

Maya's voice stayed level. "You understand systems you can influence. This isn't that. This is a solution that doesn't need permission."

Richard looked away for a moment, as if the words had landed too close to something he didn't want to touch.

His fear showed in the smallest ways. The way his fingers flexed once, like he was fighting the urge to shape the room into something safer. The way his eyes tracked Maya's face as if he was trying to memorize it in case he never saw it again.

Maya understood then. It wasn't pride.

It was terror.

He was terrified she'd become part of a system he couldn't influence. He was terrified that if the Choir could smooth a megacity, it could smooth her, too.

Maya softened her voice just enough to keep him from breaking. "You can't control this," she said. "None of us can. We can only choose how we meet it."

Richard's throat worked. He nodded once, sharp and reluctant, like agreeing cost him something.

Maya turned away from him and looked at the other Walkers in the safehouse. The ones not in the Circle. The ones trying to stay invisible.

They were already part of it.

She stepped into the center of the room and raised her voice just enough to carry, not enough to echo.

"I need three volunteers," she said. "No one's drafted. No one's owned."

A few heads lifted. Eyes watched her warily.

Maya pointed to a woman with a hood pulled low, resonance steady but tight. "You. You're good at moving without leaving a trail."

The woman hesitated, then nodded once.

Maya pointed to a man near the kitchen, hands stained with grease, who'd been quiet since she arrived. "You've been near the calm drift zones. You can feel when crowds start smoothing."

The man swallowed and nodded, eyes flicking to Alex like he needed permission from gravity.

Maya pointed to the older Walker with gray hair who'd been awake now, sitting upright on the couch. His eyes were clear, but tired. "You're going to be a relay. Not in the Weave. On the street. If signals go dark, you keep a line open."

He stared at her for a long moment. Then he nodded. "I can do that."

Maya held their eyes. "You can say no. Any time."

None of them spoke. But the Weave around them shifted, a slight tightening that wasn't fear.

Choice had weight.

Alex moved to her side. "I can't keep everybody steady if we all go," he said quietly.

Maya glanced at him. She could see it in the slight tremor in his hands. He was already doing too much.

Alex continued, voice firm. "I go with you to the node. Proximity matters. You know it does."

Maya nodded. "It does."

Joe looked at Alex, then at Maya, then at Elara. The lines of the split were forming whether anyone liked it or not.

Joe spoke carefully. "Richard and I track the rail corridor. We follow Alliance movement. We don't engage unless we have to."

Elara's eyes narrowed. "You'll have to."

Joe didn't deny it.

Maya looked at the board one last time. Two fires. Two fronts.

No clean choice. Only deliberate ones.

They moved quickly after that. Not frantic. Efficient. Quiet. The way people moved when they'd accepted that the worst was coming and they'd decided to meet it standing.

Joe and Richard left first.

They didn't walk out like heroes. They moved like ghosts, slipping through stairwells and service corridors, avoiding cameras and patterns. Joe carried a small bag and a calm face. Richard carried nothing visible, which meant he carried danger inside his skin.

At the door, Elara stopped Joe with a hand on his sleeve. Not a grip. A touch.

Joe turned.

They shared a look that wasn't a promise. It wasn't even hope.

It was an admission.

They might not get another conversation.

Joe's mouth tightened. "Stay with Maya," he said softly.

Elara's voice barely carried. "Come back."

Joe nodded once and left.

Maya, Alex, and Elara left differently.

They didn't need to ghost through the city. The Choir's pull was already doing that for them. It smoothed traffic. It softened attention. It made people look away without knowing why.

Maya felt it in her chest as soon as they hit the street. A slope beneath the world. A gravity well of attention that bypassed fear and went straight to focus.

Alex walked close at her side, grounding her without touching. Elara stayed a half step behind, fire coiled under her skin like a restrained animal.

As they moved, Maya felt the Weave stretch between the teams.

Not break.

Stretch.

Threads connecting Joe's far movement to her own, thin but present, like nerves learning their shape.

The network was starting to behave like a nervous system.

And then, as they reached the corner where the city opened toward the district beneath where the node waited, Maya felt something change aboveground.

A wave of calm swept across the street in front of them, too smooth to be natural.

Two men who'd been shouting at each other stopped mid-word. One blinked as if he'd forgotten why his fists were clenched. A woman hurried across the crosswalk, then slowed, then walked as if she had all the time in the world.

The Choir had reached higher.

It wasn't just under the city now.

It was in the air.

Maya's stomach tightened.

Alex felt it too. "It's already smoothing," he said.

Elara's voice was a low rasp. "That means it's already winning."

Maya didn't answer.

She stared down the street toward the district where the pull steepened and the world's edges began to feel too clean.

Winning wasn't the right word.

The Choir didn't want victory.

It wanted completion.

Somewhere across the city, Joe's awareness flared for half a second with a distant reach, sharp and clean.

Alliance contact confirmed.

Maya felt it as a brief tightening in the Weave, a signal passing along nerves that didn't exist a week ago.

Two fires.

Both real.

And the day had only started.

18

The Alliances True Agenda

The rail corridor woke slowly, like it didn't want to admit the day had started. Joe watched from the shadowed lip of an overpass, elbows resting on cold concrete, breath steady and controlled. Below them, a stretch of rented industrial land unfolded in neat, forgettable blocks. Warehouses with fresh paint and no signage. Temporary lighting rigs humming at half power. Portable offices set back just far enough to feel accidental.

No fences. No guard towers. No guns on display.

That was the first tell.

"This isn't a base," Joe murmured.

Richard stood a step behind him, hands in the pockets of a plain jacket that made him look like a tired consultant waiting on a late train. "No," he said. "It's a handoff."

Unmarked freight trucks rolled in and out at measured intervals. Not convoys. Singles and pairs. Drivers climbed down, scanned clipboards, signed nothing, said little. They moved with the dull efficiency of people paid to stop noticing details.

Bored, not secretive.

Joe let his gaze drift, not looking for faces or tells or the subtle fractures he used to hunt in interviews. There were no lies down there. Not in the way his gift recognized them.

Instead, he watched spacing.

Two men leaned against a loading bay door, posture loose, attention wandering. When a truck arrived, one of them straightened. Not alert. Adjusted. He shifted half a step closer to the bay. Another man on the far side mirrored the movement, closing a gap Joe hadn't noticed until it vanished.

No orders exchanged. No signals given.

Just pattern.

"They're correcting for flow," Joe said quietly. "Not guarding against intrusion. They're managing tempo."

Richard leaned forward slightly. "They expect compliance."

"Yeah," Joe said. "And they're usually right."

A forklift whined as it crossed the concrete, carrying a sealed crate that looked like every other crate in every other yard in the country. But the sound lingered wrong in Joe's ears. A low harmonic under the engine noise, steady and controlled.

"That hum," Joe said. "You hear that?"

Richard nodded. "I feel it."

Joe focused on it. It wasn't active suppression tech. He'd been around enough of that to recognize the aggressive bite, the way it pushed back against perception. This was smoother. Tuned. Like a system meant to coexist with interference rather than crush it.

"Whatever they're moving," Joe said, "they expect it to resist."

Richard's eyes narrowed as he studied the layout. The lines of the loading bays. The angles of the temporary barriers. The placement of lighting poles and access ramps. To Joe it looked arbitrary. To Richard, it wasn't.

"That's containment geometry," Richard said. Not impressed. Not angry. Just precise. "Not mystical. Structural. You see how everything curves just a few degrees off square?"

Joe followed his gaze. The bay doors weren't aligned perfectly with the buildings. The ramps bent slightly as they rose. Even the painted traffic lines weren't straight.

"It's subtle," Richard continued. "Enough to guide movement without forcing it. Enough to keep pressure from pooling."

Joe exhaled slowly. "So they're not using the Weave."

"No," Richard said. "They're designing around it."

That landed heavier than Joe expected.

A group of workers crossed the yard, laughing at something one of them said. The sound carried, then faded as they passed into the shadow of a warehouse. A moment later, the laughter stopped. Not abruptly. It just... resolved. Voices dropped. Footsteps slowed.

Joe frowned. "That was odd."

"Yes," Richard said. "That's environmental correction."

Joe shifted his weight, scanning again. He noticed things he would've missed before. The way arguments never quite started. The way a man raised his voice on a phone call, then lowered it without finishing his sentence. The way attention slid off the site unless someone made an effort to keep looking.

"They're not hiding," Joe said.

Richard's mouth tightened. "They don't need to."

Joe felt it then. Not through the Weave exactly. Not a reach or a resonance. Just the weight of repetition. This place wasn't unique. It was replicable. Modular. Something that could be dropped anywhere rail met road and nobody would ask why.

Normalization.

"This is logistics doctrine," Joe said. "Scaled to look like infrastructure."

"And infrastructure doesn't get questioned," Richard replied. "It gets routed around."

A truck pulled away, merging onto a side road that fed into the city's waking arteries. No escort. No urgency. Just another delivery joining the morning flow.

Joe watched it go. "They're moving something alive enough to need containment, but common enough they don't fear exposure."

Richard didn't answer right away. He was staring at the geometry again, jaw set, eyes tracking invisible lines.

"Whatever comes next," Richard said finally, "this is how it starts. Not with sirens. With paperwork and zoning permits."

Joe nodded. His stomach felt hollow.

The Alliance wasn't building monsters in the dark.

They were teaching the world to live with them.

The service corridor didn't look like an entrance.

That was the point.

Joe followed Richard down a narrow maintenance passage that smelled faintly of ozone and old dust, the kind of space designed to be ignored by everyone except the people paid to keep lights on and doors opening. The walls were painted an institutional gray that absorbed attention. No cameras were visible. No guards stood watch.

Security assumed compliance.

Joe clocked it immediately. Every system in place was built around the idea that no one without authorization would even think to be here. That assumption did more work than any lock ever could.

Richard stopped beside what appeared to be a solid section of wall between two utility panels. No markings. No access plate. Just uninterrupted concrete.

Joe waited for effort. For the familiar signs of strain he'd seen when Richard pushed too hard. The subtle tremor in his hands. The air tightening as reality resisted being told it was wrong.

None of that happened.

Richard tilted his head slightly, like he was listening to a rhythm only he could hear. He raised one hand and rested his fingertips against the wall.

There was no light. No distortion. No dramatic reshaping.

The surface simply... failed.

A seam appeared where there hadn't been one, not tearing open but admitting its own mistake. The concrete parted as if it had always been designed to do so, revealing a dark gap just wide enough for a person to slip through.

Joe's stomach tightened.

That was worse than spectacle.

"That's it?" Joe asked quietly.

Richard didn't look at him. "That's all it takes when you stop arguing with the material."

Joe stepped closer, peering at the opening. The edges weren't jagged. They weren't melted or cracked. They were smooth in a way that didn't belong to anything man-made.

Wrongness without violence.

They moved through one at a time. Joe half expected alarms. Pressure changes. Anything to announce intrusion.

Nothing happened.

On the other side, the corridor continued, identical to the one they'd left. Same paint. Same humming lights. Same anonymous utility doors spaced at regular intervals.

Joe let out a slow breath. "No alert."

Richard closed the wall behind them with the same minimal gesture. The seam vanished, leaving only uninterrupted concrete.

"No breach registered," Joe continued. "No secondary response. They didn't even assume an anomaly."

"Why would they?" Richard said. "This place is designed around the idea that everything abnormal is already accounted for."

They walked.

Joe felt it then. Not a spike. Not a warning. Just a thickness to the air, like humidity that didn't touch the skin but pressed against the senses. His Truthsense brushed it and slid off without catching.

Echo residue.

Controlled. Metered. Present at a density low enough not to trigger alarms, high enough to matter.

It reminded him of old crime scenes where someone thought gloves made them invisible. Where danger wasn't denied, just minimized enough to be tolerable.

"Feels like radiation," Joe said. "The kind people convince themselves they're safe around."

Richard nodded once. "They've convinced themselves it's contained."

Joe scanned the corridor as they moved, noting how unremarkable everything was. The lighting was even. The acoustics dampened. Footsteps didn't echo the way they should. It was all built to keep events from standing out.

Magic wasn't loud here.

That was the second tell.

He'd expected something sharper. A pushback. The Weave reacting to intrusion, even muted. Instead, the space felt curated. Managed. Like someone had tuned the environment to accept stress without reacting.

"Security assumes everyone inside belongs," Joe said. "No challenge points. No escalation triggers."

"Compliance architecture," Richard replied. "If you're here, you're supposed to be."

Joe shook his head slightly. "I'm not sure if that's arrogance or overconfidence."

They passed a junction where another corridor branched off, marked only by a small stenciled number. A man in coveralls walked past them pushing a cart stacked with sealed containers. He didn't look up. Didn't hesitate. Didn't feel the need to check badges.

Joe felt for deception and found none.

The man believed the system.

As they continued, the Echo residue thickened just enough for Joe to notice the way his thoughts smoothed at the edges. Not dulled. Just... guided. Emotional spikes softened before they could form.

He didn't like it.

"This place isn't hostile," Joe said. "It's anesthetized."

"That's how you get people to do things they'd question anywhere else," Richard said. "You remove friction."

Joe glanced at him. "You ever build something like this?"

Richard didn't answer right away.

"No," he said finally. "But I argued it should be possible."

Joe felt that settle between them like a weight.

They reached another intersection. No guards. No cameras that mattered. Just more corridors, more doors, more quiet normalization of something that should've screamed wrong.

Joe realized then what unsettled him most.

They hadn't snuck in.

They'd been absorbed.

And whatever waited deeper inside this place wasn't counting on secrecy or force.

It was counting on people deciding, without quite noticing when, that this was just how things were done now.

The observation gallery overlooked the training floor through a pane of reinforced glass that muted sound but not movement.

Below them, Division Gray soldiers ran drills in clean, precise lines. Boots struck the floor in steady cadence. Commands were short, unadorned. Bodies moved with the efficiency of people who'd trained together long enough to trust muscle memory more than thought.

At first glance, they looked exactly like what they claimed to be.

Human. Disciplined. Professional.

Joe watched without reaching, letting his instincts settle before he tested them. He'd learned the hard way that Truth didn't like being rushed.

The first pass told him nothing.

The second pass tightened something in his chest.

The third made his jaw set.

Their timing was too clean. Not sharp. Clean. Movements aligned a fraction past what shared training could explain. Reaction speed hovered just ahead of anticipation, like each soldier was responding not to what was happening, but to what had already been resolved.

Joe reached gently with his Truthsense.

Wrongness slid under his skin.

Not lies. Not deception. The soldiers weren't pretending to be anything they weren't. The distortion sat deeper than belief, woven into response itself. A delay where there shouldn't be one. A smoothing of intent that made action arrive without hesitation.

"They're synchronized," Joe murmured. "Too much."

Richard leaned forward, eyes narrowing. He hadn't reached into the Weave. He didn't need to.

"I see it," he said quietly. "There's a lag. Tiny. Between impulse and expression."

Joe glanced at him.

"Micro-resonance," Richard continued. "Like something's riding the response loop and arriving just after the decision, not before it."

Below them, one of the soldiers took a training strike meant to knock him off balance. The impact landed solidly. It should've staggered him.

It didn't.

His body absorbed the force and adjusted in the same motion, weight shifting, stance recalibrating, counter already forming before the strike finished landing. No pain reaction. No anger spike. Just adaptation.

Joe felt it then, clear and cold.

The Echo pattern wasn't overriding the human.

It was learning from it.

"Those aren't puppets," Joe said softly.

Richard's mouth tightened. "No."

"They're not possessed," Joe continued. "There's no outside hand."

"They're augmented," Richard finished.

Below them, the drill continued. Orders barked. Bodies moved. Sweat darkened uniforms. A dozen men and women training for a future that had already crossed a line.

Joe watched the soldiers run their course again and felt the Truth settle into place with a weight that didn't need explanation.

This wasn't corruption.

It was improvement.

And that was worse.

The data archive room was colder than the rest of the facility, not in temperature but in intent.

Richard felt it the moment he stepped inside. Rows of sealed terminals lined the walls, their screens dark until he brushed one awake. No alarms. No challenge. The system assumed anyone here belonged.

That assumption made his skin itch.

He accessed the files without ceremony. He didn't need to break encryption. The permissions were layered for efficiency, not paranoia. This wasn't a secret meant to be hidden. It was a process meant to be repeated.

The first header made his breath slow.

Resonant Integration Trials.

Below it, subfolders bloomed with methodical precision. Phase markers. Exposure windows. Response curves. The language was clean. Careful. Sterile in the way only people who believed themselves necessary could manage.

Another header.

Controlled Echo Imprinting.

Richard scrolled.

Subjects were listed by number. No names. No histories. Just identifiers and baseline metrics. Neural elasticity. Emotional volatility. Susceptibility thresholds. Columns of data arranged to suggest neutrality where none existed.

He knew this structure.

He'd built versions of it himself.

Success metrics followed, laid out like achievements in a report meant for promotion review.

Reduced Walker susceptibility.

Partial immunity to Truthfinder interference.

Resistance to grounding effects.

Each line hit harder than the last. They weren't just adapting Echo patterns into soldiers. They were building counters to the Circle specifically. To Joe. To Alex. To anyone who tried to stabilize instead of dominate.

Richard swallowed and kept reading.

Failure metrics came next.

Neural collapse.

Identity loss.

Permanent Echo bleed.

The words were clinical. Bloodless. They didn't say screaming. They didn't say confusion or terror or the moment when a person realized they were no longer alone inside their own head.

Richard could imagine it anyway.

He stared at the screen until the numbers blurred. The logic was flawless. Efficient. Elegant in its own way. Variables isolated. Outcomes measured. Losses categorized as acceptable variance.

This was his thinking.

Not his intent. Not his choices.

But his frameworks, stripped of hesitation and ethics and restraint.

He'd believed order could be imposed without cruelty if the system was clean enough. He'd told himself that discipline was mercy when chaos was the alternative.

Here was the end state of that belief.

Not containment.

Not protection.

Manufactured survivability at the cost of personhood.

Richard closed his eyes and let the weight settle. There was no absolution waiting for him in this room. No way to pretend this wasn't connected to the world he'd helped justify.

This wasn't a misunderstanding.

It was a continuation.

And for the first time since he'd learned to reshape stone with a thought, Richard felt something in him fracture that couldn't be transfigured back into place.

The alarm cut across the training floor without urgency.

It wasn't sharp. It didn't scream danger. It sounded procedural, like a timer reaching zero. Conversations along the perimeter didn't stop. No one ran. The soldiers in gray adjusted their stances by a fraction and waited.

Joe felt it then. Not threat. Not discovery.

Calibration.

A door opened at the far end of the floor and someone was pushed through it.

The Walker stumbled forward, barely catching himself. Young. Too young. His eyes were wide and unfocused, breath coming fast and shallow like he'd been running from something he couldn't see. His resonance flared wild and uneven, static tearing at the edges of the Weave around him.

He didn't know where he was.

He knew he was about to die.

Joe's jaw tightened.

The Walker raised his hands instinctively and the air around him rippled. Not control. Panic given shape. The distortion bent light for a split second, enough to make the watching technicians lean forward, not with concern, but with interest.

Division Gray moved.

They didn't rush him. They didn't fan out or raise weapons. They adjusted. One step here. A turn there. Their spacing changed in response to the Walker's resonance, not his position.

Joe felt the wrongness immediately.

He reached for truth.

The lie beneath the Walker's fear was simple and human. I'm alone. I'm trapped. I can't survive this.

Joe stripped it away.

The effect should have been immediate. Panic collapsing into clarity. Breath slowing. The moment where survival became possible again.

Instead, something pushed back.

Not rejection. Not refusal.

Delay.

Joe felt his Truthsense hit something soft and elastic, like pressing into dense fog. The distortion thinned but didn't vanish. It diffused sideways, caught and redistributed through the soldiers instead of collapsing.

Their movements changed again.

Faster now. Cleaner. They adjusted before the Walker finished his next motion. One of them took the brunt of a kinetic surge that should have sent him sprawling.

He didn't fall.

He compensated.

Joe felt it then and his stomach dropped.

The Echo inside the soldiers wasn't just present.

It was listening.

His Truth didn't vanish. It echoed. The hybrids absorbed the correction and adapted their internal resonance to account for it. The next time he reached, the buffering was smoother. Faster. As if the system had already learned the shape of him.

The Walker screamed.

Division Gray closed in, not with force but with inevitability. Their resonance aligned around him like a net that didn't tighten. It smoothed. His panic bled off into them and disappeared.

Joe pulled back hard, breath catching.

This wasn't suppression.

It was evolution.

The alarm cut off. The soldiers reset. The technicians spoke quietly into headsets, voices carrying the tone of successful trials.

On the floor, the Walker dropped to his knees, breathing but hollowed out, eyes glassy and unfocused.

Joe stared down at the scene, heart pounding.

They weren't just resisting him.

They were learning from him.

And that meant the next time, there wouldn't be any buffering at all.

Richard stood at the edge of the observation platform and stopped seeing individuals.

He saw vectors.

What they were doing below wasn't improvisation or even experimentation. It was convergence. Echo patterns stitched into human nervous systems, not as possession but as augmentation. A forced equilibrium. A system that learned faster than fear could react.

Echo Walker convergence.

Artificial stabilization.

Choir logic, stripped of its indifference and given hands.

The shape of it snapped into place with brutal clarity. Not just soldiers. Not just Division Gray. This was scalable. Trainable. Repeatable. Doctrine waiting for a signature.

It wouldn't stop with volunteers. It wouldn't stop with enemies. Once the model proved viable, it would become policy. Resistance rewritten as inefficiency. Choice recoded as risk.

Richard felt something give way inside him, not with pain, but with precision.

This was his language. His architecture. Order imposed without consent, optimized until nothing unpredictable remained. He'd defended versions of this logic his entire life, believing restraint could be engineered later.

There was no later.

This wasn't containment.

It was rehearsal.

They left without alarms chasing them.

No lockdown. No shouted orders. No sense of urgency behind their steps.

That was what frightened Joe the most.

The corridor felt the same as it had on entry. Clean. Quiet. Confident. The Alliance didn't need to stop them yet. Nothing they'd seen required secrecy anymore.

Joe moved fast but not rushed, cataloging as he went. The data was real. The patterns were consistent. The scale wasn't accidental. This wasn't a rogue project or a desperate gamble.

It was intentional.

Behind him, Richard paused and pressed his palm to the wall. The passage sealed with a soft wrongness, matter folding back into compliance. Joe felt the ripple of cost in it, a drag through the Weave that Richard pretended not to notice.

Neither of them spoke until they were clear.

Dawn broke pale and indifferent over the city.

Joe leaned against a concrete barrier and said it plainly, because anything else would've been a lie. "They're building troops that can fight Walkers. Echoes aren't accidents anymore. They're tools."

Richard stared at the light creeping over the rooftops. His voice was low when he answered. "They're trying to finish the world before it changes them."

Joe felt the truth of it settle into place.

The Choir sought stability without choice.

The Alliance sought control without consent.

Different paths. Same destination.

Joe straightened and turned away from the horizon.

The human side wasn't reacting anymore.

They were preparing.

19

Node Intervention

The city should've been loud. Mid-morning always brought friction. Horns. Voices. A thousand small collisions of mood and hurry. But as Maya and the others moved down the sidewalk toward the district, the world felt like someone had put a hand over its mouth.

Traffic flowed too smoothly. Cars merged without the usual stutter of hesitation. A bus drifted into a lane and nobody fought it. A man stepped off the curb without looking, and the driver who should've slammed the brakes simply slowed, calm as a clock.

Conversations softened before they could turn sharp. Maya watched a couple walking fast, shoulders tense, mouths already forming the start of an argument. Then their pace eased. Their voices dropped. The man blinked, like he'd forgotten what he was angry about. The woman exhaled and looked away, suddenly tired instead of furious.

People moved as if guided by invisible handrails. It wasn't surrender. It was comfort. That was the poison in it.

Maya felt the node under everything, not as a roar, not as static, but as persuasion. It wasn't loud. It didn't demand. It invited. It pulled attention the way gravity pulled rainwater toward the lowest place, quiet and relentless, until you didn't notice you were being guided.

A gravity of emotional resolution.

Alex walked close at her side, his posture steady, his jaw set. He wasn't fighting the field. Maya could feel that. He was doing something harder. He was keeping them distinct inside it. Holding the edges of who they were, so the smoothness couldn't sand them down into something compliant.

He breathed a little too carefully, like he was measuring every inhale.

Elara stayed a half step behind, eyes scanning, hands flexing at her sides. Heat lived under her skin. Maya could sense it like a coiled thread, restless but contained.

Elara hated this. Maya could feel it in the way Elara's shoulders stayed tight even as the world tried to loosen them.

Because the calm felt good.

And that was the worst part.

"This is a zone," Maya said quietly.

Alex nodded without looking at her. "It's an influence."

Elara's voice came out low and rough. "It's a trap that feels like relief."

Maya didn't disagree. She couldn't. The Weave around them was too smooth, too eager to settle. The city wasn't a battlefield.

It was being rewritten into an influence zone, one softened choice at a time.

At the edge of the district, the slope steepened.

Maya felt it in her bones first. The way her attention wanted to slide forward. The way her thoughts tried to take the shortest path to quiet. It would've been easy to let it happen. Easy to stop questioning. Easy to stop hurting.

Elara stopped walking.

Maya turned. Elara stood with her feet planted, shoulders squared, her gaze fixed ahead like she was staring down something with teeth. Her hands were relaxed, but the air around her felt hotter, not enough to shimmer, just enough to warn.

Elara could burn a hole through it. Not destroy the field, but punch motion back into the calm for a few seconds. Maya knew that the way you knew a storm could break a tree. Fire responded to the Choir like dry grass to heat. A flare, a push, a hot clean corridor carved through the smoothness. Elara could burn the field back into motion.

Elara's throat worked as she swallowed. Her eyes flicked once toward Maya, then away, like looking too long might make the decision for her.

"I can feel how easy it would be," Elara said.

Alex's voice was calm, but there was strain under it. "Easy doesn't mean safe."

Elara gave a bitter little laugh that held no humor. "Safe. Yeah. That's what this feels like."

Maya stepped closer, careful not to let the slope pull her forward without permission. "Don't."

Elara's jaw tightened. "You think talking to it is better?"

"I think burning it means we learn nothing," Maya said. "And we keep making the same mistake."

Elara's fingers twitched. A thin line of heat trembled along her knuckles, like a warning she didn't want to make real.

Fire wanted clarity. Fire wanted a clean answer.

But clarity through erasure was still silence.

Elara stared ahead for a long moment, then let her hands fall fully to her sides. The heat didn't vanish. It settled.

"Fine," she said, and it sounded like it cost her. "You try it your way."

Maya nodded once. Not gratitude. Recognition.

Restraint wasn't passive. It was a decision made against instinct.

They crossed into the perimeter together.

The air felt thicker, not humid, not heavy with heat, just dense with presence. The city itself seemed to lean toward stillness. Even birdsong sounded muted, like the notes had been pressed flat.

Maya didn't reach out.

Reaching out implied a sender and a receiver. It implied intent like a spear.

This wasn't that.

She stepped into alignment.

She lowered resistance the way you lowered your shoulders when you walked into a strong wind. She let the Weave touch her without pushing back. She let the slope exist in her awareness without letting it decide for her.

Alex moved closer. He didn't grab her. He didn't anchor her with force. He simply became a steady point in the field, a human weight that reminded her body it belonged to itself.

Elara stayed ready, flame tight in her chest like a held breath.

Maya closed her eyes.

The Choir was there. Not as a voice. Not as a face. A field of self-correcting calm that wanted everything sharp to become smooth.

Maya didn't demand an answer.

She listened for state.

The first response wasn't words.

It was grief.

Sudden, total, not hers.

It hit her like a wave that didn't belong to the ocean, cold and unstoppable. Her breath caught. Her chest tightened. Tears stung her eyes for no reason her mind could name.

She opened her eyes fast, blinking hard.

Alex's hand touched her elbow, light as a question.

"I'm here," he said, and the words mattered less than the steadiness behind them.

Maya swallowed and let the grief exist without drowning her.

This was the channel.

Not dialogue.

State-sharing.

The Weave didn't transmit language.

It transmitted what was held.

The world slipped sideways.

Maya stood on the street, but she also wasn't there. The node's field laid an overlay across her senses, like a second reality pressed against the first.

A hospital hallway at 3 a.m.

Fluorescent lights. The smell of bleach and fear. A man in scrubs leaning against a wall, eyes glassy, hands shaking. A woman sitting on the floor with her head against her knees, rocking silently because if she made a sound she'd break.

A mother screaming in a car that wouldn't start.

Her hands slammed the steering wheel. Her voice tore apart into raw animal sound. Rain hammered the windshield. A child in the back seat cried until the crying turned into gasps.

A soldier frozen behind cover while others died.

Dust in the air. The crack of gunfire. A radio squawking names that stopped answering. His finger wouldn't move. His body wouldn't obey. He watched a friend fall and couldn't even scream.

A child alone in a room where shouting never stopped.

The walls were thin. The voices were thick with anger and helplessness. The child sat in a corner with hands over ears, eyes squeezed shut, breathing as quietly as possible, trying to disappear into the floor.

Maya's knees went weak. The fragments came fast, not as memories being shown, but as patterns being held.

Not one story.

A thousand.

Pain repeating itself through different bodies, different languages, different years, all sharing the same unresolved shape.

Alex made a small sound, like he'd taken a blow. Maya felt his strain spike, not because he was resisting, but because he was holding the edges of them while the weight pressed in.

Grounding didn't quiet it.

It let it exist without collapse.

Elara's breath came in sharper, controlled pulls. Heat flared once, then tightened again, like she was forcing herself not to lash out at the suffering itself.

Maya's throat burned. "This isn't... it's not showing me," she whispered.

Alex's voice was tight. "It's holding it."

Maya nodded, swallowing against the ache. "It's holding it like it can't let go."

The fragments shifted.

The modern images blurred, layered, then peeled away like thin paint. Something older surfaced beneath.

Not a place Maya recognized.

Not a time.

The air tasted different. Thinner, charged with a pressure that didn't belong to weather. People stood in a wide ring carved into stone, hands lifted, mouths moving in unison. Their eyes were wild with need.

Maya felt their fear like a second skin.

Fear of death.

Fear of loss.

Fear of insignificance.

It wasn't one person panicking. It was a crowd feeding itself. Terror multiplied until it became doctrine. Until it became certainty that if they didn't force the world to give them more, they would vanish.

They reached for ascension like drowning people reached for air.

The Weave trembled under it.

Threads stretched beyond tolerance. Reality thinned like cloth pulled too hard. Maya felt the moment the lattice began to fail, not because power struck it, but because fear demanded it obey.

The fracture wasn't caused by strength.

It was caused by terror at scale.

Maya's breath came out in a shaky exhale as the vision broke apart. She swayed on her feet in the present, eyes open now, seeing the street again, seeing the people walking calmly as if nothing was wrong.

Her hands trembled.

It was the same pattern.

Different era.

Same wound.

Maya stepped forward again, closer to the heart of the slope, closer to the place where the field felt thickest. The node's calm pressed against her like a hand on her forehead, gentle and relentless.

She didn't fight it.

She didn't submit.

She held herself steady inside it, with Alex behind her like a foundation and Elara beside her like a threat held in check.

The truth arrived without drama. It didn't come as an epiphany. It came as alignment.

The Choir wasn't alien.

It wasn't engineered.

It wasn't malicious.

It was emergent.

It was the Unmaking shaped.

Given form by humanity's unresolved pain.

Pain wanted stillness because stillness felt like an ending.

The Choir sought equilibrium the way a fever sought a lower temperature. It didn't hate the body. It didn't love it either. It only knew deviation and correction.

Maya swallowed, then spoke into the field, not expecting it to hear words, but needing to set the state.

"You aren't here to destroy us," she said, voice low. "You're here because we never healed."

The calm didn't change.

Not because it rejected her.

Because rejection required choice.

But something shifted anyway. Not in tone. In orientation. Like a weight in the dark turning slightly toward a new pressure.

Maya felt it.

Not an answer.

A reconfiguration.

It had been seen.

The field reacted to acknowledgment the way an unstable structure reacted to a new load.

The smooth calm fractured.

Not into chaos. Into bleed.

Grief rose in the air like mist. Civilians nearby slowed, not from comfort now, but from sudden emotion without context. A man stopped walking and pressed a hand to his mouth, eyes wide, as if he'd remembered something he couldn't bear. A woman on a bench began to cry quietly, shoulders shaking, not knowing why.

The node destabilized just enough to become dangerous.

Alex stepped forward hard, feet planted, jaw clenched. Maya felt him ground like a spike driven into earth. The effort hit him immediately. His breath shortened. His shoulders tightened. Sweat beaded at his temples though the air wasn't hot.

He was holding the line between feeling and drowning.

His voice came out strained. "Maya, pull back. Now."

Maya tried. The slope didn't want to let her go. Not violently. Persuasively. Like slipping into sleep when you were exhausted and someone told you to stay awake.

Elara moved, a half step, heat rising without flame. "Alex."

"I've got it," Alex said through clenched teeth, and Maya heard the lie he was telling himself.

He grounded harder. The Weave around them steadied just enough for Maya to take a step back, then another. The grief haze thinned, not gone, but less overwhelming, like wind dispersing smoke.

Alex swayed once, caught himself, held.

He was close to overload.

He didn't stop.

Understanding had consequences.

Even seeing the pattern changed the pressure.

Elara took the lead as they retreated.

Not running. Leaving. The difference mattered.

She lifted one hand and let heat pour out, not as an inferno, not as a purge. A corridor of motion, just enough to push the air and the Weave back into flow. The calm didn't break. It shifted aside, like water parting around a stone.

Fire didn't destroy the Choir.

It made space to move.

They reached the edge of the influence zone and the slope eased, not gone, but less steep. Maya's lungs finally filled properly. Her heartbeat slowed into something she recognized as her own.

She turned, looking back down the street where the world still moved too smoothly.

"We didn't fix anything," Maya said.

Alex's voice was rough. "We changed something."

Elara stared toward the district, eyes narrowed, face hard. Her hands were steady now, heat still there but contained.

"It saw us," she said quietly.

Maya felt it too, a subtle reorientation in the field beneath the city. Not retreat. Not advance.

Adaptation.

The Choir now knew it was understood.

And understanding didn't make it weaker.

It made it more precise.

2 0

Ethan's Warning

Alex stood at the edge of the district where the slope finally loosened its grip, boots planted on cracked pavement that still felt too warm with borrowed emotion. The node had quieted, but it hadn't emptied. Grief lingered in the air like humidity after a storm. It didn't press anymore. It clung.

He kept grounding anyway. Not forcefully. Not aggressively. Just enough to keep the residue from pooling. Just enough to stop passersby from slowing with tears they couldn't explain. The effort pulled at him in small, constant ways. A tightness behind the eyes. A tremor in the breath he didn't let reach his shoulders.

He was stretched thinner than he admitted. Even to himself.

Maya stood several steps away, speaking quietly with Elara. Close enough to feel. Far enough not to lean. Alex noticed that too. Maya had learned to give him space when he was anchoring. She knew attention carried weight now.

Alex adjusted his stance and felt something shift.

Not more pressure. Different pressure.

This wasn't the Choir's smoothing calm. It didn't invite stillness or resolution. It didn't want him to settle. It pulled sideways, not down, like a hand on his sleeve asking him to turn.

Alex frowned and grounded harder, expecting the sensation to fade. It didn't. The realization came slow and cold. This wasn't overload. It was summoning.

Alex didn't see Ethan at first. That was the strange part. The street stayed the street. Traffic passed. People moved. Maya laughed once at something Elara said, the sound real and unaltered. The world didn't pause to make room.

Ethan was just there. Not standing. Not hovering. Overlaying the space like a reflection that didn't belong to any surface. Alex caught him out of the corner of his awareness, a presence that resolved only when he stopped trying to name it.

Alex turned his head slowly.

Ethan looked the same and not at all.

His features were intact, familiar, but softened at the edges, like they were being held by something larger than a body. His eyes were clear and tired in a way that went past exhaustion and into diffusion.

He didn't feel trapped. He felt spread thin. Alex's throat tightened. "Ethan."

Ethan's mouth curved, not quite a smile. "You're the right one," he said quietly. "That's a relief."

The world kept moving around them, but the moment between Alex and Ethan went still.

Alex didn't waste time. He couldn't afford to. "Did it fail?" he asked. "What you did. Did it fail?"

Ethan considered the question like it deserved respect.

"No," he said. "It worked."

Alex held his breath.

"It just didn't finish the job."

Ethan's presence shifted, not closer, but denser. "I absorbed strain that would've torn the lattice further. I slowed the collapse. I bought time. Real time."

Alex felt the truth of it settle into his bones. The way the world had staggered instead of shattered. The way the fracture had held, imperfect but intact.

"But the imbalance is still there," Alex said.

Ethan nodded. "Yes."

Alex's hands curled at his sides. "So you didn't fix it."

Ethan's gaze didn't waver. "I proved something could be broken to make a patch."

The words landed hard.

Martyrdom wasn't salvation. It was scaffolding.

Temporary. Load bearing. Dangerous to repeat.

They slipped deeper, not into a vision, but into a resonance layer where cause showed its seams.

"The danger isn't what I did," Ethan said. "It's what the system learned from it."

Alex listened, grounding on instinct even as the pressure increased.

"The Weave didn't register my sacrifice as failure," Ethan continued. "It registered it as viable. Compatible. Incomplete."

Alex's stomach dropped.

"It's iterating now," Ethan said. "Searching for a better fit. Greater capacity. Longer endurance."

Alex thought of Maya before Ethan said her name.

"She understands it," Ethan went on. "She listens instead of fighting. She can hold complexity without flinching."

Alex felt a cold spread through his chest.

"She fits the criteria," Ethan said softly.

This wasn't jealousy. This wasn't fear.

This was structure.

Maya wasn't in danger because she was loved.

She was in danger because she was effective.

Ethan didn't raise his voice. He didn't gesture. He spoke the way a final data point spoke when there were no variables left to test.

"It won't see her as a risk," he said. "It'll see her as a solution."

Alex shook his head once, sharp. "Then I'll stop it."

Ethan's expression didn't change. "You can't stop the Weave by force. You know that."

Alex swallowed.

"My sacrifice taught it something," Ethan said. "That singular load works. That removal can stabilize."

His gaze held Alex's. "Don't let her become the improved version of my mistake."

"How?" Alex asked. "How do I prevent it?"

Ethan exhaled, a sound like wind through many places at once. "You don't block it. You don't fight it."

Alex felt the answer forming before it was spoken.

"You change its math," Ethan said.

Alex waited.

"You prevent singular load," Ethan continued. "You maintain distinction. You force distribution."

Understanding snapped into place.

Alex wasn't meant to save Maya by standing in front of her.

He was meant to make it impossible for the system to isolate her at all.

"You're not her shield," Ethan said. "You're the reason there won't be a pedestal."

Ethan's outline wavered.

Not because he was leaving.

Because something else was noticing.

The pressure around them tightened, curious rather than hostile.

"The Choir wants stillness," Ethan said quickly. "The Weave wants resolution. Neither cares who pays the cost if it works."

Alex felt the pull intensify.

Ethan leaned closer, voice steady but urgent. "Find a pattern that doesn't end with one of you missing."

The words barely landed before Ethan thinned, presence stretching until there was nothing left to focus on.

Only weight.

The street snapped back into full clarity.

Noise. Motion. Breath.

Alex staggered once and caught himself, grounding hard, harder than before. Not to stabilize the Weave.

To keep Maya separate from it.

Maya turned toward him immediately, concern sharp in her eyes. "Alex?"

"I'm okay," he said. It was true enough.

He didn't tell her what he'd learned. Not yet.

But something in him had locked into place.

No more singular solutions.

No more substitutions dressed up as balance.

He watched Maya like someone watching a horizon that might decide to swallow a city.

Not protective.

Vigilant.

Ethan hadn't saved the world.

He'd warned it.

And Alex would not let the system try again.

21

The First Hybrid Attack

The training cell smelled like burnt coffee and old fabric. It was tucked into the lower levels of a repurposed community building, far enough from the node to avoid bleed, close enough that the Weave still felt raw. The windows were taped in neat crosses, more habit than necessity, and the lights hummed just a little too loud, the way cheap fixtures always did. Someone had brewed another pot without asking, and it sat on a folding table beside a stack of donated blankets, steam curling weakly from the spout.

It was safe. As safe as anything could be now.

Maya stood near the back wall with her arms folded, watching the trainees work through breathing drills. No theatrics. No reaching. Just inhale, feel the lattice brush the edges of awareness, exhale, let it pass. Don't chase the feeling. Don't pull. Don't prove anything.

They were learning, slowly and carefully.

The Weave lay low in the room, a quiet pressure under everything. Not beautiful. Not luminous. Functional. Like current running through reinforced cable instead of silk thread.

Alex moved among them without touching, correcting posture with a glance and steadying breath with proximity alone. He didn't teach technique. He taught endurance. Maya liked watching him work. He made people feel like they weren't about to break.

Someone laughed softly when they lost focus. Someone else swore under their breath and reset. It felt human. Ordinary in a way that mattered.

Then Alex stopped.

He didn't stiffen or reach. He just went still, eyes lifting as if he'd heard something that hadn't made a sound. Maya felt it a second later. The air flattened. Not silence. Not panic. Something else. A subtle pressure that erased depth, like a room losing its corners.

Alex turned his head slowly. "That's not the Choir," he said.

Maya nodded, skin prickling. "No."

Whatever this was, it didn't want them afraid.

The pressure rolled in like bad weather. Not sudden. Not violent. Just inevitable.

It sharpened the air and made breathing feel thin. Alex reached for grounding out of reflex and felt resistance, like trying to press a hand against a surface that refused to give. The Weave felt farther away. Not gone. Distant. Like speaking through glass.

One of the trainees gasped as their resonance flared and then collapsed in on itself. Another tried to stabilize and overcorrected, power spiking before dying out completely. Alex's jaw tightened.

This wasn't overload. It wasn't emotional bleed or echo drift. This was tuned. Designed.

"Everyone still," he said, voice calm and loud enough to cut through the room. "No hero moves."

They froze. Even the ones who wanted to run. Good. Panic would make it worse.

The pressure didn't ease. It settled.

The breach didn't announce itself. No sirens. No shouted commands. Just a clean, methodical intrusion, like someone unlocking a door they already knew how to open.

Maya felt it through the floor first. A shift. A displacement of intention.

The exterior door came down in controlled segments, hinges cut and frame compromised without noise. Figures moved through the opening with disciplined efficiency.

Soldiers.

Not rushing. Not cautious. Executing.

They moved like they expected resistance and had already planned for it. Maya reached for a short blink, just enough to pull one trainee out of the room.

The world caught.

For a fraction of a second, reality stuttered like a skipped frame, then snapped back into place. She was exactly where she'd started, breath catching hard in her chest.

"Elara," she said.

Elara lifted a hand and released a controlled flare. Heat rolled forward in a tight arc, clean and precise, and struck something invisible. The flame guttered sideways, twisting wrong and bleeding off into smoke that smelled sharp and metallic.

Not blocked. Misfired.

Teleportation and fire weren't solving this.

The fire hit hard. It should've scorched. It should've forced retreat.

Instead it washed over them like they were built to expect it.

Elara saw it clearly now, the way the heat bent not around armor but around bodies. As if the soldiers carried a second pattern under their skin. One of them turned his head, and she caught it, a brief shimmer just beneath the surface. Wrong. Flickering.

A trainee screamed and threw raw power into the room. It rebounded.

Elara reacted without thinking, snapping a wall of heat between the blast and the others and forcing it upward where it burned itself out against the ceiling. She wanted to burn the soldiers. She couldn't.

Protecting instead of attacking made her furious, and fear crept in beneath it.

These weren't just armored humans.

They were tuned.

Joe knew the moment he stepped inside the room. Wrongness layered like paint. The soldiers didn't read as false. There was no lie to catch, no deception to strip away. Their resonance was clean in a way that made his teeth ache.

They were constructed.

He focused and saw the pattern. Echo signatures woven through muscle and nerve, not overlaying them but integrated, like a second nervous system humming just under conscious control. The field pressed against his senses, bending truth-state just enough to make Walker output slip sideways.

It wasn't blocking power.

It was spoofing reality.

Joe swallowed and pushed his Truthsense outward, not to accuse or confront, but to clarify. He reached for the space between signal and mask and held it steady.

Truth didn't strike. It resolved.

Joe anchored on the nearest hybrid and separated what had been fused. Human resonance. Echo overlay. Dampening scaffold. The layers peeled apart like wet paper.

The soldier faltered, not physically at first, but harmonically. The stutter rippled outward, a shared glitch moving through the squad as their constructed coherence lost alignment.

The field wavered.

Just for a breath.

In that breath, Maya blinked and someone vanished from the room. Elara's fire found a clean path and forced two soldiers back a step. Joe sagged, the effort burning behind his eyes.

That was all they were getting.

"Extract," Maya said. "Now."

They weren't winning this. They were surviving it.

Alex moved with her, close enough that the Weave steadied when she reached for it. Short jumps. Brutal precision. No elegance. Elara laid smoke and heat in layers, forcing space and shaping corridors instead of infernos.

One of the hybrids recovered faster than the others. Adjusted. Changed rhythm mid-motion.

Maya felt it and knew.

They were learning.

They pulled the last of the trainees into the stairwell and vanished into the alley beyond, night air cold and sharp against skin that still hummed with interference.

The fallback site was quiet in the way only shock could make it. Injuries were treated. Breathing slowed. Fear shook loose in aftershocks.

Alex grounded until his hands trembled, but the dampening residue clung. Static on clothes. Pressure that refused to fully dissipate.

Joe leaned against the wall, pale and steady. "They weren't resisting us," he said. "They were built to survive us."

Maya closed her eyes. The Alliance could scale this. The realization settled like a weight on her chest.

They hadn't come to wipe out the cell.

They'd come to measure it.

The war hadn't escalated.

It had changed categories.

And somewhere out there, someone was already adjusting the next test.

22

Elara's Revelation

The fallback site smelled like antiseptic and burned dust.

It wasn't a place meant for staying. It was a place meant for breathing long enough to decide what came next. Folding cots lined the walls. Someone had scavenged medical kits from three different sources and laid them out on a table that had once been used for potlucks or craft fairs. Bandages were wrapped with hands that still shook. Voices stayed low, not because anyone had asked them to, but because raising them felt wrong.

Elara stood near the far wall and tried to cool down.

The fire hadn't left her.

It clung beneath her skin like an afterimage, the way light lingered when you stared too long at the sun. She rolled her shoulders, flexed her hands, drew slow breaths through her nose and let them out through her mouth the way she'd been taught. Inhale, ground, release. Again. Slower.

The heat didn't respond.

It didn't surge, either. That was worse.

Fire she could understand. Fire was honest. It rose when it was fed. It burned when it was given room. It died when it ran out of things to take. This wasn't that. This was heat without hunger, pressure without release.

Alex moved through the room, grounding where he could, steadying the worst of the aftershocks with quiet words and presence alone. He passed near Elara once, close enough that she felt his stabilizing pull brush her field.

It slid off.

Not violently. Not rejected. Just ignored.

Alex paused, eyes flicking to her for half a second longer than normal. He didn't say anything. He didn't reach. Elara was grateful for that. Whatever was happening inside her wasn't something she wanted anchored yet.

She focused on her breathing again and felt sweat bead along her spine.

The fire wasn't fading.

It was waiting.

The surge hit without warning.

One moment Elara was standing still, counting breaths, and the next the heat tore free of restraint like it had been looking for an excuse. Flame spilled outward in a rush that scorched the air and sent people scrambling back with startled shouts. Light flared against the walls. The temperature jumped hard enough to make metal creak.

Elara gasped and tried to pull it back.

The fire didn't listen.

It wasn't rage. It wasn't fear. There was no spike of emotion driving it, no surge of adrenaline she could ride down. This was response without permission, output without intent. The room became a hazard in seconds, heat rolling across the ceiling, licking along the floor.

Alex planted himself between Elara and the others and grounded hard. She felt him hit the Weave like a weight dropped into water. The pressure around her tightened, tried to hold.

The fire pushed back.

Not aggressively. Persistently.

Elara's eyes widened. She'd never felt that before. Not resistance to grounding. Not refusal. Something adjacent. As if the fire wasn't hers alone in this moment.

"This isn't me," she said hoarsely, even as the words sounded like denial.

Alex's jaw clenched. "Elara, I need you to pull it down."

"I'm trying."

And she was. She reached inward, not to command the flame, but to contain it, to fold it back into the space where it usually lived. Her hands shook with the effort. Sweat poured down her temples. The heat only thickened, warping the air around her into shimmering waves.

Something else was moving inside the blaze.

Elara felt it then. Not heat. Not light.

Attention.

Her stomach dropped.

"Get them out," she said, forcing the words through clenched teeth. "Now."

Alex hesitated for half a second, then nodded. He started issuing calm, precise instructions, moving people back, opening distance. Elara waited until they were clear, until she felt the empty space around her expand.

Then she turned and ran.

She didn't flee in panic. She chose isolation.

The moment she crossed the threshold into open air, the fire surged higher, rolling off her in sheets of heat and light. The world distorted around her, the ground shimmering, the night bending under pressure. She ran until there was nothing nearby to burn, nothing close enough to hurt.

Then she stopped.

Flame wrapped her like a living thing, spiraling upward, roaring without sound. Elara stood at its heart, breath ragged, heart hammering, heat so intense it felt like it should be tearing her apart.

Instead, it held.

She should've felt powerful.

She felt afraid.

Inside the blaze, something shifted.

It wasn't a voice. There were no words. No commands. No intrusion.

It was presence.

And it was terrified.

The realization hit her harder than the heat ever could. Elara froze, breath catching as she felt it clearly now. Not a threat. Not an enemy.

Fear.

Not sharp panic, but a deep, sustained terror, the kind that lived in systems that remembered extinction. It pressed against her awareness, raw and unfiltered, a resonance shaped by survival at any cost.

The Unmaking wasn't speaking.

It was reacting.

It wasn't trying to consume her fire. It wasn't challenging it. It was recoiling and reaching at the same time, like something cornered that didn't know whether to flee or brace.

It was afraid of being extinguished.

Elara's knees nearly buckled.

Images flickered through her perception. Not visions. Patterns. Pressure memories etched into the Weave itself. Creation surging unchecked. Threads pulled too tight. Power forced into forms that couldn't hold it. Something essential nearly erased in the attempt to make the world stable by brute force.

This wasn't hunger.

This was defense.

The Shadow Current existed because someone had once decided imbalance had to be burned away completely. It had been born from refusal. From the belief that erasure was cleaner than endurance.

Fire didn't just destroy.

Fire renewed.

Fire cleared space for change when nothing else could move.

Elara swallowed hard as understanding settled into place.

Her flame wasn't opposite the Unmaking.

It mirrored it.

Both were answers shaped by trauma. Both were forces that didn't negotiate, only responded. Both existed because something had once been pushed too far and learned never to let that happen again.

This wasn't a war between good and evil.

It was a system trying to correct pain with force because it didn't know another language.

Elara's breath shuddered as the fire surged higher, feeding on the realization, resonance peaking until it felt like she might dissolve into it entirely. The Unmaking pressed closer, not attacking, not merging, just present in shared recognition.

If she let the fire decide, it would burn until there was nothing left to threaten it.

Just like the Shadow Current would.

"No," Elara whispered.

The word barely existed against the roar, but she meant it with everything she had. She didn't command the fire to stop. She refused to let it consume everything.

She folded inward instead.

The effort was agony. It felt like trying to collapse a star with bare hands. Every instinct screamed to release, to let the flame finish what it had started. Her muscles locked. Her vision tunneled. Pain flared white-hot behind her eyes.

She held anyway.

Not dominance.

Choice.

The fire recoiled, confused, collapsing back toward her center in ragged waves. Heat slammed into her ribs, her spine, her lungs. She cried out and dropped to one knee, hands braced against scorched earth as the blaze folded inward and vanished.

The night rushed back in, cold and empty.

Elara collapsed forward, chest heaving, skin slick with sweat. The fire was gone.

The awareness was not.

When she staggered back toward the others, her legs trembled beneath her. Alex was the first to reach her, grounding gently, carefully, like approaching a wild animal that had just learned something dangerous about itself.

"You're clear," he said quietly.

Elara shook her head. "No."

He didn't argue.

She looked at the others, at the fear and relief tangled in their expressions, and forced herself to speak.

"The Unmaking isn't something you kill," she said. Her voice sounded strange to her own ears. Steadier than she felt. "It's something you survive alongside."

Silence answered her.

Later, lying awake on a borrowed cot, the heat finally gone, Elara stared at the ceiling and felt her mind race. The hybrids came back to her then. The way they'd adapted. The way they'd learned from fire even as it hit them.

Attention changed systems.

The Unmaking learned the same way.

Fire wasn't the answer.

But neither was silence.

Elara closed her eyes, knowing one thing with absolute clarity.

Balance was going to demand something harder than power.

Choice.

And it was going to hurt.

23

The Convergence Clock

J oe had come back less than an hour earlier.

He hadn't knocked. He'd just walked in, dirt still on his boots, eyes tired in a way that had nothing to do with sleep. Richard hadn't followed him. When Maya asked where he was, Joe had only said that Richard needed to confirm something on his own.

No one argued. Whatever Joe and Richard had found with the Alliance had already crossed from theory into consequence. You could feel it in the way Joe moved through the room, setting his bag down, scanning faces, grounding himself before he spoke to anyone at all.

Malcolm Fraser arrived without fanfare.

No surge rippled through the Weave when he crossed the perimeter. No alarm flared. No one felt him coming until he was already there, standing just beyond the reach of the outer sentries, hands visible, posture careful in the way of someone who understood exactly how dangerous misunderstanding had become.

It was late. The kind of hour when exhaustion softened vigilance but did not quite allow rest. The fallback site had settled into low, murmuring activity, people moving quietly between stations, voices hushed not by command but by shared strain.

Alex sensed him first.

Not power. Not threat.

Presence.

Alex lifted his head, grounding reflexively, eyes narrowing toward the far edge of the lot where the shadows thinned under a single flickering security light. A man stood there, coat pulled tight against the cold, hair dark and wind-tossed, face drawn with the look of someone who had not slept well in a very long time.

He was not carrying a weapon.

He was carrying a satchel.

Alex raised a hand, signaling the others to hold, and walked forward a few steps. "You're inside a restricted zone," he said calmly. "If you didn't mean to be, you need to turn around."

The man swallowed. His accent marked him immediately, soft Highland cadence worn thin by nerves.

"I know where I am," he said. "I've been seeing this place for months."

That got Alex's full attention.

Before he could respond, Maya felt it.

Not a pull. Not a flare.

Recognition.

She straightened where she sat at the table, the Arcana still open beneath her hands, and looked up sharply. Her breath caught as her eyes found the man standing under the light.

She had seen him before.

Not clearly. Not all at once. A figure standing at the edge of vision, never close enough to touch, always present in moments where choice narrowed and pressure thickened. A watcher who never spoke.

Her pulse quickened.

"That's him," she said quietly.

Alex glanced back at her. "You know him?"

"No," Maya replied, standing slowly. "But the Weave does."

That was enough.

Alex gestured once, and the tension shifted subtly as the sentries eased back, weapons lowered but not slung. The man exhaled shakily, relief flickering across his face before he caught himself and squared his shoulders.

"My name's Malcolm Fraser," he said. "I'm not here to ask for protection. I'm here because I was told to bring something back into the light."

He hesitated, then reached into the satchel and withdrew a wrapped object, careful as if it might break simply by being seen. The cloth was old, not decorative, its fibers softened by time and handling.

He placed it gently on the table between them.

Maya felt the room change.

Not with power.

With weight.

She reached out before she quite realized she was moving and drew the cloth aside. Beneath it lay a journal. Leather-bound, cracked with age, edges worn smooth by hands long turned to dust. There was no glow. No shift. No response to her presence.

Just ink and paper.

And something else.

History.

"I didn't know what it was at first," Malcolm said, voice tight. "Just that it mattered. The visions started after the auroras. Faces. Places. Pressure building and nowhere to put it. And always you."

He met Maya's eyes, apologetic. "I'm sorry. I didn't know your name until yesterday."

Maya swallowed. "Where did you find it?"

"In a sanctum," Malcolm replied. "Carved into stone beneath the Highlands. The Weave showed me where to look. I didn't understand why until I saw him."

Alex frowned. "Him?"

Malcolm nodded. "The skeleton. On a stone bed. Hands folded around the journal like he was afraid someone might take it before he was done."

Silence settled hard over the room.

Maya's fingers trembled as she opened the cover.

The handwriting inside was dense, deliberate, unmistakably human. No symbols. No sigils. No attempts at instruction. Just observation, reflection, doubt.

After glancing at a few pages she didn't need the Weave to tell her whose hand had written it. The hand was too careful. Too burdened.

"Merlin," she whispered.

Malcolm released a breath that sounded like he'd been holding it for centuries. "I'm descended from him. Or so the visions finally made clear. That was never meant to matter until now."

Joe, who had been watching from the edge of the room, stepped closer. "Why bring it to us?"

Malcolm's gaze moved across them, taking in their exhaustion, their injuries, the strain threaded through the space like wire pulled too tight.

"Because he didn't leave instructions," Malcolm said quietly. "He left proof. And because whatever comes next can't be decided by ghosts."

Maya closed the journal slowly.

For the first time since the Codex had turned to ash, she did not feel abandoned.

She felt challenged.

And somewhere deep in the Weave, something old and patient seemed to acknowledge that a circle long left open had finally closed.

The Arcana of the Weave and Merlin's Journal lay open on the scarred table, their pages held down at the corners by a ceramic mug, a folded map, and a smooth stone Alex had picked up somewhere along the way. They didn't glow or hum. They didn't respond to Maya's presence the way the Codex once had. They simply existed, ink on paper, human hands made visible through careful, stubborn lines of script.

Maya turned a page slowly, fingertips dry against the parchment. Isabella's annotations crowded the margins, tight and precise, sometimes circling a phrase, sometimes arguing with it, sometimes simply writing the same word again and again as if repetition might force clarity. Pressure. Overlap. Compression. Moments that feel too full to contain themselves.

There were no instructions. No warnings. No signs telling her what to do next.

The realization sat heavy in her chest. The Codex had aligned her whether she wanted it to or not. It had shown her what she could not yet understand and dared her to survive the consequences. The Arcana did nothing of the sort. It offered witness without guidance, record without interpretation. It was a book written by someone who had stood close enough to the Weave to feel it strain and had chosen to write that feeling down rather than look away.

Maya exhaled slowly and turned another page. This was what they had now. No immortal lens. No enforced clarity. Just fragments of human observation and the burden of deciding what they meant.

Around her, the fallback site had been stripped of anything resembling comfort and repurposed into something like a command space. Maps covered the walls, layered over each other and pinned with mismatched tacks. Screens glowed with satellite feeds and data streams that flickered as if they were still uncertain whether the rules applied anymore. Someone had drawn ley geometries in dry erase marker directly onto a whiteboard meant for schedules and grocery lists.

Joe stood in the center of it all, jacket discarded, sleeves rolled up, eyes sharp despite the exhaustion that pulled at his posture. He moved between the maps and the screens, compiling and discarding, testing connections the way he once tested alibis. Node activations. Echo density. Hybrid deployments. Civilian attunement spikes. Each category alone was alarming. Together, they were something else entirely.

He began overlaying Arcana timestamps with modern events, marking centuries-old entries against live data. At first, the matches felt coincidental, the kind of pattern the human brain was desperate to impose when chaos refused to resolve. Then the coincidences stacked. A compression event recorded in the margins of a journal written by a woman who never knew the word Convergence aligned precisely with a present-day surge in Echo density halfway across the world.

Joe stepped back from the wall and rubbed a hand over his face. "They're not independent," he said quietly.

Alex looked up from where he had been grounding a pair of shaken Tier II Walkers, his attention sharpening. "Say that again."

"The nodes," Joe said. "They're not acting like separate failures. They're reacting to each other. When one stabilizes, pressure doesn't disappear. It moves. Somewhere else spikes harder."

Maya closed the Arcana and rested her palm on the cover. The book felt exactly what it was. Human. Finite. Honest in its limitations.

"That's load sharing," she said. "Like a network rerouting around damage."

Joe nodded. "Which means we don't get to put out fires anymore. Every time we do, we're lighting one somewhere else."

The room fell quiet, not with panic but with recognition. This was the difference between chaos and structure. Chaos felt random. Structure demanded accountability.

The air shifted before anyone saw Beagron.

There was no full manifestation, no towering presence of stone and weight. Instead, pressure settled into the room, low and steady, like gravity remembering itself. The Weave tightened, threads aligning just enough to carry something more than absence.

Beagron did not look surprised by what he found.

"You have reached the phase we feared most," his voice resonated, not from a single point but through the lattice itself. "Not collapse. Not revelation. Synchronization."

Maya lifted her head. "So it's true," she said. "This was never about stopping it."

"No," Beagron replied. "The sealing delayed synchronization. It did not prevent it. The Veil has thinned beyond concealment, and delay has ended."

Joe folded his arms, jaw tight. "So Convergence isn't a switch. It's a staircase."

Beagron's presence pressed closer, acknowledging the accuracy. "It is threshold-based. Each crossing alters the system. Each alteration narrows the range of possible outcomes."

Maya felt the truth of it unfold inside her perception. She closed her eyes and let the Weave show her what words struggled to hold. Convergence was not a line moving forward. It was a series of curves, overlapping and accelerating, each feeding the others. Public awareness rose, and with it Walker density. Shadow adaptation followed attention, while institutional interference distorted flow instead of stabilizing it.

None of the curves reset. They only bent.

"If we slow one," she said softly, "we accelerate the others."

"Yes," Beagron said. "This is why no single victory can resolve what is coming."

Alex moved to the center of the room, grounding without touching anyone, his presence steadying the spike of fear that followed the realization. Joe pulled data together, refining projections, stripping away hope-driven variables until only constraint remained.

"How long," Alex asked.

The silence that followed was not empty. It was careful.

"Approximately one year," Beagron said at last. "Not exact. Not guaranteed. But narrowing."

The words landed hard, not because they promised doom, but because they refused certainty. A year was long enough to plan and short enough to fail.

Joe shook his head once, already anticipating the misinterpretation. "This isn't an apocalypse countdown," he said. "There's no day circled on the calendar where everything falls apart. This is the last window where choice still matters. After that, the system optimizes whether we like it or not."

Elara stood near one of the maps, watching heat signatures pulse faintly where pressure had recently spiked. "And every time we hit it," she said quietly, "we make it worse."

No one argued.

"Fire, suppression, forced containment," she continued. "All of it feeds pressure. The Unmaking isn't driving the clock. Reaction to it is."

Maya felt the pieces lock together, not with relief, but with clarity. She looked down at the Arcana, at the careful, frightened handwriting of a woman who had felt the world grow too tight and had written anyway.

"There's a final threshold," she said. "Once it's crossed, Guardians have to exist or the system collapses into entropy. There isn't a third state."

Joe exhaled slowly. "So we're not racing to stop Convergence."

"No," Maya said. "We're racing to meet it correctly."

The model stabilized as if in response, patterns settling into something that was not doom, but direction. The room did not feel safer. It felt oriented.

The clock had not started tonight.

They had only just learned how to read it.

Malcolm Fraser left before dawn, when the sky was still deciding whether it would belong to night or morning. The fallback site was quiet in that hollow, exhausted way that followed too many decisions made too quickly. He didn't wake anyone. He didn't say goodbye. He adjusted the strap of his satchel, now lighter than it had been when he arrived, and stepped past the outer boundary without resistance. No pressure followed him. No resonance tugged at his awareness. For the first time in months, the air felt like air again.

As he walked, the visions didn't return. The faces that had crowded the edges of his sight were gone. The weight that had lived behind his eyes had eased into something that felt almost like silence. Not absence. Completion. He understood then that the Weave hadn't called him to stay. It had called him to *deliver*, and now that task was finished. Whatever came next would not be decided by bloodlines or buried sanctums. It would be decided by the living.

By the time the sun broke the horizon, Malcolm was already on the road that would take him north, then east, then across the water. Scotland waited, unchanged and entirely different, a land that would soon feel the same pressures as everywhere else. He didn't know what role, if any, he would play again. He only knew that if the visions ever returned, he would listen. Until then, he walked on, carrying nothing but the knowledge that history had been placed back in human hands.

24

The Immortals' Fracture

Maya drifted toward sleep the way she always did now, not falling so much as easing sideways into it, awareness thinning while the Weave pressed gently at the edges of her mind. She lay on her back on a borrowed cot, hands folded over her stomach, eyes closed, listening to the quiet breaths and distant movements of the others. The fallback site had gone still in that fragile way that followed crisis, when exhaustion pretended to be peace.

She did not reach for the Weave.

It reached for her.

There was no sensation of movement, no feeling of being pulled from her body or lifted into another place. Instead, pressure gathered around her awareness, subtle at first, then insistent, as if the air itself had grown heavier. Her breath caught, not from fear, but from the sudden certainty that she was no longer entirely where she had been.

She was not somewhere else.

She was between.

The Weave did not open into form or color. There were no threads to follow, no geometry to orient herself by. What surrounded her was density, overlapping layers of intent that pressed against one another without resolution. The sensation was like standing in the center of a storm made of thought rather than wind.

She felt them before she understood them.

Immortal signatures flared through the pressure field, vast and unmistakable, each carrying a harmonic weight that dwarfed anything mortal. They did not speak in words. They did not need to. Their presence collided and recoiled in waves of resonance that carried meaning as clearly as shouted argument.

This was not a summons.

This was not a vision meant for her.

This was something breaking containment.

Cylian's presence cut first through the pressure, sharp and luminous, her resonance bending inward with urgency rather than authority. Maya felt the force of her intent like a hand braced against a failing wall.

Restraint is accelerating collapse.

The meaning came without sound, precise and relentless. Cylian's awareness pressed outward, mapping consequences, tracing fractures already forming beneath the surface of the lattice. She did not argue from emotion. She argued from observation.

The Covenant assumed stability that no longer exists.

Maya sensed her insistence on that point, the way it anchored everything else Cylian brought forward. The Immortals had bound themselves to non-intervention on the assumption that the system would hold long enough for mortals to adapt gradually, safely, without guidance becoming dependence.

That assumption was failing.

Non-intervention is not neutrality, Cylian pressed. It is passive harm when collapse is measurable.

Her resonance shifted then, not toward dominance, but toward a narrow band of possibility. Selective intervention. Guided, restrained, temporary. Not correction, not command, but presence that acknowledged the scale of what was unfolding.

They are learning blind, she insisted. Blind learning breaks systems before it builds them.

Maya felt the truth of it resonate uncomfortably close to her own experience, the memory of the Codex now reduced to ash, of alignment gained and then taken away without replacement. Cylian's argument was not a plea for power. It was a refusal to abandon responsibility simply because responsibility carried risk.

Antec's presence answered her, vast and immovable, his resonance carrying the weight of memory so dense it nearly collapsed the surrounding field. Where Cylian's awareness pressed forward, Antec's held ground.

He did not counter with theory.

He countered with history.

I remember the last time we intervened, his resonance conveyed, slow and deliberate. Not as warning, but as fact. I remember how guidance became correction. How correction became enforcement. How enforcement became certainty that we knew better than those we claimed to protect.

Maya felt images ripple beneath his meaning, impressions of ancient moments when Immortal hands had shaped outcomes with perfect intention and catastrophic consequence. Systems had stabilized, yes. They had also calcified.

Intervention always escalates authority, Antec continued. Even when it begins with restraint. Even when it swears it will stop.

His resistance was not fear of failure. It was fear of success achieved the wrong way, success that carried seeds of corruption because it replaced choice with certainty.

Restraint is not cowardice, his presence insisted. It is memory that refuses to repeat itself.

The pressure between them intensified, not into violence, but into strain. Their resonances did not clash destructively. They locked, neither yielding, neither overpowering the other. Maya felt the Weave itself begin to tremble under the unresolved tension.

Beagron's presence emerged then, deeper than the others, not forceful but unavoidable, like stone shifting under accumulated weight. His resonance did not align with either side of the argument at first. It settled beneath them, anchoring the space simply by existing.

You are arguing as if time remains, Beagron conveyed, and the words carried an exhaustion that startled Maya more than the conflict itself.

The others paused, not in silence, but in recalibration, their attention bending toward him.

Each surge weakens us, Beagron continued. Not symbolically. Structurally. Our coherence requires harmonic separation that the world no longer sustains.

Maya felt the truth of it resonate through the lattice, a low vibration that carried no accusation, only inevitability. The Immortals were not being attacked. They were not being overthrown or displaced by force.

They were being outpaced.

The Covenant assumed time was infinite, Beagron pressed, and for the first time there was no mistaking the sorrow embedded in his awareness. It never was.

The implication settled like cold weight in Maya's chest. The Immortals were fading not because they had failed in their duty, but because the world that had once required their role was transforming into something that no longer sustained it. Their forms depended on distinctions that Convergence was erasing.

The old order was not under siege.

It was becoming obsolete.

The pressure around Maya shifted then, not because the argument ended, but because it widened. She realized with a jolt of unease that she was not meant to be hearing any of this. The Immortals were not addressing her. They were not even aware of her in any focused way.

Their resonance was leaking.

Under strain, the boundaries that once filtered mortal perception were thinning, allowing fragments of Immortal deliberation to bleed outward. Maya felt their exhaustion now, the fragmentation beneath their immense presence, the subtle thinning that came with every surge of Convergence.

They were not gods arguing from power.

They were custodians arguing from depletion.

The realization left her breathless.

Vilya's presence rose quietly through the layered pressure, less forceful than the others, but no less profound. Where Beagron anchored and Cylian pressed forward, Vilya observed, holding memory the way others held weapons.

The Covenant was never meant to be eternal, his resonance conveyed, gentle and inexorable. It was meant to hold until successors emerged.

Maya felt something shift at those words, a reorientation that reframed everything she had assumed about the Immortals' role. Longevity had masqueraded as permanence. Survival had been mistaken for destiny.

Mortals were always the continuation, not the threat, Vilya pressed, and there was neither judgment nor absolution in the truth. Only clarity.

The Immortals had not failed by weakening. They had failed only by forgetting that they were a bridge, not an endpoint.

The argument did not resolve.

There was no vote, no consensus, no declaration that would bind them back into harmony. The Weave itself began to destabilize under the competing harmonic intents, resonance slipping into interference as unresolved pressure sought release.

Maya felt the boundary around her awareness collapse abruptly. The Weave recoiled, ejecting her from the shared space with a force that stole the air from her lungs.

She gasped awake, heart hammering, the dim ceiling of the fallback site snapping into focus above her. Her body trembled, not from injury, but from the shock of having crossed a line she had never intended to approach.

She had not listened where she was forbidden.

She had listened where no one remained strong enough to stop her.

The knowledge settled heavily as she lay there, staring into the quiet dark. The Immortals were not deciding whether mortals would take their place.

They were deciding whether they would endure long enough to witness it.

And in that realization, Maya understood with painful clarity that the old order was already ending, not with rebellion or catastrophe, but with the slow, irreversible erosion of authority that could no longer adapt to the world it had once shaped.

Mortals were no longer being tested.

They were being prepared.

25

The Battle of Perception

Joe had learned long ago that outrage was useless.

It burned hot and fast, made noise, drew eyes, and gave people something to point at while they decided nothing. Joe sat alone at the edge of the temporary command space, sleeves rolled up, jacket draped over the back of a chair he had not sat in all morning, and watched the world react exactly the way it always did when it was scared.

Screens glowed across the far wall, muted but dense with motion. Headlines scrolled past in half a dozen languages. Hybrid footage looped endlessly. Blurred figures. Fire. Bodies moving wrong. Voices raised high enough to crack into distortion. The feeds competed for attention, each one louder than the last.

Joe didn't watch them.

He filtered instead.

He muted volume, stripped away commentary, isolated response curves and delay intervals. He tracked where statements slowed before being released and where official channels hesitated just long enough to suggest disagreement behind closed doors. He marked pauses. Retractions. Carefully hedged phrases that said everything by refusing to say anything at all.

Fear was predictable. Authority hesitating was not.

Joe leaned closer to the data, fingers moving in short, precise motions as he reorganized the streams. He pulled regional statements from allied governments and laid them beside internal Alliance briefings that had not been meant to see daylight. The contradictions were subtle but unmistakable. A denial issued two hours after a confirmation request. A threat softened into a warning. A call for decisive action delayed under the guise of review.

That was the crack.

Public belief didn't shift because someone revealed the truth. It shifted when the people who were supposed to know what they were doing stopped acting like they did.

Joe tapped the side of the tablet and brought up a new layer. Civilian reactions. Not the trending outrage that burned itself out in minutes, but the slower responses. The ones that asked questions. The ones that waited.

Hesitation spread quietly. It didn't announce itself. It didn't chant or riot. It simply refused to move when pushed.

Joe smiled faintly and got to work.

He didn't dump information. He never did. A flood drowned context and washed away credibility with it. Instead, he queued releases the way a surgeon staged incisions, spaced far enough apart to let each one be seen for what it was.

Verified fragments only. No commentary. No framing.

He released internal documents detailing hybrid field failures, stripped of technical jargon but clear in their implications. He followed with procurement records that showed where oversight had been bypassed and who had signed off anyway. Then came testimonies. Not Walker accounts. Civilian voices, shaken but coherent, describing what it felt like to be near something that wore a human shape and moved like a machine built to survive pain.

Joe let the facts sit.

Outrage surged, just as he knew it would. It flared across networks and feeds, angry and hungry and directionless. Calls for retaliation spiked. Demands for control hardened. But beneath it all, something else began to take hold.

Doubt.

Leaders were forced to answer questions they had not prepared for. Not about the Walkers, but about the hybrids. Not about containment, but about consent. Not about power, but about responsibility.

Joe watched escalation stall at the points that mattered most.

Outrage burned fast. Doubt lasted longer.

Maya stood behind him as the next phase unfolded, her presence steady and watchful. She didn't interfere. She understood enough now to know when restraint mattered more than action.

The feeds shifted from data to motion as Walker interventions went live. Not attacks. Not rescues staged for cameras. Carefully chosen moments where refusal would be conspicuous. A bridge collapse stabilized without spectacle. A chemical fire suppressed without injury. A hospital grid brought back online just long enough for evacuation to complete.

No displays of dominance. No punishment. No sermons.

The Walkers did what needed to be done and left before anyone could ask them to stay.

Maya watched faces on the screens change as events resolved without escalation. Confusion gave way to something quieter. Relief, perhaps. Or recalibration. She felt the Weave stir faintly with each intervention, not easing, but redistributing pressure the way it always did now.

Mediation changed perception more than victory ever could.

Alex took it all in from the far side of the room, arms folded, grounding gently as tension rippled through the space. Statements from political leaders began to fracture, no longer aligned even within the same administrations. Some voices sharpened, leaning into fear and force. Others delayed, calling for further review, further data, further time.

Alex noted the shift and said nothing at first.

When he finally spoke, his voice was calm. "They aren't agreeing with us," he said. "They're failing to agree with each other."

Joe glanced up, satisfied. "That's enough."

Resistance didn't have to collapse to be weakened. It only had to hesitate long enough for alternatives to exist.

By late afternoon, outrage reached its ceiling.

Public fury over the hybrids intensified, but the calls for escalation stalled before they reached authorization. Internal leaks began to surface inside Alliance aligned institutions, small at first, then clustering as individuals sensed which way the wind was bending. The narrative shifted, slowly and unevenly, away from containing the Walkers and toward explaining the hybrids.

When authority had to explain itself, it was already losing control.

Joe stood at the strategy table as the data stabilized into a pattern that was not victory, but leverage. He didn't allow himself to relax. He knew better than that. Momentum was a fragile thing, especially when built on restraint.

Maya joined him quietly, her gaze lingering on the feeds. She saw what Joe saw and something more besides.

"They're watching us now," she said. "Not just reacting. Measuring."

Joe nodded. "That was always going to happen."

"How long before mediation becomes expectation," she asked, "and expectation turns into demand."

Joe considered her question carefully before answering. "That is the risk of being seen clearly," he said. "But silence does not protect you from that. It only lets someone else define you first."

He met her eyes, not unkindly. "Truth doesn't need to be loud. It just needs enough cracks to get through."

Night fell without ceremony.

The command space dimmed as feeds shifted to quieter coverage. Less shouting. More speculation. Some civilians defended Walkers openly now, pointing to interventions that had prevented loss rather than caused it. Others doubled down on fear, insisting that restraint was simply another form of manipulation.

The Circle understood the balance they stood on.

They had not changed the world.

They had changed the direction it was leaning.

Joe logged the final metrics before shutting down the displays. Institutional delays were lengthening. Emergency authorizations were being reviewed instead of signed. The machinery of escalation was slowing, not stopping, but slowing enough to matter.

Maya felt the Weave respond, not with relief, but with movement. Pressure redistributed again, sliding into new fault lines, seeking expression elsewhere. The system didn't rest simply because people paused.

Perception had shifted just enough to matter.

And not nearly enough to be safe.

Joe shut off the last screen and leaned back, exhaustion finally settling into his bones. Tomorrow, the world would wake up still afraid, still divided, still uncertain. But uncertainty had edges, and edges could be shaped.

For now, that would have to be enough.

26

The Silence Storm

Maya had learned not to rush Merlin's Journal.

It was tempting, especially now, to flip pages looking for something useful. A warning. A diagram. A sentence that ended with certainty instead of implication. But the Journal did not reward urgency. It resisted it, not through magic, but through tone. Every page assumed the reader would linger. Every paragraph felt written by someone who had learned the cost of moving too fast.

She sat at the scarred table near the edge of the fallback site, early morning light still gray beyond the narrow windows. The building wasn't much, just a repurposed municipal facility outside the worst node corridors, chosen for distance and redundancy and the fact that no one looked twice at it. It smelled like dust and old carpet and the bitter edge of cheap coffee.

The Arcana lay closed beside her, its familiar weight steady but inert. Merlin's Journal was different. Older. Thinner in places where the parchment had been handled too often. The leather binding creaked faintly when she adjusted it, a sound that felt indecently loud in the quiet room.

The others were waking into motion behind her. Quiet footsteps. Low voices. The scrape of a chair. Joe had already been up for an hour, maybe two, because Joe treated sleep the way he treated lies. As something that happened to other people when the world was behaving.

Maya did not search for instructions.

Merlin had not left any. That was the point. The Journal did not read like a handbook. It read like a confession written by a man who had seen too much and decided the only honest legacy he could leave was proof that certainty was dangerous.

She read for shape.

Merlin wrote like a man trying to describe pressure without language designed for it. He circled concepts rather than naming them, returning again and again to the same sensations, the same failures of metaphor. Maya noticed the shift halfway down a page she had already read twice.

The language changed.

Earlier entries were dense with struggle. Words like strain, resistance, correction. Descriptions of the Weave under stress, of imbalance pressing back against containment. But here, the tone flattened. Not emotionally. Structurally, like a song losing its melody and leaving only the thinnest vibration of rhythm.

There are failures that do not announce themselves.

No flare. No fracture. No violence.

There is silence without peace.

There is pressure that leaves nothing behind.

There is resonance that does not answer.

Maya stopped reading.

She let her fingers rest on the page. The paper was cool beneath her skin. She felt the Weave at the edges of her perception, not bright or loud, just present, the way it always was now. A lattice that hummed behind everything. She read the passage again, slower. She didn't just read the words. She listened for what he had been trying to communicate beneath them.

Merlin was not describing Shadow.

He was not describing the Unmaking.

He was describing absence.

The thought settled wrong in her chest. She turned the page and found the same language again, separated by years of entries that spoke of other things. Experiments. Observations. Failures that burned and twisted and scarred. Then, without warning, the same quiet phrases returned.

Silence without peace.

Pressure that leaves nothing behind.

Resonance that does not answer.

He had catalogued it.

Not when it happened. Not where.

How it began.

Maya closed the Journal and sat with the weight of that for a moment. The air in the room felt thicker. Not mystical. Not ominous in a way that would make a good story later. It felt thick the way air felt before a storm, when the world seemed to hold its breath even if you told yourself it was just humidity.

She stood and carried the Journal across the room.

Joe's command space was a corner carved out of necessity. Folding tables. Two laptops. A whiteboard crowded with lines and circles and names written and rewritten. A radio set that had no right to work as well as it did. No glowing government wall display. No bunker. No uniformed staff. Just an exhausted truthfinder who'd taught himself crisis coordination because no one else had the right mix of skepticism and nerve.

He had a spreadsheet open on one screen, a map on the other, and a third device that looked like a cheap environmental sensor station. He was comparing notes, not because he trusted any one thing, but because patterns only emerged when you stacked imperfect truths.

He looked up as Maya approached, the way he always did when she moved with purpose.

"I think we're watching for the wrong thing," she said quietly.

Joe didn't respond right away. He finished a line of notes and then turned fully toward her. His expression was alert but not dramatic. That was Joe. Even his fear tended to look like calculation.

"Say that again."

She opened the Journal to the marked passage and slid it to him. "Merlin wasn't writing about surges here. Or breaches. He was writing about failures that don't escalate. They go quiet."

Joe read quickly, eyes moving faster than hers had. His brows drew together. Then, instead of dismissing it, he did what he always did when something didn't fit his existing model. He adjusted the model.

"Quiet how," he asked, eyes still on the page.

"Flattening," Maya said. "Loss of response. Absence where something should be."

Joe's gaze flicked to his screens. "If that's the case, we're filtering wrong."

He turned back to his workstation and began reconfiguring his displays. He muted alert thresholds designed to flag spikes. He stripped away the automated smoothing that made graphs look clean. He pulled raw feeds forward and layered them over their own baselines, then over baselines from other regions. He started looking for what machines and people ignored because it didn't look like danger.

Maya watched him work and felt a quiet dread settle deeper. Because the thing about Joe was that when he got it, he got it fast.

He stopped and leaned closer to the screen.

"That shouldn't be possible," he said.

"What," Maya asked.

Joe pointed. "Background electromagnetic variance. See the noise here. The normal mess. It's flattening."

Maya stared at the graph. It didn't spike. It didn't crash. It simply smoothed, as if something had reached into the living turbulence of the world and pressed down until it behaved.

Joe pulled up another layer. Atmospheric micro-variations. Seismic noise. A proxy system they'd built to track civilian attunement clusters without pretending to understand the Weave itself. He called them Echo proxies because calling them anything else invited bad assumptions.

All of them showed the same subtle shift.

Quiet.

Maya felt it too, not in the data but in her bones. The Weave didn't surge. It withdrew. Like a hand pulling away from a surface that had turned cold.

"This isn't overload," Joe said slowly. "This is withdrawal."

Maya's throat tightened. "Where."

Joe didn't answer immediately. He dragged a map into the main view. Colored overlays. Lines of stress. Node corridors. Human population density. It looked like a weather model and a war plan stitched together.

A small region in northern Arizona had begun to lose its normal background activity.

Sedona.

Maya felt her own pulse jump. "Sedona isn't a primary node."

"No," Joe agreed. "It's overlap."

He clicked again, bringing up the corridor intersections that ran through it. Minor nodes braided together. Not enough to attract attention. Enough to become dangerous if pressure rose and no one noticed because they were busy watching the obvious threats.

Joe's fingers hovered over the keys.

Then he said, very softly, "It's already inside its failure curve."

Maya looked at him sharply. "How much time."

Joe's jaw worked once. "None."

The feeds went silent a heartbeat later.

Not cut. Not jammed. Silent.

Maya felt it as the Weave slipped sideways, a sudden hollowness where something had been. It was like stepping into a room you knew well and finding it empty of furniture. The shape was still there, but the purpose was gone.

Joe didn't curse. He didn't shout for anyone to do anything. He stood utterly still for half a second as the truth hit him, and then he moved.

"Alex," he said into the radio, voice controlled. "We've got a collapse event. Sedona. It's not a surge."

Static crackled. Alex's voice came back, tight with immediate focus. "Define not a surge."

"It's flattening," Joe said. "It's withdrawal. It's absence."

There was a pause. Not disbelief. Recalibration.

Maya turned away from the screens and looked toward the open doorway where Elara and a couple others had been half listening, half pretending they weren't. Elara's eyes met hers, and Maya saw the same thing she felt in her own chest.

This was different.

This wasn't another echo event. This wasn't the Shadow Current rising like a tide that could be pushed back with effort and sacrifice.

This was the Weave failing to answer.

And they were already late.

Sedona went silent at 8:42 a.m. local time.

It didn't feel like quiet the way snow muffled sound or distance thinned it. It felt like someone had reached inside the world and removed a function.

A woman standing at a crosswalk watched a dog trot past her and realized she couldn't hear its nails on the pavement. Her mind tried to supply the sound, because the human brain hated absence. It failed. She blinked hard, confused, and then the confusion became fear when she realized she couldn't hear the traffic either.

Her heart thudded in her ears.

Then she realized she couldn't hear that, either.

She opened her mouth to call out and felt air move but no vibration. No sound left her throat. She pressed a hand to her neck, convinced for one sick second that she was choking. Her lungs still drew breath. Her body still worked.

The world had simply stopped responding.

Across town, in a café that catered to tourists and locals alike, a man laughed at something on his phone and startled because he saw his own face laughing without hearing it. He looked around. Others were doing the same thing, mouths open, eyebrows lifted, looking for the moment the sound would return.

It didn't.

A mug slipped from a waitress's hand and shattered on the tile. The sight of ceramic breaking without sound made her stomach flip. She froze, unable to reconcile the visual with the absence of impact.

Panic spread without a single audible cue.

People ran and could not hear their own footsteps. They collided and recoiled, mouths open, eyes wide, communicating through expression alone. A child cried silently, face scrunched in confusion as tears fell without the familiar comfort of sound.

Wind stopped.

Not just the noise of it. The motion. Leaves on trees hung in a stillness that didn't feel natural. Hair stopped lifting. Clothing stopped fluttering. Even heat felt different, as if the atmosphere had become a sealed container.

Then the lights went out.

Cars stalled in the street. Engines died mid turn. Phones went black. Digital screens froze and then collapsed into dead glass. The modern world blinked out of existence in the space of a breath.

It wasn't a dramatic failure. No sparks. No explosions. No fire. Machines simply stopped behaving as machines.

A man tried to restart his car and found the ignition dead. Not drained. Dead, as if the concept of electrical response had been pulled away.

And then memory took its place.

A woman in a boutique found herself standing in a hospital corridor that smelled of antiseptic and grief. Her hands were smaller. Her voice was younger. She could see her mother, alive and dying at once, because memory didn't respect linear time. The moment played through with the brutal clarity of the first time, and when it ended she blinked and found herself back in the boutique.

For a fraction of a second she thought it was over.

Then it began again.

A man in his fifties clutched at his chest and found himself back in the desert, heat rippling off sand, the sound of distant combat absent but the terror present anyway. He did not have his weapon. He did not have his comrades. He did not have the years of recovery he'd spent convincing himself he was safe.

He had the moment.

Again and again.

The loops did not pick only trauma. They picked defining moments. The memory that had shaped you. The moment your life bent and you did not become who you thought you'd be. The moment you loved someone so hard it hurt. The moment you failed. The moment you survived.

Sedona became a city of silent faces reliving the core of themselves on repeat.

Time lost meaning inside the storm.

Maya arrived at the perimeter with the taste of copper in her mouth.

Blinking into crisis always carried disorientation, but this was different. It wasn't the usual snap of location change, the reorientation of senses as the Weave stitched her into a new coordinate. This felt like stepping into a place where the stitching thread had been removed.

She stood on a highway turnout a few miles outside Sedona with Alex and Elara and two other Walkers who'd become part of the Circle's wider orbit over the last months. Vehicles clustered there, their drivers standing beside them, gesturing in frantic confusion. Some were crying. Some were staring toward the city with the blank expression of people who'd seen something they couldn't name.

Maya opened her awareness.

The Weave did not answer the way it should have. There was no resistance. No push. No pull.

Nothing.

She had never felt nothing before. Even the Shadow Current had a texture. Even damage had a texture. Nothing had no texture.

It made her dizzy.

Elara stepped closer, her gaze locked on the distant skyline. "I can't feel it," she said.

Maya swallowed. "I can."

Elara looked at her sharply.

"Not the way you mean," Maya added. "I can feel where it isn't."

Alex's jaw tightened. "A hole."

Maya nodded slowly. "A void."

Joe's voice crackled through the radio from the fallback site. It was faint but usable. "Maya. Talk to me."

She glanced at Alex, then spoke. "We're at the edge. The Weave doesn't respond inside."

A pause. Joe's voice came back, controlled but strained. "Is it Shadow dominance?"

"No," Maya said. "Shadow is... present. Even when it's terrible, it's present. This isn't presence."

Alex shifted his stance, scanning the horizon. "Can you go in."

Maya tried to reach for her blink.

Her power was not gone. She could feel the pathways she normally used. But when she aimed it toward the city, her perception slid off. Like trying to grab a rope made of smoke.

"I can't anchor," she said.

Elara's hands curled. A faint shimmer of heat rippled around her, more reflex than intention. "So we just stand here."

Maya watched a man stumble at the edge of the perimeter and drop to his knees. His mouth was open in a silent howl. His eyes were wide and unfocused, as if he was watching something only he could see.

Memory bleed.

The gradient was already spreading beyond the city.

"We don't stand," Maya said. "We build a line."

From orbit, Sedona appeared as a dark circle punched through the aurora grid.

Alex saw it on a remote feed twenty minutes later when a satellite pass aligned with the region. The aurora patterns that had haunted the world since the first visible thresholds were faint now, not always present to the naked eye, but instruments still read them as a living net of resonance.

Sedona was a dead spot.

A clean edged void where the grid simply stopped.

Alex stared at it, and something cold moved through him. Not fear. Recognition. The kind that made your body prepare for a punch before it landed.

"It's stable," he said into the radio.

Joe's voice was tight. "Define stable."

"It isn't moving," Alex said. "It's... set. Like it reached a radius and decided that's what it is."

Elara laughed once, sharp and humorless. "That's worse."

Alex didn't disagree.

He stepped closer to the perimeter and did what he was built to do. He grounded.

He spread his awareness outward, not into the void itself but into the edges where people were still reachable. He felt the storm like a pressure gradient, not a force pushing outward, but a lack pulling things inward. People's minds slid toward their loops because there was nothing in the Weave to catch them.

Alex became that catch.

He didn't stop the storm. He couldn't. But he could hold the line where the world still had enough structure to respond.

He felt the strain begin almost immediately. Not in his muscles. In his cognition. In the way his mind had to keep returning to the simplest truths.

You are here.

You are now.

You are not back there.

It wasn't just for him. It was for everyone close enough to be influenced by his presence. He watched a woman at the edge blink hard, her face twisting with sudden grief, and then her eyes cleared for a moment as if she'd been pulled out of deep water.

Alex exhaled slowly.

This was what he could do.

Containment without victory.

Flagstaff began to fail in pieces.

Not total silence. Not full loops.

Intermittent loss.

A paramedic leaned over a patient and spoke a triage question, only to watch the patient's eyes widen in fear because the words never arrived. Then, half a second later, the sound hit like a delayed echo, distorted and wrong.

Traffic lights blinked unpredictably. Radios crackled with nonsense. A hospital computer froze, then recovered, then displayed corrupted data that made no sense to anyone.

Emergency services called it a cyberattack for the first ten minutes because that was the closest language they had.

Then responders started reporting the same thing from different districts. People standing in the street staring into nothing. People weeping without sound. People screaming silently while their hands shook like they were trapped in the worst moment of their lives.

A dispatcher tried to keep order while her own memory bled into her awareness. She saw, for half a second, the face of her father in a coffin from ten years ago with perfect clarity. She blinked hard and forced herself back to the present because if she didn't the entire system would collapse into human grief.

Some people escaped the gradient.

Others didn't.

A family driving north hit a patch where sound cut out entirely for three seconds. In those three seconds the mother saw her daughter at age five running into the street. The memory hit so hard she swerved. The car clipped a barrier. No one died. But the father stared at his shaking hands afterward and knew something was happening that seatbelts couldn't prevent.

Distance from the node determined survivability, not preparedness.

Maya felt that truth in her bones as the perimeter expanded.

Joe worked with two phones that barely held signal and a radio that squealed every time someone near the storm tried to transmit.

He hated helplessness. He hated it the way other people hated violence. He'd built his whole life around the idea that the truth, once dragged into daylight, had power. Even ugly truth had power.

But this wasn't a lie. It wasn't a coverup. It wasn't even an enemy in a shape he could pursue.

It was a structural failure.

He issued evacuation routes, not because he believed in order but because order bought time. He coordinated with local authorities without telling them what was really happening because no one would believe it, and belief itself was part of the problem now.

He kept his language mundane.

"Signal failure."

"Regional outage."

"Atmospheric interference."

"Unknown event, prioritize evacuation."

Every word was a bridge between realities.

He watched the map redraw as reports came in. Sedona was a blacked out zone. Flagstaff was a smeared gradient, unpredictable but still breathable. Beyond that, the world was normal enough to pretend it was still the old world.

Joe stopped pretending.

He picked up Merlin's Journal again and read the passage a third time. Not because he needed to understand it. Because he needed to anchor himself to the fact that this had been possible all along.

Maya's voice came through the radio. "Joe. It's not fighting. It's absence."

Joe closed his eyes for half a second. "We can't solve absence."

"No," Maya agreed. "But we can keep people from falling into it."

Joe opened his eyes and looked at the map.

"Then we build a ring," he said. "We don't try to save the center. We save what the center will otherwise take with it."

There were protests from someone in the room. Not from the Walkers. From a civilian volunteer who had been helping coordinate relief efforts. Her face was pale, her eyes wide.

"We can't just abandon them," she said.

Joe looked at her, and his voice softened without losing its edge. "We aren't abandoning them. We're being honest about what we can reach."

He tapped the map. "If we push into the core, we lose responders. If we lose responders, we lose the edge. If we lose the edge, we lose Flagstaff. If we lose Flagstaff, we lose everything north of it that thinks this is still a contained event."

He didn't need his Truthfinder ability to know fear was building. It was in every movement. Every breath. Every person trying to speak around the fact that no one understood what they were watching.

Joe leaned toward the radio. "Alex. Hold the line. Do not cross into the core."

Alex's response was immediate. "I'm already doing that."

"Good," Joe said. "Maya. You're going to hate this."

Maya's voice was quiet. "Say it."

"We're not going to fix Sedona today," Joe said. "We're going to keep it from reaching Phoenix."

There was silence. Not the storm's silence. The human kind. The kind where everyone heard the truth at the same time and didn't want to say it out loud.

Then Maya said, "Understood."

Joe exhaled slowly. He didn't feel relief. He felt responsibility settle heavier.

Elara stood at the perimeter and stared into nothing.

Fire was her language. Heat, motion, reaction. Even her fear tended to express itself as a flare. Inside the storm, there was no reaction to push against.

She held out a hand and let a small tongue of flame ignite at her fingertips.

The flame burned.

It did not reach.

It didn't even flicker toward the void as if drawn. It was as if the void didn't exist as a thing fire could recognize.

Elara swallowed.

The Unmaking, though, reacted.

She felt it the way she felt pressure changes in her own blood. The Shadow Current, always eager to stir when attention lingered, recoiled from the edge of the storm like an animal avoiding a trap.

Elara's mouth went dry. "It's scared."

Maya turned toward her. "The Unmaking."

Elara nodded once. "Or at least... it doesn't want to touch it. It doesn't want to be there."

Alex's gaze narrowed. "Entropy doesn't get scared."

Elara almost smiled. "Then it gets cautious."

She looked back at the void.

"This isn't Shadow dominance," she said, voice low. "Shadow is still something. It's still a force. It still moves."

She flexed her fingers and let the flame die.

"This is erasure."

Maya's eyes tightened. "Say that again."

Elara didn't look away. "Not Shadow. Not Weave. Just nothing. Forced nothing."

The words landed like a weight.

Maya whispered, "Silence without peace."

Elara nodded. "Yeah."

Alex's hands clenched at his sides. He was holding his line, but even he looked unsettled now, like the storm had found the one thing he couldn't ground.

Meaning.

By afternoon, the refugee zone outside Flagstaff had become a city of tents and exhausted faces.

Maya walked through it slowly, not because she was trying to be seen as a leader, but because she couldn't bear staying still. If she stayed still, she would feel the storm too clearly.

People looked at her with a mixture of hope and suspicion. Some recognized her now, not by name, but by the way the air shifted around her when she moved. Attuned people, even Tier I, noticed more than they wanted to admit.

A woman sat on a folding chair staring at her hands as if she didn't trust them. Her lips moved silently, repeating something to herself. Maya knelt near her and waited until the woman's eyes lifted.

"I keep seeing him," the woman mouthed. No sound came out because the gradient was still unstable here, but Maya could read her lips well enough.

"Who," Maya asked softly.

The woman's face crumpled. "My brother. He died. Years ago. But I keep seeing him like it's happening right now."

Maya nodded. "You're not crazy."

The woman's eyes filled with tears at that, and Maya hated how much relief the sentence gave her. She shouldn't have needed it. But human beings always needed permission to believe their own minds when reality shifted.

Maya moved on.

She found a teenage boy sitting apart from the others, eyes fixed on nothing. His posture was too still, like a statue pretending to be human. Maya approached slowly.

"Hey," she said. "Can you hear me."

The boy's eyes flicked toward her. "Sometimes," he said, voice faint and delayed, as if the sound had to fight its way into existence.

"What's your name."

"Dylan."

"Dylan," Maya repeated. "What's happening to you?"

He swallowed. "I keep hearing... stuff. Like... like echoes of people talking. But nobody's talking."

Maya felt the Weave twitch around him, faint and unstable. Not full Walker resonance. Not nothing either.

A survivor signature.

A new class of wound.

She sat on the ground near him, keeping her posture low and non-threatening. "Do you see things too?"

He nodded. "When it hits, I'm not here anymore. I'm in my dad's truck. He's yelling. I'm twelve. I can smell the cigarettes. I can feel the seatbelt digging into my neck."

Maya closed her eyes for a moment, not to block it out, but to keep her own emotions from spilling into the air.

"When you come back," she said, "how do you do it?"

Dylan blinked. "I don't know. Sometimes I just... look at something real. Like... the dirt. My shoes. The way the sun hits the tent."

Alex's grounding principle, spoken by a boy who didn't know Alex existed.

Maya nodded slowly. "That's good. That's exactly what you should do."

Dylan stared at her. "Is this going to happen again?"

Maya didn't lie. Not to him.

"Yes," she said. "But you're still here. You're still you. That matters."

He swallowed hard. "Why me?"

Maya looked toward the horizon where Sedona sat like a bruise on the world.

"Because you were close," she said. "That's all. It isn't fair. It isn't personal. It's proximity."

The boy's eyes narrowed. "So I'm... what. Broken?"

Maya held his gaze. "Wounded," she corrected. "Not broken."

She stood and kept walking.

Behind her, the refugee camp murmured with delayed voices and intermittent silence and the kind of collective fear that could become a weapon if it found the wrong story to attach itself to.

Maya felt it.

The storm wasn't just erasing a city.

It was rewriting people.

Night fell.

The Silence Storm did not recede.

Sedona remained a dead zone. A void in the aurora grid. A hole in the world that was not a crater of destruction but a crater of meaning.

Joe stood in the command space with the map open, watching the lines settle into something no one had the courage to call permanent out loud.

Alex sat with his back against a wall, eyes closed, breathing slow, recovering from hours of holding a line that should not have been his responsibility alone.

Elara stared at her hands, not because she was afraid of fire, but because she was afraid of what it meant that fire had been useless.

Maya sat at the table again with Merlin's Journal open, not reading, just looking at the words as if they were a wound she needed to understand.

Joe came to stand beside her.

He didn't speak for a long moment. Then he said quietly, "Sedona sat at a multi-node overlap."

Maya didn't look up. "I know."

Joe's voice was careful. "There are others."

Maya finally lifted her eyes.

The room felt still.

No one talked about reversing it.

No one talked about saving the center.

They talked about lines. Evacuation. Supplies. What to do when the next one hit, because everyone in that room understood the truth now.

This wasn't a warning.

It was a demonstration.

Maya's voice came out low. "No more illusions of control."

Joe nodded once. "Yeah."

Maya closed the Journal gently.

Outside, the world kept turning. People still checked their phones in cities far away. Cars still started. Lights still worked. Normality continued by inertia, because most of humanity had not been forced to stare directly into absence.

Yet.

Maya looked at the map again, at the dark circle that would not fade, and she felt something harden inside her that had once been softer.

Inaction was no longer neutrality.

It was a choice with casualties.

<h1 style="text-align:center">27</h1>

<h1 style="text-align:center">Refugees of Silence</h1>

Dawn came slowly to the high desert outside Flagstaff, a pale wash of light that didn't quite feel like morning. The air was cold and thin, carrying the smell of dust, antiseptic, and something scorched that no one could quite identify. Maya stood at the edge of the intake zone and watched the survivors arrive.

They didn't come as crowds.

They came in pieces.

A man walking alone down the shoulder of the road, shoes in his hands, eyes unfocused but determined. A family of three holding hands too tightly, the youngest child dragging her feet as if gravity had grown heavier around her ankles. Two women leaning on each other, moving in step without speaking, their faces slack with exhaustion rather than fear.

There was no screaming. No hysteria. No surge of panic the way Maya had come to expect after disaster.

Just movement. Slow, uneven, disoriented movement.

Medical teams waved them forward, voices gentle, gestures exaggerated to make up for how little anyone seemed to respond to sound. Clipboards filled quickly with notes that didn't fit standard categories. Disorientation. Fatigue. Memory disruption. Sensory anomalies. No clear trauma markers. No consistent neurological pattern.

Maya felt it before she understood it.

Unstable resonance flickered through the line, faint and erratic, like sparks caught under skin. Some signatures pulsed briefly and vanished. Others clung stubbornly, refusing to settle. None of it followed a rhythm she recognized. It wasn't power. It wasn't awakening.

It was reaction.

A woman near the front of the line glanced up suddenly and met Maya's eyes. She blinked, startled, then visibly relaxed, shoulders lowering as if someone had turned down a noise only she could hear. She didn't know why. Neither did Maya.

The damage wasn't visible at first.

It revealed itself through proximity.

The medical shelter buzzed with low activity, generators humming, monitors flickering, stretchers lining the walls in uneven rows. Maya moved between cots, listening more than she spoke.

"They're not real sounds," one man told her, gripping the blanket around his shoulders. "I know that. But they feel like they should be. Like something's trying to remember how noise works."

Another woman described hearing her name spoken just behind her left ear, always just out of reach. A teenager pressed his palms to his temples and asked Maya why the silence kept echoing.

Scans showed nothing wrong. No lesions. No abnormal neural activity. No chemical imbalance that explained the symptoms.

Maya closed her eyes briefly and let her awareness widen, just enough to feel the edges of the Weave without touching it.

The Weave didn't answer.

But it brushed them.

She understood then with a clarity that made her stomach tighten. These people weren't hearing things. They were sensing resonance without access. Feeling pressure without permission. The system acknowledged them but refused to engage.

Exposure had created sensitivity without control.

She moved on, pulse steady but unease growing heavier with every step.

The stabilization corridor was louder than the shelter, voices sharper, tension tighter. Alex stood near the center, grounding gently, hands open, posture calm.

The disruption came fast.

A man near the far wall flinched as a medic raised her voice, the sound cutting through his awareness like a blade. Something snapped outward from him, not power but reflex. The air warped briefly, a shimmer that bent light and then vanished.

The man stared at his hands in horror.

"I didn't mean to," he said, voice breaking. "I didn't do anything."

Alex was there in an instant, grounding hard enough to anchor the corridor without touching anyone. The shimmer faded, but not completely. Residual instability clung to the man's outline like static.

The man sagged, legs giving out as the fear caught up to him.

Alex caught him before he hit the floor.

"This isn't activation," Alex said quietly to the medic watching with wide eyes. "This is damage."

The man sobbed into Alex's shoulder, shaking, terrified not of what he'd felt, but of what he'd almost become.

These people hadn't awakened.

They'd been scarred open.

Elara stood apart from the others, watching a different group entirely.

They sat upright on their cots, backs straight, eyes attentive. They answered questions clearly. They followed instructions. They showed no signs of confusion or distress.

They were intact.

And empty.

Elara reached out through the weave, careful, precise.

Nothing answered.

No recoil. No resistance. No echo of fear or memory or instinct. Fire didn't recognize them. Silence didn't cling to them either. They existed in a narrow, perfect absence.

"They're intact," Elara said softly to Maya when she approached. "But empty."

Maya looked at the man closest to them. He met her gaze politely and nodded, as if waiting for her to finish whatever she'd come to say.

Silence could hollow people without killing them.

The thought settled like ash.

Joe sat hunched over a folding table in the command tent, screens arranged in a rough arc around him. He wasn't watching faces. He was watching maps.

Exposure radii. Arrival points. Symptom clusters. Proximity overlays.

The data refused to behave.

Symptoms didn't correlate with time spent inside Sedona. Some people who had fled early showed severe instability. Others pulled from the center of the storm showed none at all. Effects rippled outward beyond city limits, brushing Flagstaff unevenly, touching some neighborhoods and skipping others entirely.

Joe leaned back and rubbed his eyes.

Preparedness didn't predict outcome.

Distance didn't guarantee safety.

Survivability wasn't controllable.

It was probabilistic.

He flagged the realization and sent it to the team without commentary.

Maya sat beside a young woman on a cot near the edge of the shelter. The woman's hands shook continuously, breath shallow, eyes darting as if tracking something just beyond the visible world.

Maya didn't reach for the Weave. She didn't try to fix anything.

She stayed.

The shaking slowed. The woman's breathing deepened. Her gaze steadied, confusion easing into something like relief.

"It's quieter," the woman whispered. "Don't move."

Maya froze.

She hadn't acted.

She'd been present.

After a moment, Maya shifted slightly, just enough to test the boundary. The woman's hands began to tremble again, the quiet slipping away.

Maya felt cold spread through her chest.

Walkers altered people now just by existing nearby.

Ethical distance wasn't a choice anymore.

They gathered later in a makeshift briefing space, exhaustion etched into every face.

"They aren't Walkers," someone said.

"That doesn't help," Joe replied.

"Apprentices," another offered, then shook their head. "No. That implies choice."

Silence stretched as they searched for language that didn't lie.

"Proto-apprentices," Alex said at last. "Not awakened. Not trained. Just altered."

No one liked it.

That was why it stuck.

Humanity was changing faster than language could adapt.

Night fell quietly.

Maya walked alone through the rows of sleeping refugees. Some glowed faintly in the low light, resonance leaking without form. Others lay still, untouched, human in ways that suddenly felt fragile.

There had been no consent. No warning. No choice.

She looked at her hands and wondered, for the first time, whether the Covenant had ever been protection at all.

Responsibility had arrived ahead of intention.

That terrified her.

Joe watched the feeds as the first footage leaked. Blurred images. Unstable survivors. Headlines grasping for words that didn't exist yet.

Contaminated. Evolved. Dangerous. Blessed.

Fear would find new targets.

Outside, the Silence Storm remained, a permanent scar on the map. Inside, the Circle understood the truth settling over them.

The storm hadn't just destroyed a city.

It had created a population that couldn't go back.

Convergence no longer needed permission.

It had begun rewriting people.

28

Saints and Terrorists

Joe had learned to listen to language the way some people listened to weather.

Not for what it said, but for how it shifted.

Three days after Sedona went silent, the words began to change.

He stood in the temporary command space just outside Flagstaff, coffee gone cold in his hand, eyes moving across a wall of muted feeds and text summaries. Refugee numbers ticked upward in one corner of the display. Supply inventories scrolled in another. But Joe wasn't watching those. Not yet.

He was watching statements.

At first, governments had spoken the way they always did after catastrophe. Careful phrases. Passive constructions. Incidents under review. Anomalous events. Ongoing assessments. There had been sympathy, concern, the promise of coordination that never quite materialized.

That language was gone.

Now the words carried edges.

Containment protocols. Unauthorized actors. Destabilizing elements.

Joe straightened slightly, the faintest tension threading through his shoulders.

The Walkers were no longer being described as phenomena. They weren't anomalies or unknown variables anymore. They were being framed as agents. Actors with intent. Forces that could be named, categorized, opposed.

He pulled two statements side by side and read them slowly.

One referred to the Silence Storm as a natural escalation of uncontrolled resonance. The other described it as the foreseeable consequence of unregulated interference.

Neither mentioned Sedona's node overlap. Neither mentioned Alliance research sites buried in the same geographies. Neither acknowledged the hybrids.

Joe exhaled through his nose.

Governments decided who you were before they decided what you'd done. Once the label stuck, facts became optional.

By midday, the fracture widened.

The first designation didn't come from a superpower. It came from a mid-tier state with a strong internal security doctrine and a long history of aligning early with whoever looked most decisive.

The Weave Circle was formally classified as a terrorist organization.

Joe read the justification twice, then a third time.

Extra-state actors operating beyond oversight. Unregulated use of force with mass casualty proximity. Destabilization of civil order through unauthorized intervention.

It was vague by design. Just specific enough to justify action. Just abstract enough to adapt later.

Within hours, other governments echoed parts of the language without committing fully. Temporary classifications. Pending reviews. Conditional threat status.

Imitation without consensus.

Fear moving faster than evidence ever could.

Joe forwarded the designation to the team without commentary. He didn't need to explain it. Anyone who'd ever watched power consolidate under pressure knew what came next.

Neutral ground was already eroding.

Maya learned about the other side of it in a quieter way.

She was in a side room off the main compound, seated at a folding table cluttered with maps and handwritten notes, when the first message came through. It wasn't addressed to her directly. It didn't come from a known channel.

It came through an intermediary who never quite said who they represented.

There were no seals. No formal requests. No signatures that could be traced.

Just questions.

Could she stabilize a site without appearing on record. Could she advise local responders without crossing borders. Could she come closer without being seen.

Maya stared at the screen for a long moment, a familiar weight settling in her chest.

These governments didn't defend the Circle publicly. They condemned them, hedged, or stayed silent. But when their own systems strained, when their own populations edged toward panic, they reached anyway.

Authority always did.

She typed no commitments. Offered no promises. She asked only what they were seeing.

The answers came quickly.

Unstable regions. Echo bleed. Infrastructure behaving strangely even where nothing visible had happened yet.

Maya closed her eyes.

She hadn't asked for this role. She hadn't agreed to it. But the shape of it was undeniable now. She was becoming a point of contact not because anyone had voted or appointed her, but because there was no one else who could answer the questions they were afraid to ask out loud.

She wondered how long it would be before that made her a target everywhere instead of a resource anywhere.

Alex saw the shape of it from the perimeter.

By the fourth night after Sedona, he stood near the outer edge of the compound, tablet in hand, eyes scanning movement reports that had nothing to do with combat and everything to do with readiness.

Troops weren't mobilizing. They weren't deploying en masse or crossing borders.

They were repositioning.

Readiness levels ticked up. Surveillance assets shifted. Recon flights increased. Satellite attention narrowed.

No strikes. No engagement orders. No one wanted to be first.

Everyone wanted to be ready.

Alex didn't need experience to recognize the shape of it. He'd designed systems like this for years. States held just below activation. Tension accumulating without release. A world paused at the edge of escalation. The tension of deterrence. The brittle calm that preceded either restraint or catastrophe.

This wasn't war.

It was the shape of a cold one forming.

By the end of the week, the fracture reached the public.

Headlines split sharply along lines that felt less ideological than emotional.

Walkers Prevent Further Collapse.

Uncontrolled Entities Endanger Humanity.

Footage looped endlessly. Walker interventions spliced beside images of Sedona's silent streets. Survivors speaking haltingly about what they'd lost, about what they'd felt near the Circle, about the strange quiet that followed them even now.

Protests appeared in cities half a world away. Some carried signs demanding protection. Others demanded containment. Counter-protests followed within hours.

Survivors of the Silence Storm became symbols before they could become people again.

Joe watched the feeds late into the night, cataloging patterns that made his jaw tighten.

Symbols were negotiable. Safety was not.

On the sixth night, he finally spoke plainly to the Circle.

They gathered in the command space, exhaustion etched into every face. Maps lined the walls. Refugee numbers updated in quiet increments. Outside, generators hummed steadily, a sound that had become almost comforting in its persistence.

"This isn't consensus," Joe said, hands braced on the table. "It's alignment by fear. They don't need to agree about us. They just need to act like they might."

He looked at Maya as he said it, not accusing, just honest.

"Every escalation accelerates pressure in the system. Every attempt to control us feeds the same dynamics that caused Sedona. And the survivors are becoming leverage. Whether they want to be or not."

No one argued.

Maya stepped outside later, the desert night cool against her skin. The stars looked unchanged. That almost made it worse.

Neutrality had been an illusion. Silence had been mistaken for safety. Staying unseen now only meant letting someone else decide who she was and what she represented.

She understood the trap clearly enough to feel its edges closing.

Speaking publicly would escalate everything. Not speaking would do the same, just slower and without her voice in it.

Doing nothing was no longer moral ground.

It was surrender.

By the end of the week, the Circle occupied a space no one had planned for and no one could step away from.

Terrorist designations multiplied. Quiet coordination requests increased. Refugees continued to arrive.

They were hunted and relied upon at the same time.

They were no longer outside the world's systems.

They were the pressure point inside them.

The question was no longer whether the world would respond.

It was who would speak first.

29

Maya Goes Public

The desert woke slowly.

Maya stood just beyond the outer edge of the compound while the sky lightened from black to a thin, uncertain gray. Morning crept in without confidence, as if the world itself wasn't sure it wanted to be seen yet. Generators hummed behind her. Somewhere farther out, a truck backfired and then fell silent again. The air smelled like dust, cold metal, and old smoke that never quite went away.

She listened.

Not to the Weave. Not yet.

She listened to the world waking up.

Feeds scrolled quietly on a tablet propped against a crate beside her. Time stamps jumped between continents. Emergency banners crawled beneath familiar logos. The words were changing again. She could feel it even before she read them.

Unauthorized actors.

Threat environment escalation.

Preemptive containment measures.

The labels multiplied faster than the explanations ever had.

She swiped past a statement from one government and straight into a denial from another. The denials didn't deny the same things.

That mattered. She'd learned that from Joe. When fear outran coordination, truth fractured first.

Behind her, the refugee tents stretched in uneven rows, dim shapes against the sand. People slept in fragments there too. Not deeply. Not well. Some glowed faintly in ways that no camera ever quite captured right. Others lay dark and quiet, breathing steadily, human in ways that suddenly felt fragile.

They were here because silence had reached out and changed them.

And because she had been near enough to matter.

Maya closed the tablet and let her arms hang at her sides. She could feel the pull of it now, the pressure she'd been holding at bay for days. The world wasn't waiting anymore. It was leaning. Toward fear. Toward someone else speaking first.

Silence wasn't restraint now.

It was abdication.

She turned back toward the compound and walked inside.

Joe looked up the moment she entered the command space. He didn't ask how she'd slept. No one did anymore. The room was already awake, maps layered on screens, feeds muted, data sliding quietly from one state of almost-order into another.

"I'm going public," Maya said.

No preamble. No apology.

The room went still in a way she'd learned to recognize. Not shock. Calculation.

Joe exhaled slowly through his nose. "That's escalation."

"Yes," she said. "It is."

Alex straightened from where he'd been leaning against a table. His expression tightened, not in anger but concern. "Once you do that, there's no way to control what comes back at us. They won't just label us anymore. They'll act."

Elara stood near the far counter, one hand curled around a mug that had long since gone cold. She frowned, eyes distant, and without looking down, she brushed the ceramic with her thumb. The coffee inside steamed faintly, warming as if the thought had occurred to it. She didn't seem to notice she'd done it.

"It will accelerate things," Elara said quietly. "Pressure responds to attention. You know that."

Maya nodded. She hadn't expected agreement. She hadn't even expected permission.

"I know," she said. "But they're already defining what we are. Every hour we stay quiet, that version hardens."

Joe crossed his arms. "Once you speak, you can't take it back. You won't just be explaining. You'll be choosing sides for everyone who hears you."

Maya met his eyes. "They already chose. We just weren't in the room."

Alex looked between them. "This paints a target on you. On all of us."

"Yes," Maya said again.

Elara set the mug down and finally looked up. "And if Convergence accelerates because of this?"

Maya didn't answer immediately. She took a breath and felt the truth settle into her chest where fear had been trying to live.

"Then it accelerates honestly," she said. "Not behind closed doors. Not through rumors and mislabels. If we don't speak, we're consenting to the version where we're monsters and they're righteous."

No one interrupted her.

"Silence doesn't keep people safe anymore," Maya continued. "It just lets someone else decide what safety means."

Joe held her gaze for a long moment. Then he nodded once.

"All right," he said. "Then we do it right."

The communications hub was already hot with activity when Joe stepped inside. He waved off a tech who started to speak and pulled up a layered display of global feeds, relays, and redundancies.

"We don't accept an interview," he said, thinking aloud. "Too much control on their end. We don't leak statements either. That gets reframed before it lands."

He zoomed in on a narrow overlap in broadcast infrastructure. Emergency channels. Commercial relays. Government advisories. For a few seconds at a time, they all passed through the same spine.

"There," Joe said. "That window."

Alex frowned. "That's not domination."

"No," Joe replied. "It's insertion."

He glanced back toward Maya. "You won't own the signal. You'll just be present in it long enough to be heard."

"That's all I need," Maya said.

The broadcast space was barely a space at all. A cleared corner of the compound. A neutral backdrop. No insignia. No flags. No symbols except the ones people would project on their own.

The cameras came online without ceremony.

Joe stood just off-frame, watching the timers tick down. "Once it starts," he said quietly, "they'll try to cut it."

Maya nodded. She stood where the light fell evenly across her face, hands relaxed at her sides. No armor. No posture. Just a woman in worn boots and a jacket that smelled faintly of smoke and dust.

"This isn't a performance," she said.

Joe gave a tight smile. "Good. Because the world's tired of those."

The feed went live.

Maya looked into the camera and felt the weight of it settle across continents.

"My name is Maya Rodriguez," she said. "I'm a Walker."

The words carried farther than any power ever had.

"I know a lot of you are afraid," she continued. "I would be too. Things are happening that don't fit the rules you were taught to trust. Silence doesn't behave like weather. People change without asking to. Governments don't agree on what's happening, but they agree on who they want to blame."

She paused, letting the space exist.

"I'm not here to ask you to trust me. I'm here to tell you what I know and what I don't."

She explained the Weave as she would to someone sitting across from her at a table. Not a force. A structure. A connective tissue that had always been there, whether anyone acknowledged it or not. She described the Unmaking not as an enemy, but as imbalance, pressure without release. A system failing to distribute what it carried.

"And Convergence," she said, "is what happens when the system stops pretending it can stay hidden."

She didn't soften the truth.

"Silence Storms aren't attacks," Maya said. "They're failures. Places where resonance collapses instead of flaring. Where there's nothing to fight because there's nothing left to answer."

She admitted uncertainty. Named limits. Refused certainty where none existed.

Credibility grew in the space she left unfilled.

When she raised her hand, it was slowly, deliberately. A faint distortion shimmered in the air beside her, a visible knot of instability she'd prepared earlier. She steadied it with care, letting it settle, not vanish.

"This is control," she said. "Not dominance. And it doesn't always work. Stopping everything isn't possible. Anyone who tells you otherwise is lying."

She lowered her hand.

"This isn't about believing me," Maya said. "It's about deciding what kind of world you're willing to build with what's coming. Denial has a cost. Cooperation has a cost. There isn't a version of this without consequence."

The signal cut mid-sentence.

Joe swore softly and turned back to his screens. "Too late," he said. "It's everywhere."

Mirrors bloomed instantly. Clips looped. Subtitles appeared in languages Maya didn't speak. The world grabbed the words and ran with them.

Governments reacted in minutes. Markets in seconds. Military readiness ticked upward again, cautious and sharp. Some officials condemned her outright. Others stayed silent long enough to be noticed.

Civilians replayed the footage until the pauses mattered as much as the words.

Later, when the sky had settled into full daylight again, Maya stepped outside once more. The air felt unchanged. That didn't comfort her the way it used to.

Joe joined her, hands in his pockets.

"There's no going back," he said.

She nodded. "I know."

"Every move we make from now on will be watched."

"I know."

Joe studied her face. "Any regrets?"

Maya looked toward the tents, toward the people who'd been changed without asking, toward a world that no longer had the luxury of pretending it didn't see.

"No," she said.

She hadn't started a war.

She'd ended the lie that there wasn't one.

Somewhere far away, the world decided how it felt about that.

And somewhere closer, the Weave tightened, not in anger or approval, but in recognition.

The door had closed.

Now the world would have to choose whether to listen.

30

Backlash and Belief

The world answered Maya's words all at once.

Not with understanding. Not with restraint.

With motion.

Within minutes of the broadcast ending, the feeds fractured into thousands of competing truths. Footage poured in from every direction, raw and unfiltered, stripped of context by speed alone. Streets filled faster than authorities could respond. In one city, people tore down barricades they had built only days earlier and lit fires in their place. In another, crowds knelt in public squares, candles trembling in their hands as they whispered prayers they had never learned how to speak.

Chants rose and collided. Some carried Maya's name like a promise. Others spat it like an accusation.

There was no single reaction. There never was.

A riot in one hemisphere shared the same hour as a vigil in another. A shrine went up beside a courthouse while a mob smashed the windows of a transit station half a world away. People who had never cared about power suddenly demanded it. People who had never trusted institutions begged them to act.

Revelation did not unify response.

It multiplied it.

At the Circle compound outside Flagstaff, the command space felt too small to hold what was unfolding. Screens flickered with overlapping footage, none of it lingering long enough to settle before the next clip replaced it. Joe stood at the center of the room, hands braced on the table, jaw tight, eyes moving constantly.

"Slow it down," he said. "I don't need everything."

A tech muted half the feeds. Another filtered by region. It barely helped.

On one screen, a group of people stood in a plaza, arms raised, palms glowing faintly as they tried to imitate what they had seen Maya do. The light was wrong. Unstable. Two of them collapsed moments later, clutching their chests in panic as bystanders screamed.

On another, a crowd surged toward a government building, signs held high demanding protection from Walkers. Someone threw a bottle. Someone else fired a weapon into the air. The feed cut before anyone could tell what happened next.

In a third window, candles lined the steps of a hospital. Survivors of the Silence Storm stood together, faces drawn, holding photos of people who had not made it out. A woman spoke quietly to a camera, tears streaking down her face.

"She told the truth," the woman said. "That doesn't mean she's right. It just means she stopped lying."

Joe exhaled slowly and marked the clip for later.

Maya watched from the edge of the room, arms folded tightly across her chest, feeling distant from her own image as it replayed across the world. She had expected anger. She had expected fear.

She had not expected worship.

The first clips had appeared less than an hour after the broadcast ended. Small gatherings at first. A handful of people kneeling in living rooms, heads bowed toward screens that replayed her words on a loop. Someone had printed her name on a scrap of cardboard and taped it to a wall like an icon.

By midnight, it had escalated.

Children stood in alleyways, hands outstretched, mimicking the gesture she had used to steady the distortion. Their parents watched with expressions caught between awe and terror. Graffiti bloomed overnight on concrete walls and abandoned storefronts.

SAINT OF BALANCE

ANGEL OF THE WEAVE

CHOSEN

Maya felt her stomach twist.

"I never asked for this," she said quietly, though she wasn't sure who she was speaking to.

Faith did not wait for permission.

It never had.

She turned away from the screen when a clip appeared of a man praying directly to her image, voice shaking as he begged her to save his family. The desperation in his eyes cut deeper than any accusation ever could.

She had told the truth.

That didn't mean she could carry what people put on it.

Joe barely looked up as another wave of messages flooded the communications hub. They came in through every channel they had not shut down and several they thought were secure. Some were official. Most were not.

Requests piled up faster than could be categorized.

Training.

Protection.

Access.

A government liaison asked if a Walker could be embedded with their emergency response units. Another demanded exclusive cooperation in exchange for political cover that Joe knew would evaporate the moment it was no longer convenient.

Private actors were worse. Corporations offering resources in exchange for proprietary access. Militias declaring allegiance and asking for blessing. Individuals demanding proof they were worthy.

Joe sorted without comment, tagging each message as it came in.

Entitlement.

Fear.

Leverage.

Transparency had turned what was rare into something everyone fought over. Everyone wanted what they believed the Circle had. No one wanted to wait.

By early morning, Elara stood alone near the outer edge of the compound, watching footage projected faintly onto a portable screen. Protesters marched through a city square, holding signs that read SEAL IT ALL and END THE WEAVE. Survivors of Sedona appeared in interviews, voices raw, begging for the world they had lost.

"I don't want miracles," one man said. "I just want it to stop."

Elara looked down at her hand. Fire flickered weakly across her palm, responding to instinct and nothing else. She closed her fingers slowly, extinguishing it.

They wanted reversal.

They wanted an undo that didn't exist.

Balance had moved too far. There was no seal strong enough to put the world back the way it had been. Elara felt the truth of that settle into her bones, heavy and irreversible.

People did not fear change.

They feared permanence.

Alex watched a different set of feeds, his focus drawn to the edges where belief curdled into action. Armed groups began to appear, self-declared guardians and hunters alike. Some wore symbols meant to resemble the Weave. Others painted targets.

A video surfaced of a man trying to demonstrate resonance for a crowd. The energy spiked unpredictably and lashed back into him. He fell screaming, the people nearest him scattering in panic.

Alex grimaced and flagged the clip.

Belief without understanding became violence faster than anything else.

By the second evening, shrines appeared near the refugee camp. Small at first. A stack of personal items. A photograph. A candle. A child's shoe placed carefully at the base of a makeshift marker.

Maya walked through them slowly, hands clasped in front of her, heart heavy.

Some people asked her to bless them. Others wanted her to admit to causing everything.

She did neither.

She stood. She listened. She stayed present without touching the Weave at all.

It was enough to change the space.

People calmed when she was near. Arguments softened. The air felt different, steadier, even when no one could explain why. Maya felt the weight of it settle on her shoulders.

Being seen changed the world whether she acted or not.

That night, the Circle gathered around the strategy table, exhaustion etched into every face. The metrics were grim.

Violence was up. Coordination was down.

But something else had shifted too.

The lies had stopped spreading.

Joe leaned back in his chair and rubbed a hand over his face. "We traded one kind of chaos for another," he said. "But at least now it's honest."

No one disagreed.

By the end of the third day, the feeds stabilized into factions. Not consensus. Not peace. Alignment.

The world was no longer asking what was true.

It was choosing sides.

Joe noted the emerging patterns quietly. Organized ideology forming faster than policy ever could. Elara felt pressure building again, subtle but unmistakable. Maya understood the truth with a clarity that left no room for denial.

Belief itself had become a force in the Weave.

The war was not over power.
It was over meaning.

31

Richard's Hard Choice

Joe knew the message wasn't a request the moment he read it.

It wasn't formatted like an order. It didn't carry the clipped authority of a directive or the hedged language of a negotiation. There were no titles attached, no identifiers beyond a secure channel he hadn't seen light up in years.

I need to speak to all of you in person.

That was it.

Joe stared at the line longer than he needed to. Outside the command space, generators hummed steadily and voices carried in low, exhausted tones. The compound had not slept properly in days. Neither had the world.

When power asked permission, it wasn't looking for approval. It was signaling that the decision already existed. What remained was whether anyone else would be allowed to witness it.

Joe sent the acknowledgment without commentary and began preparing the room.

Richard arrived that afternoon.

Maya watched him from the perimeter as the vehicle rolled to a stop on the gravel access road. No motorcade. No visible security detail. Just a single transport and a man stepping out into high desert light that showed every line on his face without mercy.

He looked older than she remembered, even though only a couple of weeks had passed.

Not frail. Not diminished. Just worn in a way that had nothing to do with age and everything to do with carrying weight that never truly set down.

Richard paused before approaching the compound, his gaze drifting toward the refugee tents scattered across the scrubland. Canvas rippled in the wind. People moved slowly between them, careful, altered, fragile in ways that didn't show up on medical charts.

He took it in without flinching.

He knew exactly what his proposal would cost.

Maya didn't greet him. She didn't stop him either. He passed her with a nod that acknowledged her presence without presuming familiarity, then followed the guards inside.

This wasn't a villain entering the room.

It was a man carrying a knife he believed would have to be used.

The strategy room felt smaller with Richard in it.

Joe took one side of the table. Maya stood rather than sat. Alex leaned against the far wall, arms folded. Elara claimed a chair but didn't relax into it, her attention inward, listening for things that never stayed quiet anymore.

Richard didn't waste time.

He brought up the maps himself, projecting layered data across the central display. Node networks. Overlap densities. Failure probabilities rendered in muted color gradients that made destruction look almost reasonable.

"This isn't random anymore," Richard said. His voice was steady, measured, and carefully stripped of rhetoric. "Sedona wasn't an anomaly. It was a pattern asserting itself."

He gestured, and the image shifted.

"Certain node overlaps are structurally unstable under current Convergence pressure. They will fail again. Others can be reinforced. Not indefinitely, but long enough to matter."

Maya felt her jaw tighten.

"And the ones that fail," she said. "You're proposing we let them."

Richard met her gaze without evasion. "I'm proposing we choose them."

The room went still.

"Controlled collapse," Richard continued. "Preemptive isolation. We abandon specific nodes and the regions anchored to them so the pressure redistributes before it tears the entire system apart."

Alex pushed off the wall slightly. "You're talking about killing people."

"I'm talking about saving most of them," Richard said. "By accepting that we cannot save all of them."

He didn't raise his voice. He didn't soften it either.

"Amputate to save the body."

The words landed like a blade laid gently on the table.

This was triage, not cruelty. And that was what made it unbearable.

Maya reacted before the echo of the sentence faded.

"No," she said.

Not loudly. Not calmly either. The word came out sharp, instinctive, anchored in something older than strategy.

"These aren't numbers. They're not pressure valves or failure zones. They're people."

Richard didn't interrupt her.

"You're taking inevitability and turning it into policy," Maya said, stepping closer to the table. "You're deciding in advance who gets erased so you can call it order."

Her voice shook now, but she didn't pull it back.

"If you decide who dies before the storm arrives, you don't stop it. You become it."

The maps hovered between them, glowing softly, indifferent.

Elara spoke next.

She had listened longer than Maya. Watched the data settle. Felt the shape beneath the proposal.

When she finally lifted her head, her expression was colder than anger.

"You're wrong about what this stabilizes," she said.

Richard turned toward her.

"Forced erasure feeds the Unmaking," Elara continued. "Intentional Silence is worse than collapse. Accidental failure leaves imbalance. Planned voids invite it."

Her fingers curled slightly against the table, heat flickering faintly beneath her skin before she suppressed it.

"You might slow the surface effects. Buy time. But metaphysically, you'd be cutting holes that nothing fills. Balance enforced through sacrifice isn't balance. It's debt."

Richard absorbed that without defensiveness.

"And if we do nothing," he asked, "how many more Sedonas do we get?"

Elara didn't answer.

Alex found himself speaking before he'd decided to.

"I see the curves," he said quietly. "The survivability math. Some of these failures are already locked in."

Maya looked at him, pain flashing across her face.

Alex held her gaze. "I'm not agreeing with him. I'm asking the question we keep avoiding."

He turned to Richard.

"What if refusing to choose just means more people die later?"

The room held its breath.

Alex wasn't endorsing the plan. But he wasn't rejecting it either. And that space between was worse than certainty.

Not choosing was still a choice.

Joe cleared his throat.

"There's a piece you're not saying out loud," he said to Richard. "So I'll say it."

He brought up a second overlay. Military readiness shifts. Emergency authorities. Quiet policy drafts circulating faster than public statements ever could.

"They're already planning this," Joe said. "Governments. The Alliance. Anyone who thinks they can manage fallout with fewer questions asked."

He looked around the table.

"They'll do it without us. Without compassion. Without limits. Without accountability."

His gaze returned to Richard.

"The real question isn't whether sacrifice happens. It's who sets the boundaries."

Power didn't wait for moral consensus. It never had.

Voices rose after that.

Not shouting. Breaking.

The Circle fractured along lines that had always been there, just never exposed under this kind of light. Ethics collided with strategy. Metaphysics with politics. Love with arithmetic.

No solution emerged that everyone could live with.

Trust strained, not from betrayal, but from incompatible truths that refused to reconcile.

Unity could not survive unanswered sacrifice.

Richard didn't force the decision.

When the room finally fell silent again, he stood and shut off the display himself.

"Time will decide if you don't," he said. "And it will be crueler than I am."

He moved toward the door, then stopped.

"I will move forward," he said, not threatening, not pleading. "With or without you."

He turned back.

"But I would rather be wrong with you than right alone."

Then he left.

The Circle stayed where they were.

No one spoke.

Maya stared at the blank wall where the maps had been, her mind filling in the outlines anyway. Red zones. Sacrifice corridors. Places where the world would simply end because someone decided it had to.

The Covenant had never been about protection.

It had been about choosing who bore the cost.

Joe's tablet chimed softly.

He glanced down, then closed his eyes for a moment before speaking.

"The Alliance is experimenting with forced node collapse," he said. "Early stage. Not theoretical."

The room absorbed that quietly.

The question was no longer whether sacrifice would occur.

It was who would get to decide.

And how much of themselves they were willing to lose in the process.

32

The Truth Bomb

Joe had learned that evil rarely announced itself with a snarl.

It arrived dressed in procedure. It came with forms and approvals. It brought committees to soften the blade and vocabulary to make the cut sound clean. It filed itself into binders and archived itself behind classifications that sounded like safety.

Late at night, in the command space outside Flagstaff, the glow of a dozen screens painted Joe's hands the color of bruised ice. Generators hummed beyond the tent walls, steady as breath. Somewhere in the refugee rows, a baby cried once and was quieted almost immediately. Even grief had learned to keep its voice down.

Joe scrolled through the latest policy drafts tied to Richard's proposal. They weren't signed. They didn't need to be. The language had a familiar flavor, the bureaucratic way of describing a massacre without ever saying the word.

Selective abandonment zones. Managed depopulation corridors. Containment prioritization. Controlled node isolation.

Sanitized violence.

He read the paragraphs and could see the people they were trying not to mention. He could see families packed into cars, eyes wide, gas gauges low, nowhere to go. He could see the ones who wouldn't make it out because a spreadsheet had decided the math was acceptable. He could see the ones who'd be left behind because the world was tired and wanted to pretend the necessary had been done by someone else.

Richard had at least carried his knife into the room and made everyone look at it.

These people wanted to use the knife and still keep their hands clean.

Joe leaned back, rubbing his thumb against the edge of his coffee cup until the cardboard softened. His eyelids felt gritty. The world had been awake too long. He'd been awake with it.

On another screen, a live feed ran silent footage of Sedona. A drone camera drifting above streets that looked normal until you remembered what was missing. No wind moving tree limbs. No birds. No stray dogs. No distant traffic. A city preserved in a kind of quiet that didn't belong on Earth.

His stomach tightened the way it always did when he looked at it.

Sedona wasn't a natural disaster. Not really. Not anymore. Not with what Joe had in his possession.

He minimized the feed and pulled up a folder that didn't exist in the system's visible architecture. It was tucked inside a secured enclave he'd built by hand over months, hiding it the way you hid a loaded weapon from a child. He'd told himself he was waiting for the right time.

It had always been a lie.

He'd been waiting for courage.

On the folder's face was a single label, not for clarity but as a reminder to himself.

HANDS DIRTY.

Joe stared at that label for a long moment, his mind drifting through the last weeks, the first emergence of Walkers, the lies that had piled up around them like sandbags in rising floodwater. The Alliance had always been there, shaping, steering, redirecting. They hadn't been subtle. They hadn't needed to be.

They had simply assumed no one could prove it.

Joe clicked the folder open.

Inside were subfolders stamped with internal designations, each one a coffin with a neat tag. Some of the files had been harvested before Sedona. Some had been pulled during the storm's chaotic aftermath. Some had come from sources Joe wouldn't name aloud even if he were alone.

He didn't feel triumph at having them.

He felt sick.

Truth delayed became leverage. Truth released became a weapon.

Joe hovered his cursor over the first folder.

Then he stopped hovering.

He clicked.

The screen filled with documents. Not vague summaries. Not claims. Not interpretations. Raw system logs. Chain-of-custody packets. Engineering notes. Test results. Video captures. Audio transcripts. Human names attached to human outcomes, reduced to clinical phrasing by people who had convinced themselves that cruelty became moral when you called it research.

Joe's jaw clenched.

He began to build the package.

Not with anger. With precision.

If the world was going to turn, it wouldn't be because Joe had a speech ready. It would be because the Alliance had written their own confession and he was going to hand it to anyone who could read.

He dragged files into a clean release directory. He grouped them by category, not for narrative but for verification.

Echo-hybrid research documentation.

Human experimentation logs.

Forced resonance evacuation protocols.

Suppression algorithms designed to drain unstable nodes.

He opened a schematic and stared at it until the lines made sense in his head. It was elegant in a way that made him want to throw up. A system designed to detect resonance build and then pull it out, not by stabilizing the pattern but by stripping it. Removing response. Removing feedback. Removing the living texture of the Weave until only absence remained.

An extraction.

He pulled up the Sedona map overlay and layered the node data on top. The overlap density lit up like a bruise spreading beneath skin. Sedona wasn't just a node. It had been a knot, a convergence of convergences, an intersection of pressure points.

Joe opened the time stamps and aligned them with the suppression protocol logs.

The activation preceded the Silence Storm.

He ran it again, just to be certain.

It wasn't a coincidence.

It wasn't a cascade initiated by Convergence.

It was a deliberate interference at a multi-node overlap.

The suppression protocol didn't fail.

It succeeded too well.

It evacuated resonance completely.

Joe sat very still, his hands resting flat on the table as if they belonged to somebody else.

For days, people had said the Silence Storm was a warning. Or a demonstration. Or an inevitable consequence of forces too large to control.

They weren't wrong about the demonstration. They were wrong about whose hand had been on the lever.

Joe's throat tightened. He forced himself to keep moving.

The package needed redundancy. It needed corroboration. It needed to survive the first wave of denial and the second wave of counter-denial that would follow. It needed to live beyond the Alliance's first instinct, which would be to bury it under louder noise.

He included internal emails. Not the ones that sounded guilty on their own, but the ones that revealed casual acceptance. The kind of message where a person asked for coffee and then appended a line about evacuation thresholds as if it were equally mundane.

He included meeting minutes.

He included chain-of-command approvals.

He included the names of the people who had signed off.

He included the names of the people who had objected and been ignored.

He included one video clip he almost deleted twice because it felt like too much, because it would hurt innocent people, because the victims' faces were visible.

He kept it anyway.

Let the world see what clean language did to a human being.

Behind him, fabric rustled.

Maya stepped into the command space quietly. She didn't announce herself. She didn't need to. Joe knew her weight, the way she moved when she was trying not to be noticed.

He didn't look up immediately. He didn't want her to see his face yet.

"You're still awake," she said.

Joe gave a short, humorless breath. "So are you."

Maya moved closer. The screens reflected faintly in her eyes, turning them into little mirrors of disaster. She looked at the files, the headings, the categories.

"What is this?" she asked.

Joe finally turned his head.

"It's the part of the story they've been hiding," he said. "It's the part that makes Sedona make sense."

Maya's expression tightened. "Joe."

He saw the warning there. Not fear for him. Fear of what the information would do once it was free.

Joe nodded once. "Yeah."

Maya came around the table and leaned in, reading. Her breathing slowed, then changed. He could hear the moment the horror landed.

Not in a gasp. In a quiet stillness, the kind that came when the mind didn't want to accept what the eyes were showing it.

She scrolled through the suppression protocol overview. She stared at the language.

Resonance evacuation.

She whispered it like it didn't belong in the air.

Joe watched her face, the way her jaw set. The way her hand hovered for a moment over a diagram as if she could touch it and feel the lies.

"I recognize that shape," Maya said.

Joe frowned. "What do you mean?"

She tapped the schematic. "This isn't just machine logic. It's a mimic. It's trying to do what we do when we stabilize. When we take pressure and ease it. Only it's doing it without feedback."

Her voice lowered. "Without consent."

Joe nodded. "Without limits. Without correction."

Maya swallowed. "It's like... taking a person's breathing and stopping it because it's too loud."

Joe didn't answer. He didn't have words for it. The Alliance had always treated the Weave like infrastructure. A system. A resource.

Maya saw it like a living weave of resonance and response.

If you ripped response out of it, you didn't stabilize it.

You murdered it.

She pulled up a log file and read the entries. Her fingers trembled once, then steadied.

"They did this," she said. It wasn't a question.

Joe's mouth felt dry. "Yes."

Maya's gaze lifted to his. "They didn't fear power."

"No," Joe said.

Maya's eyes hardened. "They wanted to own it."

For a moment, the air between them felt tight, as if the tent itself had inhaled and forgotten how to let go. Joe glanced at the feed of Sedona again, the silent streets, the dark stillness.

It wasn't an accident.

It wasn't a mystery.

It was a choice made by people who thought the world was theirs to manage.

Maya looked down again, her face pale. "If you release this…"

"I know," Joe said.

She turned her head slightly, listening. Not to the Weave, not exactly, but to that sense Walkers had of pressure and consequence.

"It's going to break things," she said.

Joe nodded. "They're already broken."

Maya's voice was quiet. "And it's going to break people."

Joe's hands curled into fists and then opened again. "People are already broken too. They just don't know who did it to them."

Maya watched him for a long moment.

Then she said, "Do it right."

Joe's lips tightened. "That's what I'm trying to do."

Maya leaned closer to the screen, eyes tracking the suppression diagrams. As her attention focused, the display flickered once. Just a blink. The waveform lines sharpened, their noise collapsing into clean, brutal clarity.

Joe frowned. "I didn't touch anything."

Maya swallowed. "Neither did I."

The data hadn't changed.

It had resolved.

The Weave didn't resist being seen.

It aligned.

Maya met Joe's eyes again. "You're going to need to stay clear when you hit send."

Joe turned back to the screens.

He moved into the communications hub where their uplinks were cleanest. The hub was a converted trailer with antenna arrays that looked like skeletal trees against the night. Inside, cables ran like veins.

A tech glanced up, started to speak, then stopped when he saw Joe's expression.

"What do you need?" the tech asked.

Joe didn't raise his voice. "A window where I can push hard and fast. No throttling. No handshake delays."

The tech's eyes narrowed. "That'll light up every surveillance board that's watching us."

Joe nodded once. "Good."

He sat down and opened the distribution plan.

He didn't send it to one outlet. That could be pressured. Bought. Threatened. Drowned in distractions.

He sent it to dozens, across rival networks, across countries that hated each other, to journalists who competed viciously and would verify out of spite if nothing else. He sent it to legal watchdog organizations and academic analysts and international courts that moved slowly but didn't forget.

He sent it to people who had built their lives on proving institutions lied.

He attached verification keys.

He attached chain-of-custody proofs.

He attached raw logs that could be checked independently.

No commentary. No framing. No moral language.

Just documents, logs, timestamps, corroboration.

Joe paused with his finger hovering over the final command.

This was the point where the world changed.

He thought of Sedona. He thought of the refugees outside Flagstaff, sleeping in fragments. He thought of the words used to justify sacrifice zones and managed depopulation corridors.

He thought of how many people would die because the world wouldn't admit the truth until it was forced.

Joe pressed send.

The upload bars jumped.

For a moment, nothing happened. The world always took a breath before it screamed.

Then the mirrors began.

The package replicated itself across networks the Alliance didn't control. Copies appeared in places designed to survive deletion. Analysts began to pull it apart in public, verifying signatures, cross-checking time stamps, comparing internal terminology with leaked memos from months prior.

Within minutes, the first headlines formed, not as stories but as reactions.

SEDONA WASN'T A FAILURE.

ALLIANCE SUPPRESSION TRIGGERED SILENCE STORM.

HUMAN EXPERIMENTS CONFIRMED.

Joe watched the feeds as if he were watching a storm system grow teeth.

The narrative pivoted so fast it made his head ache. People who had been calling Walkers terrorists the day before were now replaying footage of sedated test subjects and asking who had authorized it. Survivors who had been treated like contaminated anomalies were suddenly evidence, living proof of what extraction did to a human mind.

The outrage didn't vanish. It changed direction.

Fear changed targets when guilt became provable.

Joe's screen filled with public statements, some issued so quickly they had to be prewritten.

One government announced an immediate suspension of cooperation pending review.

Another called the leaks fabricated and promised harsh retaliation against the source.

A third demanded an independent international investigation and named the Alliance directly.

Emergency meetings were announced.

Some were canceled an hour later.

Some went forward in secret.

The Alliance's official channels went quiet for twenty minutes.

Twenty minutes was an eternity in a crisis like this.

Then a statement appeared, cautious, measured, furious in its restraint. Denial without specifics. Condemnation without engagement. Promises of internal review.

Joe snorted softly. "Internal review," he muttered. "Like that fixes Sedona."

Maya came into the hub and stood behind him, watching the world tear itself open.

Her face didn't show satisfaction. It showed grief sharpened into something dangerous.

"They're going to come for you," she said.

Joe didn't look away from the screen. "They already were."

On another feed, a montage of Alliance internal chaos leaked almost immediately, as if the system had begun vomiting its own secrets now that the seal was broken. Panic messages. Contradictory orders. Blame shifting upward and downward simultaneously. Programs paused, renamed, erased.

Too late.

Control systems failed when exposed to light.

Somewhere inside the Alliance, someone screamed into a phone and got no answer. Someone deleted files and found they'd already been mirrored a thousand times. Someone realized the leash they'd held for months had snapped and lashed them across the face.

Joe didn't feel pity.

He felt tired.

The hours that followed didn't calm. They escalated in waves.

Public outrage erupted in streets that had already been burning from belief and backlash. Now the signs changed. Now the chants shifted. It wasn't saint and terrorist anymore.

It was who did this.

It was who lied.

It was who signed the forms.

At dawn, Maya stepped outside into the desert air.

The sky was a washed-out blue, the kind that made you think nothing bad could ever happen under it. The refugee tents fluttered in the wind like tired flags. Someone had built a small shrine near the camp, not to her, but to the dead. Photographs weighted with stones. A candle in a jar. A strip of cloth tied to a stake.

Maya watched a survivor interview on a portable screen propped against a crate. A woman with hollow eyes spoke in a flat, careful voice. She described the Silence Storm, how it had stolen sound and then stolen parts of her memory. She described how she could feel something brush her now, like an invisible hand hovering at the edge of her thoughts.

The interviewer asked, gently, if she blamed the Walkers.

The woman hesitated.

Then she said, "I blamed what I didn't understand. Now I blame the people who decided I didn't deserve to know."

Maya's throat tightened.

The same pain meant something different now.

The world was no longer afraid of Walkers in the same way.

It was afraid of people who acted without consent, without restraint, without witness.

The enemy was never power.

It was authority without accountability.

Back inside, the Circle gathered around the strategy table. The air smelled like warm electronics and stale food. Everyone looked wrung out. Nobody looked victorious.

Joe stood with his palms on the table and spoke plainly, not as a commander, not as a politician, but as a man who had finally shoved a rotten beam out of a wall and was watching the structure lean.

"HECATE as it was," he said, "is finished."

Alex's expression tightened. "Finished how?"

"Politically shattered," Joe said. "They can't reclaim the moral ground. Not after this. Not with proof that clean." He lifted a hand slightly, as if weighing the statement. "But the Alliance doesn't vanish because it loses legitimacy."

Elara's eyes narrowed. "It fractures."

Joe nodded. "It fractures. And that's the dangerous part. Pieces break off. They keep the tech. They keep the mindset. They lose oversight and gain urgency. Rogue elements will escalate quietly."

Maya sat down, slowly, as if the chair might disappear.

Joe continued, "This will make some things safer. Some governments will back off because they can't afford to be seen holding the knife. Some leaders will throw the Alliance under the bus to save themselves."

"And the others?" Alex asked.

Joe's voice stayed level. "They'll double down in secret. They'll call it necessary. They'll say the world can't afford transparency. They'll build new programs under new names and swear they're different."

Elara's fingers curled slightly, heat flickering under her skin and then fading. Her voice was cold. "They won't stop wanting to own it."

Joe met her gaze. "No. They won't."

Silence settled over the table, not the storm's silence. The human kind. The kind that came when you knew the cost of what you'd done and did it anyway because the cost of not doing it had been worse.

Outside, Sedona remained silent.

Nothing was undone.

Nobody was brought back.

The Circle did not celebrate.

No one called it justice.

But the lie was dead.

And that mattered, even if it didn't feel like victory.

Joe's tablet chimed. A message came in on a channel that shouldn't have been active.

He read it once.

Then again.

His mouth went dry.

"What?" Maya asked, already knowing it wasn't good.

Joe looked up. "We've got confirmation that some suppression tech has gone dark."

Alex frowned. "Dark how?"

Joe's eyes didn't blink. "As in, it's not reporting. Not communicating. Not showing up on any of the internal boards that just got exposed."

Elara's voice was barely above a whisper. "Other sites."

Joe nodded. "Other sites have gone quiet too."

Maya's hands tightened together. "Do we know who controls them now?"

Joe exhaled once, slow and controlled.

"No," he said. "And that's the point."

The truth didn't save the world.

It shattered the people who claimed they owned it.

Now the pieces were moving.

And somewhere, in the silence between nodes, someone was learning to pull resonance out of the world like breath from lungs.

33

The Quiet Choir Pays a Visit

The first sign something was wrong was not an alarm.

It was the absence of one.

Joe noticed it because he lived inside noise now. The compound never truly slept. Generators thrummed. Radios hissed. People shifted in tents. Someone coughed. Someone cried. Somewhere, always, something moved.

Tonight, the soundscape flattened.

Joe frowned at the audio monitors in the command space. Levels were steady. No dropouts. No interference. The system read normal.

It didn't feel normal.

The quiet had shape to it. Not silence like a failure. Silence like intention.

He adjusted the frequency bands manually, narrowing them down to ranges most people never noticed. Subsonic. Edge harmonics. Places where resonance left fingerprints even when it wasn't speaking.

There it was.

A low, synchronized trough across every channel. Not a spike. Not a void. A listening curve.

Joe's skin prickled.

"They're not hitting the systems," he murmured.

The tech beside him glanced up. "Then what is it?"

Joe swallowed. His Truthfinder sense pressed uncomfortably against his ribs, not flaring, not warning. Just registering presence.

"They're paying attention," he said. "To us."

Outside the command space, the compound lights hummed softly against the desert dark. The refugee tents formed a loose crescent at the perimeter, canvas catching moonlight like pale ribs. The night should have been busy with human noise.

Instead, it felt like the world was holding its breath.

Maya stepped out beyond the edge of the light spill, needing air that didn't smell like electronics and fear. The desert night wrapped around her, cool and vast.

Then she heard her name.

Not shouted. Not whispered.

Spoken.

"Maya."

Her body reacted before her mind did. A sharp intake of breath. A step backward. The Weave stirred instinctively, threads tightening in readiness.

She forced it still.

The voice came again, closer now. Familiar in a way that bypassed reason and went straight to memory.

"Maya, my child."

Her throat closed.

She hadn't heard that cadence in what felt like years. Not out loud. Not with breath behind it.

She turned slowly.

Isabella stood just beyond the reach of the lights.

Not young. Not old.

She stood as the Weave had held her. Hair pulled back simply, dark and practical, untouched by fashion or ceremony. The cut of her clothing was wrong for the century, but right for the life she'd lived. Wool and linen. A woman built for long days and quiet endurance.

Maya didn't recognize her from memory.

She recognized her from resonance.

This was the woman from the crypt. The presence she had felt before she had words for it. The witness whose silence had been pressed into paper because it could not be carried in a voice.

Isabella.

She didn't glow. She didn't flicker. She cast a shadow where the moonlight reached her feet, not because she was alive, but because the Weave remembered her as real.

The Weave did not surge.

It receded.

Space made room for memory.

Isabella looked at her with gentle familiarity. No accusation. No sorrow sharpened into blame. Just recognition.

"Thou art weary," Isabella said. "Thou hast ever pressed beyond thy strength."

Maya's heart hammered. Her fingers curled reflexively, nails biting into her palms.

"This isn't truly here," she said, more to herself than to the figure in front of her.

Isabella smiled faintly. "I was never easy with such reckonings."

Across the compound, others were seeing their own ghosts.

Alex froze between two rows of tents as figures stepped out of shadow and floodlight alike. People he had tried to hold together. People he had grounded too late. Faces twisted not in anger, but in relief.

"You see us now," one of them said softly.

Alex instinctively reached out, grounding flaring as muscle memory took over. The Weave pushed back.

Hard.

Pain lanced through his chest, sharp and immediate, dropping him to one knee. The Echo mirrored his motion, kneeling with him, expression unchanged.

"Don't," the figure said. "That hurts."

Alex stared at them, breath ragged. The words weren't an accusation.

They were a request.

Nearby, Elara stood rigid at the command perimeter as heat crawled up her spine, fire itching beneath her skin. Figures moved at the edges of her vision. Burned silhouettes. People she had saved. People she had not.

She didn't feel the Shadow Current.

She felt accumulation.

Grief layered on grief, pressed so tightly together it had learned how to sing.

"This isn't hostility," she said aloud, voice steady even as her hands trembled. "It's storage."

Maya's attention snapped back to Isabella.

Maya swallowed. "You're not here."

"Yet thou art." Isabella's voice did not rise. It did not argue. "And so am I, in the manner thou hast need of me."

Maya shook her head. "You died."

Isabella inclined her head once. Not denial. Not agreement.

"All flesh comes to rest, child. That was never the measure of what abides."

She stepped no closer. She did not reach out.

"Thou hast carried what was left unspoken. Not sin. Not failure. Only silence."

Maya's breath hitched.

"I did not ask thee to be strong," Isabella said gently. "Only to be true."

The words did not command.

They did not absolve.

They named what had always been there.

"You shouldn't be here," Maya said, the words brittle.

Isabella inclined her head. "I did not come hither. Thou didst call me forth."

The truth of it struck like a bruise.

Maya's instinct screamed at her to shut this down. To blink away. To cut the thread. To assert control.

She didn't.

She let her shoulders drop.

"I didn't stay," Maya said quietly. "I left before I knew how much time mattered."

Isabella nodded. "Thou wert always fearful of staying overlong."

"I was afraid of becoming stuck," Maya said. Her voice wavered, then steadied. "Of watching and not acting. Of recording the world while it burned."

Isabella's eyes softened. "And now?"

"Now I act," Maya said. "And people get hurt anyway."

She didn't ask forgiveness.

She didn't ask the Echo to leave.

She named the wound and let it exist between them.

"I carry what you couldn't," Maya said. "And I don't know if that makes me right."

For the first time, Isabella's image blurred slightly at the edges. Not breaking. Softening.

"That was never the question before thee," Isabella said.

Around them, the compound changed.

Refugees spoke names into the night. Some sobbed. Some laughed through tears. Some simply sat and let the weight move through them instead of away.

Alex bowed his head, hands open and empty. Elara closed her eyes and let the heat burn without shaping it.

The harmony wavered.

Echoes overlapped, losing clarity. Some figures faded like breath on glass. Others lowered their heads, expressions easing as if something long clenched had finally loosened.

In the command space, Joe watched the monitors normalize one by one. No spikes. No crashes. Just exhaustion settling in like a tide going out.

"The Choir is withdrawing," the tech said quietly.

Joe nodded. His chest felt tight. Not fear. Understanding.

"This was a test," he said. "It wanted to see what we'd do."

Outside, as dawn crept pale and uncertain over the desert, Maya stood alone again where Isabella had been.

The space was empty.

But it didn't feel hollow.

Elara joined her, gaze scanning the quiet camp. "It wasn't trying to kill us."

"No," Maya said. "It was trying to be heard."

Elara exhaled slowly. "The Quiet Choir," she said. Naming it felt like setting a boundary.

Joe's voice came over the comm, subdued. "We've got reports coming in. Similar manifestations near other suppression sites. Always where truth was buried."

Maya closed her eyes.

The world was full of unacknowledged grief now. Silence Storms had torn open places where pain had never been allowed to speak.

This enemy would not be defeated with force.

The next battle would be fought with truths people were afraid to admit.

And the Choir would be listening.

34

Alex's Near Death

The camp woke slowly, as if it were unsure the day deserved to begin.

After the Quiet Choir withdrew, nothing felt settled. People moved through routine because routine was all that remained. Fires were coaxed back to life. Water was hauled. Medical lines formed and dissolved. No one celebrated survival. No one spoke of victory. They worked with the hollow efficiency of people who had learned that relief was temporary and silence could still cut.

Alex felt wrong. Not injured. Not exhausted. Wrong in a way that didn't fit any failure mode he knew. Elara lingered close by, closer than usual, heat coiled tight beneath her skin as if she'd never fully relaxed after the Choir's visit.

He stood near the thinning edge of the compound where canvas gave way to desert, trying to ground the space around him. The instinct came easily. Spread. Absorb. Flatten the edges. It always had.

This time the response was uneven.

His Shield sense was too open. Too alert. It reached outward without permission, brushing against pain that wasn't his, grief that hadn't found words, fear that had learned to sit quietly and wait. He had spent every waking day learning how to turn that noise down. Now it pressed against him from every side.

He clenched his jaw and tried again. The pressure didn't settle. It tugged instead, pulling from multiple directions at once, as if the world wanted him to listen rather than hold.

Maya noticed before he said anything.

She stood a short distance away, watching the camp with eyes that never truly rested anymore. The Weave moved around her differently since the Choir's visit. Not louder. Narrower. More deliberate.

"You're listening outward," she said.

Alex looked at her. "I can't stop."

Before she could answer, the air changed.

Joe felt it first.

He had stepped out of the command tent for a quick bite, data pad tucked under his arm, trying to convince himself that standing still counted as rest.

Joe staggered as the truth dropped out from under him.

The Weave went quiet. Not distorted. Not masked. Gone.

Just a few steps away, Elara stiffened. The heat that usually answered her awareness went cold, flame refusing to rise even in potential. It wasn't suppression. It was absence of permission.

Maya's breath caught as the Weave tightened around her, threads drawing close until movement itself felt costly. Not blocked. Focused.

This wasn't an attack.

It was correction.

The pressure sharpened, no longer global. It aligned.

Alex felt the vector snap into place.

It was aimed at Maya.

He didn't think. Not in words. Not in plans.

The Shield in him understood before the rest of him caught up. If Maya took that load, she wouldn't die. Worse, she would fracture. The Weave would recalibrate through her, carving something permanent and wrong into the system. If he did nothing, the pressure would find another route. Collapse was efficient. It always was.

He stepped forward.

No warning. No declaration.

Just one pace, placing his body between Maya and the narrowing force.

Maya moved at the same instant, the Weave flaring instinctively.

"Don't," Joe said sharply.

She froze, breath locked in her chest.

"You push now, you tear whatever he's holding together," Joe said. His voice wasn't calm. It was precise, and that was worse.

The pressure hit.

There was no explosion. No sound. No visible force.

Alex's Shield didn't flare outward.

It folded.

The resonance he had built his life around collapsed inward, gravity reversing direction. For an instant, everything he had ever absorbed came back at once. Fear. Grief. Rage he had bled out of others and never released. Memories that weren't his, but had lived in him long enough to feel personal.

He couldn't ground it. There was nothing left to ground with.

Alex fell.

Not slowly. Not dramatically. His legs simply gave out, and he hit the dirt hard, body slack, head snapping to one side. Dust puffed up around him and settled.

He didn't move.

His eyes were open.

Wide. Fixed. Staring at nothing.

Maya stopped breathing.

For half a second, no one spoke. No one moved. Even the camp seemed to recoil, a collective step back as if the space itself understood what it was looking at.

"Elara," Maya said, her voice breaking. "Elara."

Elara was already there, one hand pressed flat to Alex's chest. She felt nothing. No rise. No heat responding. Her throat tightened.

Joe reached instinctively for certainty and found nothing there. Not dead. Not alive.

"That's not right," Joe said. His voice had lost its edge. "That's not right."

Maya dropped to her knees beside Alex, hands hovering uselessly over him, afraid to touch. "Alex," she said. Louder now. "Alex, you have to breathe."

Nothing happened.

One second.

Then another.

The Weave did not respond.

The Shadow did.

Not as rescue. Not as intent.

Absence recognized absence.

Inside Alex, the break widened. His Shield fractured along a fault he hadn't known existed, separating into two incompatible states. One resonated with the Weave, with connection and continuity. The other aligned with nothingness, with the quiet where pressure went when there was nowhere else to go.

They should have destroyed each other.

They didn't.

They locked.

The opposing states found balance not through harmony, but refusal to yield. Pressure equalized around the point where Alex existed. Not dampened. Not erased.

Held.

Alex sucked in a breath.

It was sharp. Ragged. Too loud in the sudden quiet.

His chest rose, then stuttered, then rose again.

Maya folded forward, a sound tearing out of her she didn't recognize as relief until it was already gone.

Elara swore, breath shaking. "Don't ever do that again," she said, fierce and unsteady.

Air tore back into his lungs like it had been waiting permission. His pulse returned in uneven bursts, fast and wrong but present. The pressure snapped loose, collapsing inward and dispersing. Not defeated. Rebalanced.

Maya sank to one knee, hands shaking now that there was nothing left to hold.

The Weave re-expanded around them. Altered. Strained. Still intact.

Alex tried to sit up and failed.

His limbs shook, not with weakness but overload. The grounding field around him spread without direction, tugging at everything nearby. People backed away instinctively as the space itself leaned toward him.

Elara felt it first. She leaned closer, eyes narrowed. "He's carrying both," she said. "Weave and absence."

Joe nodded slowly. "Truth and nothing aren't excluding each other around him."

Maya understood then, dread settling cold and heavy in her chest.

Alex hadn't shielded her.

He had replaced something.

They moved him to a medical tent as the sun slid toward afternoon. Maya stayed close, her presence locked and careful, like she was afraid the Weave might notice if she relaxed.

"You didn't have to," she said finally.

Alex didn't look at her. "Yes," he said. "I did."

No one argued.

That silence weighed more than anything else he was carrying.

By dusk, the camp had settled again. Not calmer. Quieter. As if it were waiting to see what shape the day would take before trusting it.

Alex sat alone near the edge of the light, staring at his palms as the sky darkened.

Nothing looked different.

Everything was.

Maya stood a short distance away, watching the horizon. She understood now that this moment hadn't been meant for her alone. The Unmaking hadn't failed.

It had learned.

Alex had stepped into the space where Guardians were forged. Not chosen. Not crowned.

Positioned.

35

Hargreave's Redemption

The office was quiet in the way only abandoned authority could be.

Victor Hargreaves sat alone behind the broad desk that had once anchored an entire network of decisions. The lights were dimmed lower than protocol allowed, casting long shadows across framed commendations that no longer felt earned. His jacket hung untouched over the back of his chair. He had not bothered to remove his tie. The habit felt pointless now, but routine still had gravity.

The screens in front of him refused to settle.

Alliance coordination feeds fractured across the wall, voices overlapping in muted arguments. Logistics officers demanded clarifications that never came. Legal advisories contradicted standing directives. Regional commanders delayed, stalled, hedged, all sensing the same thing without naming it.

Something was breaking.

The confirmation rested open on his personal tablet, unread now because it no longer needed to be.

The Hybrid deployment was real.

It was imminent.

And it would not be hidden.

Once it moved, the world would see it. There would be no controlled narrative, no quiet correction after the fact. The illusion of legitimacy would burn fast and bright, and nothing would remain beneath it.

Hargreaves leaned back slowly and closed his eyes.

For years, he had told himself that order required unpleasant tools. That fear, properly directed, could preserve stability. That someone had to be willing to make decisions others could not afford to see.

Tonight, those arguments didn't rise to meet him.

This would not restore order.

It would end it.

And he had helped build the path that led here.

Hargreaves stood and crossed the room, the carpet muffling his steps. He keyed into systems he had not accessed personally in some time. His credentials still opened doors. His authority still lingered in forgotten permissions and dormant protocols, assumed permanent because no one imagined he would ever turn them inward.

He made no attempt to cancel the deployment.

He dismantled it.

Emergency procurement overrides went live across Alliance channels, intersecting with jurisdictional disputes that should never have been active at the same time. Compliance freezes triggered automatically, then collided with legacy authorizations that nullified them on technical grounds. Orders contradicted each other faster than anyone could reconcile them.

Across Europe, a logistics hub stalled under the weight of its own approvals, shipments stranded mid-transfer with no legal path forward.

At a desert staging site, personnel stood beside sealed containers they were no longer authorized to open, watching clocks they could no longer obey.

Deep beneath Washington, a secure data vault unlocked in layers, permissions disengaging in a sequence never meant to occur.

This was not courage.

It was bureaucracy turned against itself.

By the time the first light crept over the city, Hargreaves had moved to the second phase.

Encrypted data packets released in a single coordinated surge, not as leaks but as structures laid bare all at once. Hybrid Program documentation. Echo conditioning footage. Correlation suppression tied directly to Silence Storm events.

Every file intact. Every chain of custody preserved.

And embedded deliberately in the metadata was his digital signature.

He didn't hide.

By midmorning, he stood alone at the podium in a press room that smelled faintly of stale coffee and anticipation. No aides flanked him. No prepared speech waited in his hands.

The questions came immediately, sharp and unrestrained. Accusations piled on top of each other, outrage gaining momentum with every answer he didn't deflect.

He offered no denial to what they named.

"I believed order justified cruelty," he said once, clearly. "I was wrong."

There was no attempt at mitigation. No appeal to necessity. When security finally took his arm, he went with them without resistance, eyes forward, expression stripped of anything that might be mistaken for dignity.

The fallout spread faster than the news cycle could contain it.

Alliance internal channels fractured outright. Some cells went dark, severing communication entirely. Others accelerated recklessly, convinced that collapse had already come. The Hybrid deployment unraveled globally, not cleanly, but completely.

In the refugee compound command space, Joe watched the cascade with grim focus. "This is a rupture," he said. "It had to happen. But it's going to hurt people."

Elara didn't argue. "He didn't try to minimize the cost," she said quietly. "He accepted it."

Maya felt the shape of the truth settle into place.

This had not been strategy.

It had been atonement.

That evening, she stepped into a secured holding room that smelled of concrete and antiseptic. The teleportation left her steady but cold, the air unfamiliar after the desert heat. There were no guards inside. No restraints in sight.

Hargreaves sat at a narrow table, hands folded neatly in front of him. He looked smaller now. Not broken. Stripped.

"I'm not asking for forgiveness," he said before she could speak. "I don't deserve it."

Maya took the chair across from him and waited.

"I told myself control was protection," he continued. "That if I carried the burden, others wouldn't have to see what it cost. I was wrong. I see that now. I know this doesn't undo anything."

She studied him for a long moment, searching for deflection and finding none.

"You chose differently," she said at last. "When it cost you everything."

Hargreaves nodded once. That acknowledgment was enough.

They escorted him out later that night. The corridor echoed with measured footsteps as charges were read and protections quietly withdrawn. He offered no resistance. He didn't look back.

When Maya returned to the refugee compound, the sky had gone dark.

She stood at the perimeter, watching the horizon where the desert swallowed light without ceremony. The world had not healed. The damage remained, layered and raw.

But something poisonous had stopped spreading.

She understood then that Hargreaves had never been the true enemy.

Fear was.

And tonight, fear had lost one of its strongest champions.

36

The Prime Node

The command space had the stale, recycled smell of a place that never truly slept. Screens glowed in disciplined rows. Cables lay taped down like someone had once tried to impose order on panic and then given up when the world refused to cooperate.

Outside, the refugee compound was quiet in the way a wound went quiet when the bleeding slowed. People moved again. They lined up for breakfast. They argued about blankets. They made plans that assumed tomorrow would behave like yesterday.

Inside, nothing felt healed.

Joe Biggs stood with a mug of burnt coffee cooling in his hand, staring at a scrolling band of electronic information. He had watched it for days, watched it spike and flatten, surge and recoil, like the planet itself couldn't decide whether it wanted to scream or hold its breath.

This morning it wasn't doing either.

The data wasn't fluctuating.

It was leaning.

At first it looked like stability. The graphs had stopped their frantic up and down. The readings had tightened into smooth, disciplined lines. Any other analyst would have called it a win.

Joe felt his stomach tighten, the way it did when a witness told a story too cleanly. Too practiced.

Truth didn't do clean unless someone had cut out what hurt.

He tapped the screen with a knuckle. The line held. He shifted to another feed, another region, another network stitched together from salvaged sensors and Walker-assisted workarounds. That line held too.

No spikes.

No chaos.

He just felt a subtle, consistent pressure vector pulling everything in the same direction through the Weave, rising in him as the feeds stopped contradicting one another.

Joe's eyes narrowed.

"You seeing it?" he asked, without turning.

Maya sat at the table behind him, elbows on her knees, hands loosely clasped like she was trying not to grip anything too hard. Her gaze wasn't on the monitors. It wasn't on the maps. She was looking past them, into whatever layer of the world only she could see.

She blinked once, slow.

"It's narrowing," she said. Her voice was calm, but it carried something like disbelief. "Everywhere at once."

Joe breathed out through his nose. "No fluctuation. No recovery. No random."

Maya's eyes shifted slightly, tracking something that wasn't visible. "It's not calming down."

"It's converging," Joe said.

She lifted her head. The early light from a small window caught her face and made her look younger for half a second. Then the expression settled back into what she'd become in the last month. Someone who had been forced to learn that control was not the same thing as safety.

"The absence of spikes is what scares me," she said quietly.

Because spikes meant release. Spikes meant the system was still spilling pressure in different directions. Spikes meant there were still places for it to go.

This was different.

This felt like a fist closing.

Behind them, Alex leaned against a support pillar, arms folded. He looked like he'd been awake all night, but the man rarely looked fully rested anymore. His presence in the room was a weight you could measure by the way everyone breathed a little slower around him.

Elara sat cross-legged on a folding cot pushed against the wall, hands open on her knees. Her eyes were closed, but her posture wasn't peaceful. It was restrained. Like a blade held in its sheath by will alone.

Joe's gaze flicked over them. Four people who were becoming anchors without having asked for the job.

He set the mug down, untouched now, and reached for the worn notebook that sat on the table as if it belonged there.

Merlin's Journal.

It didn't glow. It didn't hum. It didn't whisper. It was paper and ink, pages softened at the edges by age and handling. Ordinary.

That was what made it harder to look at sometimes.

All that history, all that weight, packed into something you could drop in the mud.

No one expected it to solve anything. No one expected instructions. Merlin had made that clear with every page.

He wrote like a man who had once believed he could guide the future and then learned that guidance always became control.

Still, Joe slid it across the table toward Maya.

"It's not going to change," he said.

Maya's mouth tightened at one corner. "It never has."

She opened it anyway.

The leather cover creaked. The pages fell open to a section already marked by use. The handwriting was tight, careful, as if Merlin had been trying to make sure the words survived even if his certainty didn't.

Maya read without moving her lips.

Joe leaned over her shoulder, not to invade, but because he felt the same pull she did. The need to stare at the witness record and pretend the witness might finally say something different.

Merlin didn't.

The entries held.

He wrote about load the way a mason wrote about weight distribution. Not metaphor, not poetry. Accumulation. Pressure. Harmonic narrowing.

He described a condition where stabilization could not disperse outward anymore because the pathways of dispersal collapsed into a single channel. He called it a throat.

A place where everything had to pass.

He didn't name it.

He didn't circle it on a map.

He didn't tell anyone where to stand.

Merlin never told people where to stand. He only described what happened when no one did.

Maya's finger traced a line of ink, not touching it, just hovering. "He saw this."

"He saw the shape of it," Joe said. "Not the address."

"He refused to give it," Maya murmured.

Joe nodded. "He didn't trust himself. Or anyone."

Maya looked up from the page. Her eyes were clear. Not calm. Clear.

"He thought knowing the location would become a weapon."

"He wasn't wrong," Joe said.

The room fell into silence, but not the uncomfortable kind. It was the silence of four systems aligning without needing language.

Maya's gaze unfocused again, sliding past the physical world. She swallowed once.

"I can feel a place I can't blink away from," she said.

That sentence didn't make sense to anyone who hadn't watched her vanish across impossible distances and return with blood in her nose. For Maya, blinking away was instinct. Escape. Movement. Freedom.

To say she couldn't do it was to admit the Weave itself was drawing a boundary around her.

Joe's own power rose like a pressure behind his eyes. It wasn't a vision. It wasn't a sound. It was a truth-state.

He reached for the situation the way he reached for lies.

There was no distortion.

No masking.

No obfuscation.

Just a clean, brutal certainty that made his throat feel tight.

"It's real," he said softly. "No interference. No manipulation. This isn't fear talking."

Elara's eyes opened. The air around her shifted, subtle, like a room warming by a degree you could feel in your bones. She didn't ignite anything. She didn't need to.

"It's compressing," she said. "Heat doesn't want to rise. It's drawing inward. Like it's being called."

Alex exhaled slowly. "I feel it too."

He didn't mean as a thought. He meant as weight.

He put a hand to the pillar beside him as if checking it for stability. "It's not pushing from one direction. It's settling onto me from everywhere."

Maya stared down at the Journal again, then closed it with care. She didn't treat it like a relic. She treated it like a grave marker.

Joe pulled up the data overlays, letting the screens fill with layered maps and ugly, practical correlations. If the Weave wanted to narrow, then the world would show where it could narrow without breaking first.

They didn't talk much while they worked.

That was the strange part. It wasn't strategy anymore. It was recognition.

Joe fed in tectonic stability models. Not because he believed the planet's crust controlled magic, but because he believed pressure sought what could bear it.

Maya marked long-term settlement density. Places humans had lived and endured, places the world had already asked to carry weight.

Elara flagged myth density zones. Not because she believed stories made reality, but because she'd watched belief amplify resonance like wind feeding flame.

Alex identified quiet zones, places that absorbed pressure instead of reflecting it, regions where the Weave had always felt less jagged, less reactive. Not safe. Just steady.

Layer by layer, the map stopped being a world and became a funnel.

Not a city.

Not a monument.

Not a place people visited on purpose.

A deep continental interior zone that had never failed.

Not because it was strong.

Because it bore everything.

Joe stared at the region highlighted on the screen, the boundaries rough and imperfect. The system didn't care about borders. It cared about load paths.

Maya didn't blink. She just looked, and something in her expression hardened into acceptance.

"That's it," she said.

Joe didn't ask how she knew. He didn't need to. He could feel the truth of it settle into place like a key turning.

Alex's shoulders lowered by a fraction, as if the weight had found its hook.

Elara's breath went slow, controlled. A flame held behind teeth.

Joe saved the overlay. It felt absurd, like labeling a fault line with a sticky note.

Then he pushed his chair back and stood.

"We need air," he said.

No one argued. They moved out together, leaving the humming command space behind.

Outside, the compound sprawled under a pale afternoon sky. The desert air was cool, and the light made everything look honest. Tents. Barricades. A few patched vehicles. People moving with the careful purpose of survivors.

Joe walked past them without fully seeing them. That wasn't cruelty. It was triage. He couldn't carry the whole camp in his mind and still speak what needed speaking.

They reached the perimeter where the fencing gave way to open ground. Beyond it, the land stretched out, empty and indifferent.

Joe stopped and faced the others.

He didn't dress it up. He didn't have the energy for speeches, and he didn't want the lie of inspiration.

"If that place fails during Convergence," he said, "stabilization elsewhere becomes meaningless. Anchoring at secondary nodes won't propagate. Survival becomes temporary at best."

He let it sit.

Elara nodded once. "Force won't fix it," she said. "If we try to burn through it, we'll just feed the collapse."

Maya's jaw tightened. "There's no fallback," she said.

Alex didn't speak. He didn't have to. His silence was agreement and grief at once.

Joe felt the shape of what they were moving into. Not a battle. Not even a mission.

An obligation.

They stood there in the open air, with the camp behind them and the world ahead, and no one asked for a vote. No one tried to negotiate with reality.

Because they all understood what anchoring there would cost.

Alex would become load-bearing continuously. Not as a moment. As a state.

Maya would lose the freedom of movement that had kept her alive. The Prime Node would make her choose where to stand and then punish her for leaving.

Elara would have to restrain her instinct to meet pressure with heat. She'd have to become disciplined in the most intimate way, holding back the part of her that wanted to flare.

Joe would surrender neutrality permanently. He'd spent his life as an outsider, an investigator, a man who stepped close enough to truth to expose it and then stepped away.

There would be no stepping away now.

The decision was made the way real decisions were made. Not by declaring it.

By staying present with the truth until it stopped feeling like an option and started feeling like gravity.

Joe looked at Maya. "We're going."

Maya didn't nod dramatically. She simply didn't look away.

Elara's hands curled once, then relaxed. "Yeah," she said. It wasn't bravado. It was commitment.

Alex finally spoke, voice low. "Then we move before the pressure turns into a snap."

Late afternoon bled into dusk with the quiet inevitability of a closing door.

At the edge of the camp, preparation began.

Not a ceremony. Not a rally. Not an announcement.

Just movement.

Joe spoke with the logistics crews and picked routes that avoided populated highways. The world was too raw for convoys that looked like governments.

Alex checked supplies without fuss, making sure medical kits were stocked and batteries were charged, the practical things that kept people alive when ideals failed.

Elara gathered what she needed and nothing more, her restraint visible in the way she didn't reach for spectacle even in private.

Maya moved among them like a current, listening more than speaking, eyes distant in that way that meant she was mapping something no one else could see.

They didn't tell the camp everything.

That wasn't secrecy for power. That was restraint.

This wasn't about rallying frightened people into hope. Hope was fragile when built on ignorance.

They told the leadership enough to maintain calm and continuity. The rest would come when it had to.

Night fell.

From a slight rise overlooking the compound, the four of them stood and watched the lights of the camp flicker and settle. Fires burned low. Voices drifted in thin threads of sound. A baby cried somewhere and was soothed.

The world continued as if nothing had changed.

Joe looked out into the darkness beyond the camp. The Prime Node wasn't marked on any public map. No one in the tents below knew what had been resolved in a handful of hours of quiet correlation.

No one named it aloud.

They didn't need to.

Because naming it wouldn't change what it was.

The endgame had a location now.

Not where a war would be fought.

Where collapse would either be absorbed.

Or allowed to pass through everything.

37

The First Anchor Ritual

They arrived before dawn, when the world was still undecided about waking.

The land didn't announce itself. No marker rose to meet them. No stone circle. No scar in the earth that said *this matters*. The ground stretched out in low, patient contours, rock and soil layered the way they had been for longer than anyone remembered. It looked like everywhere else people forgot to look twice.

That was the point.

The air felt heavy, but not charged. There was no hum, no pull. Just weight. The kind that settled into bone and stayed there, not asking permission.

Maya stood still after they stepped out of the transport. Not because she was listening, but because her body had already decided movement required caution. She closed her eyes, not in meditation, but in reflex, and reached for the familiar release of displacement.

She tried to blink.

The Weave resisted.

Not violently. Not enough to hurt. Just enough to make the idea of leaving feel wrong, like leaning into a current that would not yield no matter how long you waited.

278

Her eyes opened again, breath shallow before she noticed it. "It doesn't want me shifting," she said.

Joe nodded once. He didn't look at a screen. He didn't need to. The truth here felt so stable it was unsettling, like standing in a room where sound died too quickly, leaving you aware of how quiet quiet could get. "It's not pushing back," he said. "It's settled."

Alex rolled his shoulders, then stopped when the motion pulled more weight into him instead of relieving it. "Pressure's already on," he said. "Even before we do anything."

Elara crouched and pressed her palm to the ground. The air around her stayed flat, unmoving. No upward drift. No heat bloom answering her presence the way it usually did. Her brow furrowed. "Nothing wants to rise," she said. "Everything's contained."

Maya scanned the empty stretch of land, searching for some sign she could argue with. "It doesn't feel powerful."

"No," Joe said quietly. "It feels load-bearing."

That settled it. There wasn't anything else to say.

They moved inward until Maya felt resistance peak, not as a wall, but as a balance point. A place where the Weave stopped yielding without ever hardening. She stopped there. The others followed her lead without question.

This wasn't an ancient ritual. There were no words to speak, no symbols to draw, no gestures inherited from a past that pretended to know better. What they were about to do wasn't magic in the old sense.

It was alignment.

They stood close enough to feel one another's presence without touching. Close enough that distance itself felt like a decision.

Maya centered herself, not reaching outward, but narrowing perception the way she always did before danger. The Weave came into focus gradually, like eyes adjusting to darkness. She resisted the instinct to push. Pushing was how fractures started.

Alex planted his feet and let the pressure find him. He didn't brace against it. Bracing turned weight into strain. He absorbed it the way he always had, letting it settle into muscle, bone, breath. His body adjusted before his mind could comment.

Elara drew her flame inward. It resisted, not in rebellion, but in confusion. Fire wanted direction. Here, direction was denied. She compressed it anyway, forcing discipline over instinct, feeling heat fold back on itself until it became a steady presence instead of a response.

Joe closed his eyes and did what he did best. He reached for distortion and found none waiting for him. He stripped away expectation, fear, and hope until only the truth-state remained, smooth and unyielding.

They agreed on limits before they began.

No pushing.

No amplification.

Abort at the first sign of cascade.

Then they started.

There was no surge.

The Weave didn't flare or recoil the way it had everywhere else. It didn't fight them. It slowed.

Maya felt it first. Threads that had been vibrating on the edge of tension hesitated, not stopped, just delayed, as if the lattice itself had taken a breath and decided to hold it. Her head throbbed faintly, and she realized she was leaning forward again without meaning to.

Joe felt the pressure flatten. Convergence didn't vanish. It spread, quieting into something heavier and more deliberate. Endurance, not chaos. His chest tightened at the realization.

Elara felt her flame steady into something disciplined and contained. It didn't want to leap. It wanted to stay. The emotional echo followed, her reactions blunting at the edges just enough to notice.

Alex's load spiked sharply, evenly distributed, like weight added carefully to a scale. His knees flexed before he locked them. "I've got it," he said, the words more habit than certainty.

Joe opened his eyes and checked the instruments out of reflex. The change was there. Subtle. Measurable. Confirmation, not discovery.

"Convergence's slowed," he said. "Not reversed. Not stopped. But it's real."

They held it.

Seconds stretched. Then minutes.

And then the cost made itself known.

Maya felt pressure tighten behind her eyes. Futures didn't collapse. They pressed closer together, paths overlapping until choice itself felt heavier, slower, like moving through deep water instead of open air. Her breath caught, and this time she noticed.

Joe understood in the same instant, the truth landing without distortion to soften it. "Stabilization removes optionality," he said quietly. "We're trading freedom for endurance."

Elara swallowed. The internal quiet was unmistakable now. "It's quieter inside," she said. "Not gone. Just... narrower."

Alex felt the shift as something deeper than strain. This wasn't weight anymore. This was permanence pressing in, the sense that if this held too long, it wouldn't leave cleanly.

Maya opened her eyes. "This isn't wrong," she said. "But it's incomplete."

The load shifted.

Alex staggered, just enough to matter. "I can't hold this indefinitely."

"I can't maintain perception alone," Maya said at the same time.

"I can't regulate forever without burning out," Elara added.

Joe exhaled slowly. "And I can't stabilize truth without becoming fixed."

They looked at one another.

No one spoke at first.

Then understanding landed, simultaneous and undeniable.

One anchor collapsed.

Two fractured.

Three destabilized.

Four held.

Not chosen.

Required.

Maya broke the alignment first, easing pressure the way you eased a hand off a wound. "We disengage," she said. "Now."

They pulled back deliberately. The Weave resumed motion slowly, reluctantly. Convergence rebounded slightly, then settled. The Prime Node remained patient, unchanged.

Alex nearly went to one knee. Maya was there instantly, steadying him without blinking, grounding herself in the same motion. Elara contained the residual heat with a controlled breath. Joe watched the truth-state carefully.

"No increased distortion," he said. "We didn't make it worse."

They regrouped at the temporary shelter as afternoon wore on. No arguments. No debate. Just confirmation spoken in different voices.

"This isn't symbolic," Elara said at last. "It's structural."

Joe nodded. "Four permanent anchors," he said. "Anything less fails."

"And not all of them will remain mortal," Maya said softly.

No one contradicted her.

They didn't need to.

At dusk, they stood on a low rise overlooking the quiet land. The Prime Node looked unchanged. The world beyond it continued, unaware.

Convergence moved on.

Slower now.

The path forward had fewer branches.

They hadn't saved the world.

They'd made it possible to save it later.

And the cost would be permanence.

38

The Immortals' Offer

Night settled over the Prime Node like a held breath.

Nothing announced the change. No light, no sound, no visible marker that the world had crossed a line. The land simply grew quieter, the way a room did after a truth had been spoken aloud and no one knew what to say next.

Maya felt it in her chest first. The constant resistance she'd learned to live with had redistributed itself, no longer pressing back in sharp places. The Weave here still held tension, but it was balanced now. Load-bearing. Accepting.

That scared her more than chaos ever had.

Chaos could be fought. This felt like consent.

She stood at the center of the inner stability zone, boots grounded in soil that felt impossibly old. The Prime Node didn't feel powerful. It felt responsible. As if it had already agreed to something and was waiting for the rest of the world to catch up.

Alex stood several paces away, shoulders squared, posture rigid with effort. The load he carried hadn't eased, but it had changed character. Instead of crushing down from every direction, it had settled into something even and relentless. Manageable, if he never stopped paying attention.

He realized, with a cold clarity that tightened his jaw, that this was what permanence felt like.

Elara sat on a flat stone near the edge of the zone, legs crossed, palms open on her knees. Her fire had folded inward without protest, compressed so tightly it felt almost absent. That absence unsettled her more than heat ever had. Fire was how she reacted. How she expressed. Here, reaction felt... unnecessary.

If this was the future, she wondered what it would cost her to live in it.

Joe stood at the boundary of the circle, hands buried in his pockets, head tilted slightly. He wasn't listening to sound. He was listening to truth.

And the truth here was terrifying in its clarity.

No distortion. No interference. No lies to peel back. The Prime Node didn't argue. It didn't conceal. It simply existed as a fact, and Joe felt the awful certainty that facts like this didn't care whether anyone was ready for them.

"This place changed," he said quietly.

Maya nodded. "It feels like it decided."

Alex exhaled through his nose. "About damn time."

Elara's gaze lifted toward the open space a few steps away from them. "Or about who."

Maya followed her eyes.

At first, there was nothing.

Then the air thickened, not visually, but spatially. Depth resolved where emptiness had been, like the world remembering how to allow something solid to exist there. The Weave didn't tear or bend. It simply stopped being vacant.

Maya's breath caught painfully in her throat.

The outline formed slowly, carefully. Boots touched soil without sound. Fabric settled against a body. A chest rose and fell.

Ethan stood where the Weave finished resolving him.

He didn't arrive.

He completed.

Alex's muscles tensed on reflex, his body preparing for impact that never came. The world didn't push back. It accepted Ethan the way it accepted gravity.

"Jesus," Alex breathed.

Elara rose to her feet, fire instinct flaring once before she forced it down hard. "You didn't force your way in," she said, disbelief and awe tangled together.

Ethan looked down at his hands, flexed his fingers slowly. He felt solid. That alone was shocking. Every other time he'd tried to be fully present, the world had rejected him like a bad graft.

"It let me stay," he said.

Joe swallowed. The truth-state around Ethan was unlike anything he'd ever encountered. Not masked. Not distorted. Integrated. Seamless.

"You didn't bend it," Joe said. "You fit."

Ethan nodded once. "Every other time felt like friction. Like the world and I disagreed about whether I should exist."

He lifted his gaze to Maya last. "It doesn't disagree anymore."

Maya felt tears threaten and crushed them down. This wasn't reunion. This wasn't relief. This was consequence.

"You're anchored," she said.

"Partially," Ethan replied. "Enough to be... real."

The Weave thinned again, subtle as breath leaving lungs.

And suddenly, the impossible became permissible.

Kemen resolved first.

She did not step into being. She defined herself out of the dark, presence sharpening into form without light or sound. Her gaze was steady, ancient, and female in a way that carried no softness and no cruelty. Only endurance.

Vilya followed, his presence denser, more structured, the Weave accommodating him with careful precision. Beagron came next, heavy as consequence, the ground beneath him settling rather than resisting.

Cylian and Antec braided into the space last, layered and harmonic, never entirely separate.

They were not here because they chose to be.

They were here because the Circle had made room.

Maya felt that truth land like ice in her veins.

Kemen's gaze moved over them, not judging. Recognizing.

"You have crossed a threshold," she said.

Her voice didn't echo. It didn't carry. It arrived where it was meant to be heard.

"We tried to slow it," Maya said.

"You did more than try," Kemen replied. "You altered the system."

Joe's jaw tightened. "Altered how?"

"The Covenant has begun," Kemen said. "It simply isn't stable yet."

That word lodged in Maya's chest. Covenant. Not spell. Not defense. Agreement.

Vilya stepped forward, his presence clearer now that the Weave tolerated it. "We cannot hold the seal much longer," he said. "Not because we lack strength. Because the Weave no longer accepts permanence from us."

Joe felt the truth of it snap into place. "Your presence increases strain."

"Yes," Vilya said simply.

Beagron's voice followed, rough and unyielding. "We were never meant to hold eternity. Only to delay it."

Alex felt something cold settle behind his ribs. There would be no ancient hands holding the world steady forever. No safety net.

Cylian's attention settled on Maya. "The structure that follows is not ours to command," she said. "But it is ours to name."

Maya already knew what was coming. That didn't make it easier.

"Four Guardians," Cylian said.

Alex felt the word hit him like weight finding a place to land. Elara felt it as heat wanting to move and being denied. Joe felt it as truth with no exit.

"On the mortal side," Cylian continued. "Bound through sacrifice. Anchored to distinct harmonic functions."

Antec's voice joined, precise and final. "Each Guardian must train a successor. An apprentice who inherits when the Guardian merges fully."

Joe spoke what all of them were thinking. "So you're done."

"We yield," Kemen corrected. "You inherit."

Ethan stepped forward, the Weave accepting the movement without resistance.

"The first bridge," Kemen said.

Ethan's mouth tightened. "I didn't choose this."

"No," Vilya replied. "You endured it."

"Not by design," Beagron added. "By necessity."

Ethan felt the truth of that settle into him like bone. Whatever he was now, it wasn't temporary. He'd crossed something that didn't allow return.

"He's not an exception," Joe said.

"He's proof," Cylian replied.

The cost came next.

"Guardians do not retire," Kemen said.

Alex's hands curled at his sides.

"They do not step back," Kemen continued. "They dissolve into the Weave in time."

"Memory persists," Vilya added. "Identity does not. Not indefinitely."

"This is one-way," Beagron said. "No one leaves unchanged."

Maya felt the weight of it press inward. Not fear. Responsibility. The kind you couldn't outrun.

"We're not accepting this tonight," she said.

Kemen inclined her head. "We expected that."

"No vows," Maya continued. "No promises. Not until we understand exactly what this will cost."

The Immortals began to thin, not vanishing, yielding. Their weight lifted gradually, and the space they left behind felt steadier for their absence.

"We did not come to place the torch in your hands," Kemen said. "We set it down."

Then they were gone.

Not absent. Not erased.

Yielded.

The land remained quiet.

Waiting.

<h1 style="text-align:center">39</h1>

Quiet Choir's Ultimatum

The Prime Node was quiet.

Not empty. Not calm. Quiet in the way a held breath was quiet, the way a room went still when everyone sensed that something had entered it without opening a door.

Maya felt it before anything changed around them. A pressure layered beneath the familiar tension of the Weave, subtle at first, then accumulating. Not a surge. Not an impact. A density. Like grief settling where sound used to live.

The air thickened without moving.

Alex shifted his stance, then stopped when the adjustment made the weight worse instead of better. The load he carried multiplied, not abruptly, but steadily, like hands being added one at a time. His jaw set as he accepted it, breath deep and controlled.

Elara's fire dimmed.

Not extinguished. Suppressed. The heat inside her folded inward against her will, reaction muted, flame denied its instinct to answer pressure with expansion. She frowned, unsettled by how wrong it felt.

Joe's perception flattened.

Truth didn't distort. It simplified.

Edges smoothed. Variance collapsed. Possibility thinned into something frighteningly clean. He felt the warning immediately. Lies fought back. This didn't. This offered clarity by removing disagreement.

Maya's pulse quickened.

The Quiet Choir wasn't arriving.

It was aligning.

The grief that had always existed at the margins gathered, layer by layer, resonance tightening without spectacle. No faces. No voices. No illusions. Just the accumulated weight of unacknowledged loss finding a place where coherence was finally possible.

Here, at the Prime Node, silence was thin enough to shape itself.

Maya understood with sudden certainty that the Choir was closer to coherence than it had ever been. Not stronger. Not louder. More complete.

Ethan felt it too.

He recognized the Quiet Choir instantly. Not as threat. Not as enemy. As something familiar in the way shared wounds were familiar.

He understood its origin. Humanity's refusal to listen. Pain stacked until expression became necessity. Grief denied until denial became structure.

He understood its terrible coherence.

And he rejected it utterly.

Not with anger. Not with fear. With refusal.

The Choir could not contain him. Could not reconcile him. His existence contradicted its solution at the most basic level.

The silence deepened.

Meaning resolved across them all at once.

Not speech.

Not command.

A proposition.

The Weave could be severed.

The Silence could be restored.

Humanity could be spared Convergence.

The idea did not arrive as temptation. It arrived as logic.

Maya felt the pull immediately.

A world without vigilance. Without constant harm management. Without forcing humanity to adapt faster than it wanted to. No more storms. No more escalation. No more living at the edge of collapse.

Relief washed through her so strongly it made her dizzy.

Not peace.

Relief.

She saw it clearly. The Choir was not offering control. It was offering rest. The kind that came after exhaustion had burned every other option away.

The cost clarified.

The Weave would be cut off from humanity completely.

Walkers would lose all connection.

Some would not survive the severance.

Echo-scarred minds would collapse under the absence they'd been shaped around.

History would forget magic again. Not suppress it. Forget it.

No more Shadow.

No more Silence Storms.

Pain would end.

Choice would end too.

Joe felt the truth of it lock into place with brutal clarity. It would work. The system would stabilize. The pressure would stop. Humanity would endure.

Elara felt fury rise, sharp and instinctive, at mercy that required amputation. Fire wanted to rage. It found nowhere to go.

Alex imagined the weight lifting.

Just for a moment.

The thought nearly broke him.

Ethan felt the offer as annihilation.

Not death. Erasure. The removal of what he had become, what he was becoming. The Choir could not allow him to exist without unraveling its premise.

No one spoke.

No one interrupted.

The offer stood on its own merits.

Maya felt tears burn behind her eyes. She understood why the Choir had formed. She understood why this solution existed. She understood why it was tempting.

And then she saw what it could not.

Silence was not peace.

It was postponement through erasure.

"This wouldn't heal us," she said aloud, voice steady despite the grief threading through it. "It would amputate us."

The resonance wavered.

Not violently. Not defensively.

Incomplete things always did when named.

"You formed because we wouldn't listen," Maya continued. "Because we refused to acknowledge pain until it had nowhere else to go. Your solution makes sense."

The weight shifted.

"But it's still wrong."

The Circle stood with her.

Not unanimously in feeling.

Unanimously in choice.

Maya didn't condemn the Choir. She didn't attack it. She didn't deny its necessity.

She refused it.

With grief.

The Quiet Choir dispersed.

Not vanishing. Not retreating.

Unraveling. Less coherent. Less certain.

It had been heard.

And refused.

Dawn crept toward the horizon, pale and quiet.

The Prime Node remained.

Waiting.
The world would hurt.
And humanity had chosen to stay present for it.
The easy path was gone.

40

The Measure of Time

The Prime Node held.

Not easily. Not generously. It held the way a structure did when the last allowable load had already been placed and nothing else was coming off.

Pre-dawn light barely touched the horizon when they took their positions again. No circle. No marks. No inherited shape to lean on. What they were doing now was not a ritual. It was a test of endurance, stripped down to the most honest version of holding.

No amplification.

No expansion.

Only presence.

Maya narrowed her perception until the Weave sharpened without flaring. Just enough clarity to prevent surge. She didn't reach. She didn't pull. She held the edges steady and trusted the center to do what it had already agreed to do.

Alex set his feet and let the load settle into him without extending himself toward it. Every instinct he had told him to brace harder, to take more, to prove he could. He ignored it. Holding wasn't about proving anything. It was about not breaking.

Elara drew her fire inward until it barely registered as heat. Regulation at bare minimum. No shaping. No answering pressure with expression. The restraint cost her more than flame ever had.

Joe stripped distortion down to baseline truth. No filtering for comfort. No interpretation. Just the raw state of what was. It left no margin for error, and that was the point.

And Ethan stood where the system stopped negotiating.

He didn't brace. He didn't regulate. He didn't absorb.

He remained.

The Weave adjusted around him as if it had found a resolved state it no longer needed to recalculate against. Not a wall. Not an anchor driven into place. A completed equation the system could finally reference.

Time flattened around him. Urgency dulled. The effort of becoming ceased.

The Prime Node accepted it.

They held.

Seconds stretched. Then minutes. The world didn't react. It didn't reward them. It didn't punish them either.

Dawn broke slowly.

Joe checked the numbers once. Then again. He recalculated without changing inputs, just to be sure it wasn't hope distorting his hands.

He exhaled.

"Convergence slowed," he said quietly.

No one reacted.

"Not much," he added. "But it's measurable."

Alex felt it in the way the weight shifted instead of lifting. Elara felt it in the way her fire stayed contained without effort. Maya felt it in the way the Weave stopped pressing back in unpredictable places.

Joe ran the projection again.

Then he looked up.

"One year."

The words didn't echo. They didn't need to.

The world responded subtly.

Auroras thinned across the sky, not vanishing, just dimming. Communications stabilized long enough for people to believe it meant something permanent. The atmosphere felt quieter, not calm, but alert. Like an animal that had stopped running and turned to listen.

No one celebrated.

Nothing looked like it had been saved.

That was the danger.

By late morning, the cost began to assert itself.

Alex disengaged carefully, but the load didn't fully release. It stayed with him, lighter than before but persistent. He sat for a long time afterward, grounding a space that no longer needed it, just to remind himself he still could.

Elara felt fatigue settle beneath exhaustion. A deeper drain that didn't fade with rest. She watched fire burn later without shaping it, without answering it, and wondered how long restraint could last before it became erosion.

Joe noted that truth distortion was easier now. Which meant the margin was thinner. Clarity cut both ways.

Maya understood what they had bought.

Time.

Nothing else.

They stood together overlooking the Prime Node as the day climbed higher. No speeches. No planning yet. Just acknowledgment.

"We bought a year," Maya said.

She waited.

"In a year, everything changes."

Another breath.

"Or ends."

No one contradicted her.

The world kept moving.

Refugees resumed routines. Governments scrambled and postured. Alliance remnants adapted. The Quiet Choir remained present, thinner now, less coherent, but alert.

Nothing looked like an ending.

Each of them felt the clock differently.

Alex felt it as weight that would never fully come off. Elara felt it as restraint that would cost her who she used to be. Joe logged the year as a fixed variable, not a hope. Ethan felt time as something already spent.

The sky darkened again that night. The auroras remained, dimmer and controlled. The Weave was quieter than it had ever been.

Not healed.

Waiting.

The world had one year left to decide what it would become.

****

Lila felt it while she was doing nothing at all.

Not listening. Not reaching. Not trying to interpret the Weave the way she'd learned to notice it over the last few months, carefully and with restraint. She was sitting on the steps outside the temporary shelter, watching dust drift in the late afternoon light, thinking about nothing in particular. Beyond the tents, old earthen embankments curved through the trees, long past remembering the guns they'd once held.

That was when the noise stopped.

Not sound. Something underneath it. The constant low-level pressure she'd lived with since the world fractured. The sense that everything was leaning slightly wrong, like furniture set on an uneven floor. It didn't vanish.

It aligned.

Her breath caught halfway in. She frowned, not in fear, but confusion. The world felt placed. Like something heavy had finally been set down where it belonged.

Behind her, Hogan's head came up.

The dog had been asleep, chin on his paws, breathing slow and even. Now he was alert without tension, ears forward, body still. He didn't growl. He didn't bark. He simply looked in the same direction Lila had turned without knowing why.

"There you are," she whispered, though she didn't yet know who she meant.

The Weave didn't announce anything. It didn't light up or pull at her like a hook. It did something subtler. It stopped insisting she remain where she was.

Lila stood slowly. The feeling sharpened as she moved, not stronger, just clearer. Like walking out of static into clean air. Her chest felt tight in a way that had nothing to do with panic.

Hogan was already on his feet.

He didn't look at her for permission. He never had, not when it mattered. He took a few steps, stopped, then looked back once, tail still, eyes steady.

He knew.

She swallowed. "Okay," she said quietly.

They didn't pack much. Lila slung her bag over her shoulder out of habit more than necessity. Hogan waited at the edge of the path, not pacing, not anxious.

Certain.

As they walked, Lila realized something unsettling.

She wasn't searching.

There was no sense of trial and error, no branching possibilities. The world didn't feel smaller. It felt decided. Each turn they took felt like the only one that made sense, not because alternatives were blocked, but because they no longer mattered.

She tried once to step off the path. Just to test it. The Weave didn't resist her body. It resisted the idea. The moment felt wrong, like interrupting someone mid-sentence.

She stepped back onto the trail without thinking about it again.

Hogan moved easily, trotting ahead, stopping when she slowed, re-suming when she did. He wasn't tracking a scent. His focus wasn't on the ground. It was on the space ahead, as if he were following something already visible to him.

As the hours passed, Lila's thoughts circled the same absence.

Ethan.

She hadn't said his name aloud in a long time. Not because it hurt too much. Because it felt unfinished.

He was present.

Not returning. Not reaching out.

Present.

Night fell without ceremony. They kept moving.

When the lights of the camp finally came into view, Lila stopped walking.

Her throat tightened. This wasn't hope.

This was recognition.

John D. Jennett is the author of *The Covenant of Silence Saga*, a modern speculative fantasy series that blends hidden magic, global consequence, and the human cost of power. Born in Muskegon, Michigan, and raised in foster care before being adopted in Newaygo, he enlisted in the U.S. Army in 1987 and served for 24 years, including Desert Storm and multiple combat deployments during the Global War on Terror. After retiring from military service, he returned to his lifelong love of storytelling, bringing a grounded realism to extraordinary events. John lives on a rural Tennessee homestead with his wife and family. Readers can find more information about his work on his facebook page at https://www.facebook.com/Ravenwoodfarm2600